MW01434358

Are You Happy?

A novel by

CLARA POPPY GALLOT

Clara Poppy Gallot

Copyright © 2022 Clara Poppy Gallot
All rights reserved
First Edition

Fulton Books, Inc.
Meadville, PA

Published by Fulton Books 2022

ISBN 978-1-63985-170-6 (hardcover)
ISBN 978-1-63985-169-0 (digital)

Printed in the United States of America

CHAPTER 1

Moving to San Francisco

Déjà vu had been consistent. My mind was rapid, and I was sick of my boring situation. I was living life with a minimum wage every single day of my existence. I could no longer tolerate it. I had been living my life haphazardly with everything that I did. I had been a caregiver for a century that even with my eyes closed. I could change my grandmother's diaper. I just took care of an eighty-seven-year-old man that had a stroke. He couldn't move his left side. Only his right side could function. He used to be an architect, and a damn good one. I helped him with his exercises for two years straight, besides caring for my other two cerebral palsy clients who were in their wheelchairs for four years. I had to prepare their food and feed them, give them a shower, and do their laundry for them.

I must say, I was not just a caregiver. I was a caregiver. I used to be shy when asked what my profession was. But thinking about it, my job was not as easy as you think. Patience is one tough thing to have. How I wish it was as easy as online shopping and adding things you want in that cart. It was such an honor though, but I felt like my life needed an adventure. It's like a soda. After it sits on the table, the spirit disappears. It doesn't taste that good, and it's not that cold. Or it's like an elementary student. After the second month in school, they start getting hyper and making friends not just inside the classroom but also with other classes in campus. I didn't think that all kids were like that, but somehow, based on my experience, I was that way. I never figured how I acquired patience as a caregiver, yet I had none for myself. My boredom was beyond words. I wouldn't mind getting inside a spacecraft and staying there for months. Or how about kayaking to Germany from New York? But I had to fly to the East Coast first. I thought flying to New York was more work than paddling for days. Did you think that would work? I didn't think the sharks would bother me. I was just passing by anyway. But the huge wave might throw me off the kayak, so I might need a bigger boat. Oh, how about just flying? I could fly like Wonder Woman. My mind had gone extreme for months now, and to be honest, I didn't want to end up in the psych ward.

I tried my best to do gardening, but what amazed me was that everything I planted died, even succulents. How fascinating. I drank coffee at five every single morning, and work began after that. After we all grew up and finished school, it was ridiculous. I wanted to see a new environment. A change. New people. New job.

I lay on the sofa and browsed for jobs in San Francisco. I was blown away that they paid so much and that a lot of companies and stores were open twenty-four hours a day. They were hiring like crazy. I was so speechless how you could actually save and keep yourself busy. And there were so many activities in the city compared to here. But how would I move there when I didn't know anyone in that city? I could go back and forth just to give it a try. I found a client who was looking for companionship for the weekends, and it was a live-in shift. Two days for $520. I was honestly receiving $620 biweekly at the facility I was working for. And that was

ARE YOU HAPPY?

only for two days? That was unbelievable. I'd try to call. If they didn't answer, then it was not for me. I called the number that was on Craigslist, a lady name Linda. To my surprise, my phone was answered with two rings. She explained to me the job description and said it was a man with cerebral palsy. He needed help with meal preparation and laundry, and he needed a driver for when he went to his appointments. And she asked me about my background. I explained myself, and at the end of our conversation, she asked me to meet the client so he could interview me too. An hour and thirty-five minutes of driving was not bad at all.

During the entire drive, I was contemplating about my life. I never thought I would be working in San Francisco. Speaking of a change, this was it. I was in my late twenties and still single. I didn't understand what was wrong with me. But maybe it was fate? Not to be an old maid but to meet someone who was desirable in the city, and maybe he could change my life's perspective? I was overthinking too much. I was finally here, and there was no parking. Where did people park their vehicles? After thirty minutes of hunting for a spot to put my car in, I actually had to walk a half hour to get to the client's apartment. Everything so far was a challenge. I didn't go for walks, and I was always in the sofa with my beer and watching my soap opera. Not to be all disgusting, but I had been doing that for two to three months now. To my surprise, I was still not obese.

There was an intercom, and I pressed number 2. It rang. A guy answered and buzzed me into the building. I was so fascinated. Perhaps there was no such building like this in the island where I came from. The door was already open, but I still knocked. There were two guys in their thirties, and one was in a wheelchair. He had a screen, and he used his eyes to type. I was so thrilled with everything that I was seeing with my two eyes. The other health care worker demonstrated how things were done and how the client wanted everything completed during the shift. And he asked me if I had any questions through his device.

I said, "When do you want me to start? Am I hired?"

They both laughed. He sent an email to Linda and confirmed that I passed his qualifications. I received a text message from them, saying that I could start this coming weekend. Wow. Just like that? I drove straight back to where I currently lived. Perhaps I didn't really have the money to explore the city. I couldn't believe I just got hired. Saturday and Sunday in San Francisco with a client. That was amazing.

A month passed by, and everything was going smoothly with me and the client. I had more job offers with different clients, but this time it was not with a cerebral palsy patient but with a ninety-year-old lady in a retirement home. She needed someone with her for twelve hours every night. But where was I going to stay in the daytime if I took this weekday client? I lived too far from the city, and I didn't want to ruin my poor vehicle. I really wanted to take it. I wanted to get out from where I was. But one more question was, where was I going to take a shower? This was insane. With my weekend client, I guess.

I took the job, and now I was working seven days a week now. Some friends said that I was overworking myself and should only work five days a week because it was not healthy. They were all right. A person must have a life in this lifetime. Why was I overworking myself? Maybe because I didn't agree with the world's system? And I might end up longing for a boyfriend to fill that loneliness. Not every time you need your friends, they'll be present. But a partner, the both of you got to go home in the same roof and tell each other about the stuff that happened that day. It didn't get that sad compared to being single. I guess that was the benefit of being all alone. I got to move to places where I wanted and whenever I wanted.

What was the plan? To sleep in my car and see where it led me. I packed two suitcases that fit just right in the trunk of my car. I put some toiletries, even though I had no idea if I'd get to use this stuff on weekdays. I was bringing three heavy comforters and two pillows, and it would go straight to the back seat. And I had a backpack with my wallet and identification card. It felt like I was going camping for weeks. And so my manhunt began. I mean, my life's journey started now.

It took me a while to find the building where I needed to meet my client. It was my first night with her. San Francisco was a difficult place to drive in. There were so many one-way streets, and police cars were everywhere. And to my surprise, homeless people were all over the streets. I didn't understand. This beautiful city had them too? Perhaps I could consider myself the new homeless in town. I parked my car in the basement of the building after I received a permit. One thing I learned here was that this city did not give free access parking to anyone. It was either you paid hourly or you worked for the business is based in the building.

I clocked in as soon as I got inside and was sent to the fourth floor. I started at 7:00 p.m. I met this wonderful lady who was in her nineties. She was drinking her coffee and listening to symphony orchestra. A pleasant welcoming from her. It didn't feel like I was there to work but to visit my grandma. An offer of coffee was delightful. We talked and talked, and then it was 11:00 p.m. I helped her get ready for bed. She put on her pajamas and brushed her teeth. She took some of her vitamins. I tucked her in her bed. I turned the lights off and kept the symphony on, but I lowered the sound. I sat on the sofa in the living room and tried my best to stay up until next day morning. I did her laundry around three in the morning and folded them. I put it on top of her dresser for her to see that it was done.

It was 7:00 a.m., and she was still asleep. I wrote her a letter saying that I'd see her tonight, and I put it on top of her nightstand before I left. When I got inside my car, I laid down the driver's seat and stretched. I was so happy and had the biggest smile I could ever have in my entire life. I was so fortunate to have someone like Ms. Nancy as a client. She was a retired professor from Lombard Street. What did I know about Lombard Street? Besides that crooked street. I was so thankful. But I needed to leave this building, or else they'd end up giving me a ticket for being parked too long. But where was I going? There was nowhere to go and nowhere to park.

I went to the grocery store. Perhaps they thought I was one of the employees parked in front of the store. I'd slept in the driver's seat and put pillow on my left side so it wouldn't be too hard on my muscles. I cracked the window a little bit to get fresh air. I was not feeling starvation at the moment, but exhaustion from lack of sleep was attacking me. So I closed my eyes and was able to sleep for three to four hours. It was good enough. I went inside the grocery store and used the bathroom. I tilted my head in the sink and shampooed my hair. I washed my face and filled my water bottle and went to the commode. I ran some water on my small hand towel and wiped my entire body. I felt fresh. I bought some dark coffee and a sandwich. I cut it in two and saved the other part for when I got hungry again. I stayed inside my car until 6:00 p.m. and browsed for places to live in. I had no luck. Everything was expensive. After a month, I needed to go back to where I was staying and put my stuff in the storage. If I got lucky here in San Francisco. How I wish I could explore the city, except I had no idea how to, and I didn't really have the money. I had hope that that day would come for me.

It was the end of the week. I was so excited to go to my other client. I was so looking forward to that shower. Ugh, the fresh water on my skin was so soothing. I shampooed my hair twice and soaped my body twice as well. I showered in the morning and at night, just after the client went to bed, to take those nasty body odors from my weekdays.

On my second consistent week being a new homeless citizen of San Francisco, I encountered a health care worker like me named Norlin. We were both doing our separate laundry for our clients, and she was fussing about her roommate leaving the city. Now she had to pay the full amount of the bedroom she was renting. I asked her if I could rent the other bed, if we could be roommates. She looked at me from head to toe, and I did my best to sell myself on how good of a person I was. I wonder why I did not end up in the marketing department. She said yes. She gave me a key and said where the address was. She asked me how many stuff I had, and I laughed at her. I said I only had two suitcases. I thanked her with my life.

Two weeks of living in my vehicle was an experience. Someone opening their doors for you was unimaginable. The heavens were always watching over me. So far, within those weeks, I hadn't set up a tent on the street of Dolores Park with the rest of the people who lived there. I typed in the address in my phone map, and it led me to City College of San Francisco. The house Norlin lived in was in front of the college. Maybe this was my opportunity to take some units to add with my schoolwork. I went inside the house and settled all my stuff in the bedroom. The first thing I did was put all my blankets on the twin bed and slept. Right then, I wasn't thinking about anyone and anything, but I would have a nice proper rest. When I woke up, Norlin was gone and left me a text message saying that she had a schedule with a client today. I replied to her with a big thank you and that I would put my first day of rent in an envelope and leave it on top of her bed.

This was amazing. I was now a normal taxpaying citizen of San Francisco. I couldn't believe I just leveled up myself within two weeks of being a homeless person. I really do believe when you want something and try to chase it, you'll definitely get it. Should I try to be the next president of the United States? I arranged my side table and put all my moisturizers and lotions on top. My stomach was now rumbling, and because I got paid with a good amount from last week, I thought I deserved a good meal. Two blocks from the house was a Chinese restaurant. I just hoped the food was not that greasy. It was scary to eat in a place you were not familiar with because you ended up wasting money when you were not satisfied. Plus when the orange chicken was very much drowned in oil. But I had to try it. It was the only nearby Chinese restaurant.

It was an eight-minute walk to the restaurant. I sat down and ordered white rice and sweet-and-sour pork. The Chinese man brought me a teapot and a cup of ice-cold water. I was so mesmerized. I couldn't imagine living in this city. San Francisco, to be exact. Who would have thought? I was so sure this wouldn't sink in for another five years or so. There were so many people in San Francisco. It was so exciting and inviting.

The waiter put my order on the table and said, "Enjoy!" with a Chinese accent. I just wanted to give him a hug. I couldn't contain the joy that I was feeling inside my body,

ARE YOU HAPPY?

but if I did that, everyone was going to think I was a weirdo and most likely kick me out of the restaurant. I sat still, ate my food, and thanked the heavens for everything that was happening in my life. Okay. There wouldn't be any leftover orange chicken. This was just so tasty. I took this as my reward for all the hard work I had been doing since I moved to the city, plus a pat in the back. "Good job, Amelie."

Months passed by, and life had been the same. Ms. Nancy surprised Norlin and me with a *Nutcracker* ticket as our Christmas gift. She said that we worked too hard and deserved something very nice. She wasn't going with us. She wanted the both of us to experience it. I had never seen a ballet performance in my entire life. I only saw them in television. I didn't know how to thank her for this experience. I called Norlin and told her about the tickets, and she was surprised. It was one week before the performance. I browsed my wardrobe to see if I had something formal to wear. I found skinny slacks and a nice white polo shirt. I put them on my bed so that I wouldn't forget next week. And I'd be reminded I was going to the *Nutcracker* ballet.

After six months of being with my cerebral palsy client on weekends, I decided to stop caring for him, to stop working on weekends, and to look for a church. I looked for some organizations where I could get involved too. I thought I was doing well, and everything was going smoothly. Maybe I could try out some things here in the city. I could learn a new language or experience a salsa class or pottery courses. I called my bank and changed my address, and I also updated my driver's license.

It was 5:00 p.m. I met Norlin at 455 Franklin Street. I took a taxi because parking downtown was impossible. It took her fifteen minutes to find parking, but luckily, she found one before the show started. We took some nice pictures at the front of the building before we went inside, and my phone wouldn't stop clicking. The inside of the hall was spectacular. The architecture was incredible, and there were lots of people in suits and dresses with their families ready to watch those beautiful ballerinas. Norlin and I looked for our seats, and to our surprise, we were on the second-floor front seat. How could we thank Ms. Nancy enough for giving us this kind of gift? We were both mesmerized by the ceiling of the building and the front where the performers did their presentation. Everything was amusing. Here it was, finally. They dimmed the lights and opened the lovely big curtains in front of us. And the ballerinas were dancing gently and beautifully.

I received a text message from my brother all the way from Manila. Mom and Dad would be visiting him and his wife for a week, and they planned to go the beach the entire week. He was making me jealous that it would be a fun and exciting week. He also added to his message that if I went to Manila next week, he would get a case of beer. Was he a fool or what? Sibling treacheries were never-ending even when you guys were in your late twenties. I sent him a reply after an hour. "Hi. See you on Monday. Pick me up."

I bought a ticket for next week. My flight was leaving Sunday, so I should get there on a Monday. Now what I was going to say to my employer? After a week, on the day of my flight, I went to my employers' office and started giving an excuse that I had an emergency and needed to go back to my country. Perhaps something happened. Good thing I was crying the entire night because of emotional distress from this guy from the village where I came from. He was making me feel like I was wanted by someone, but I was not. Because of my own stupidity, I bit on it, which I should not have. I ended up putting myself in a hole and into his games. My pride and ego were eating me extremely. So that morning, my eyes were all red and swollen, and everyone at the office thought that someone died in my family. They did actually ask me if someone passed away. I didn't say, "Yes, someone did pass away." I just nodded at what she said. Hilarious.

So I flew to Manila and was crying the entire time inside the plane. I had a blanket cover over me. My eyes were just embarrassing. I saw my brother waiting for me at the airport, and he was giving me a lecture the entire night. It was 2:00 a.m. already. His speeches were never-ending. I've had ten bottles of beer, and I couldn't believe I was still standing and hearing him say how stupid I was. The next day, I found out my parents were actually going to Sydney for seven days. So they were spending a week in Manila and a week in Australia. My mom asked me if I wanted to go, and I straight up said, "No, thank you."

And you know what her response was? "No, you're going with us to Sydney. So you buy your flight now. Here is our flight information, and you have to match it."

My brother was giggling, and my sister-in-law was laughing. They knew that I couldn't say no to our mother. It would be nice to spend time with my parents before I head back to San Francisco and work again. My life has been interesting, and I had a lot of experiences since I moved to the city. I shared everything to my parents during our time in Sydney. They wanted to take a tour bus to the Blue Mountains, but I suggested that I'd rent a car and drive us there instead. I had never driven on the right side of a car, but I confirmed to them that I experienced it before. I couldn't be in a group of people. My anxiety would be triggered.

I went to Triple AAA in downtown Sydney. While waiting for the guy to finish up with my reservation for tomorrow first thing in the morning, I made short talk with him.

To my surprise, he offered me a full-time job. As I walked back to the hotel, I was thinking clearly if what I heard was right. "Guess what just happened. I got a job offer at the rental car full time."

My parents looked at me like I made it up. My mom went along with what I said and started asking me questions. I could feel they didn't believe me. The funny part was when I went back to pick up the rental car in the morning, my dad said, "I'll go with you so I can get my walk first thing in the morning."

I think that was a trick. Because when we got to the rental place, he asked the guy, who was actually the owner, if he really did offer me a job. I was so embarrassed and thought, *Oh my god, he's going to say no.*

He said, "Yes, I offered your daughter a full-time job and told her to send me an email or call me. She has my information." My dad was surprised and looked at me. "Hey, she wasn't lying at all." Wow, I didn't know what to say. My parents said that they could leave me behind and I could work there, but where was I going to stay? Well, there were rooms for rent in Sydney that cost $500 a month. But what about my things in San Francisco? What was I going to do with all of those things? I just moved to San Francisco. I was tired of moving here and there. But it was so tempting to stay behind. Maybe I could send Norlin a message, and she could rent my bed space out so there was income coming in for her. But I needed to leave all my stuff and would be back after a year or two. What should I do?

I didn't think Mom was also helping me. "That would be a good experience for you, to live in a different country with a full-time job. Getting an offer like this does not happen anywhere."

But I couldn't just leave my stuff in San Francisco. So far, I was having a great experience in the city, and I didn't want to leave that lifestyle yet. I flew back to the States and went back to my work as a caregiver. I started working seven days a week so I wouldn't notice my lonely life, or else I might end up packing all my stuff and flying back to Sydney for another new life journey.

CHAPTER 2

Meeting Oliver

Single life can be lonely at times. I guess everything in this existence has its negative and positive energy. Getting the material stuff you want and need without asking your parents or any family members, not anyone around you, will definitely make your heart flutter. It feels good, and you just can't explain it. And when you come to a point where you share it to some friends who you think are your real friends, the only responses you will hear are negative. And when you try to distance yourself from them, it's like you're in Hollywood. Everyone just starts talking shit about you. And here is my response to all of them: "I don't care at all."

Life is too full of love and excitement to focus on what other people think about my own decisions and the mistakes that I've done since day one. Come on. Get over it. I don't hover myself on getting detailed information about your life. And as I realize, a lot of people in the Bay Area here in California are alone because of the same mentality I have.

Because of that, I went on Match.com and started making a profile. I didn't think I wanted to be alone for the rest of my life. And on the other hand, I'd rather suck on what people thought about me because they didn't know me, and they only judged me based on what they saw at the current moment. I knew myself truly. At least I thought I did. Okay, hold on. It was asking me for a picture. I browsed for a good one, but not too much that showed skin. A little modest, but not too modest. I wanted to find someone who would respect me, but not too much. Someone who was old-school, who believed in God but at the same time was a little bit dirty. Oh my god, obviously there was something wrong with me mentally. I heard that this site had a lot of single people that ended matching with someone, and their relationship turned out well. So I was trying it out, and if I found someone who could tolerate my attitude, then that would be wonderful. If not, then that would suck for me.

I was thirty-one years old and still single. There must be something wrong with me. One problem of mine was that every time I dated or was at the point with someone that we were hitting it to the next level, I always ended up telling them that I wanted to get married. And that was probably the reason why they walked out on me. Pathetic. But this time, I wouldn't say it again and wouldn't put pressure on the guy. I promise. Okay, the site was asking me to put a summary of my interests. I just typed, "Looking for a relationship." I was a hypocrite. Well, it was always good to put straight up what you were looking for, wasn't it? So both sides wouldn't be wasting time. What if I found someone who only wanted a fling? I didn't want that at all. I was desperately looking for someone, not for entertainment but to settle down with. Wait, someone actually sent me a message. I had a victim. Who was this? Ugh, I had to pay? Nothing in life was free no more. And I fell for it. I just wasted my money on a one-month subscription. This should be worth it, or I'd go nuts for wasting my money and time.

I went straight to the inbox and opened the message after subscribing. Oliver just said hi to me. Okay, who was this Oliver? I clicked on his profile, and it said he was six feet tall. He was half African and half French with a little bit of curls in his hair. One more thing was that he was forty-eight years old. Wait, let me get my calculator out and subtract his age from my age. He was seventeen years older than I was? Let's see. I dated men in my age group, even men who were ten years older than I was, and I had not found not one mature enough to handle my character. And for whatever reason did I end up dating a lot of men? That was because I was desperate for a relationship, and when it came to its realization, they happened to be frightened and walked away from me. Embarrassing? Yes, it was. My high school classmates were mostly settled and had kids. When would it be my turn?

Oliver looked handsome in his picture. But was he handsome in real life too? Oh! This might be a scam. I needed to be careful, but at the same time, I definitely entertained him. Perhaps I had a lot of time? So I sent a response back to him and said, "Wow, that was quick. I just made my account like ten minutes ago. Definitely green light on your end." What was the best icebreaker? Because I had no idea. If he replied, then wonderful. If he didn't, then good night. In less than five minutes, he replied. Oliver and I conversed the entire night. Oh my god, I had to finish our conversation because he had to wake up at 5:00 a.m. to work. According to him, he had been an arborist for the city of San Francisco for thirty years now. Wow, wasn't that amazing?

The conversation consisted of both our interests and jobs. We exchanged numbers after a week of chatting online. I didn't know if it was a good idea that we exchanged numbers because now we are sending each other messages every second twenty-four seven. What was I complaining of? This was what I wanted. That's why I went to the online dating app. Was this too much texting, or was it because we were getting to know each other? I asked him if I could hear his voice over the phone to make sure he didn't sound weird. And after five minutes, he called me. I wanted him. Yup, I was marrying this guy. But I couldn't tell him that, right? I needed to control my vocabulary and blur out the words *relationship* and *marriage*, unless I wanted him to walk out on me. You have to understand when a woman reaches her peak in their thirties, they're desperate. At least I know I was. His voice sounded hot, but he was still seventeen years older than I was. I shouldn't be carried away. I haven't met him in person.

He said, "I love your voice. It's soft." Right. That definitely was a lie. I would not be negative about this, but we did know that when guys said things like this, it was complete bull. What could I say? "Oh, thank you. You're so kind." Now I was bullshitting myself. It was all right. I was so entertained by this.

I was inside the bedsheet, and gladly my roommate was not home. I got the chance to giggle and felt like I was back in high school. Oliver and I set a date for our first meeting. After chatting online and on text messages for two weeks, we decided to see each other. After he got off work around 3:00 p.m., he texted me and said that he would just take a shower and change his clothes. We would see each other at Jane on Fillmore Coffee Shop around 5:30 p.m. I was glad that today was my day off. I had the entire day to watch my soap operas and eat my ramen noodles with a hard-boiled egg. Today was a lazy day for me. I was in my pajamas the whole day, without washing my face and brushing my teeth. I was such a disgusting person. I felt bad for Oliver, but of course, why would I say such a thing to him? I'd definitely change my habit, only if I knew that he was a hygienic person. I know, I was full of crap.

I put on my blue converse, polo shirt, and my jeans after I showered. I brushed my teeth and made sure I ate a lot of mint leaves and mint chewing gums. I had lemon tea too. I felt like I was trying hard, and later on, I'd realize it was not worth any effort. That I wasted my time. Oh well. Who knows. It might be different. I took an Uber to Fillmore St. and California St. I sent Oliver a message saying that I just arrived. He was running late. What? It should be me who was late because I was the woman, not him. This was one red flag. Nope. First meeting and he was making the girl wait. I found a bench in front of the coffee shop and sat for a moment while waiting for him. He texted me and said that he was on Fillmore St. and he was approaching.

My phone rang. "Where are you, Amelie?"

I walked toward the intersection and stood at the side of the crosswalk and told him exactly where I was, and he said he was in a Toyota truck turning left. He asked if it was okay for me to hop into his truck because there was no parking. He had been driving around for fifteen minutes, looking for a place to park his vehicle. He asked for us to go straight to the beach. There he was. I could see him on the other street on a red light, talking over the phone. Oh no, another red flag for him. The light turned green, and he was about to turn left, and he saw me at the corner. I waved at him, and he smiled back at me. He stopped in the middle of the street and stared at me. Everything stopped, and we only saw each other at that moment. Was it love at first sight? I was feeling it, and thought I was in a movie with a background love song, until all the honking started because now Oliver was blocking the intersection.

ARE YOU HAPPY?

The people on the street saw what happened. Some were laughing, but some were giggling because they thought it was romantic. Was it? I didn't know. Let's see. He pulled over on the side of California Street, and I hopped in. He put the emergency light on temporarily so we could double park while we stared at each other and said hi. We were literally staring at each other, and we both had huge smiles with no words. He looked so different from his picture. He looked a mess and a bit dirty in his picture, but he was handsome and tall in person, with brown skin and long legs. So this was the combination of black and white? Yikes.

He started driving toward Lands' End Beach, and we were still staring at each other. Honestly, he was hot. Thank you, Match.com, for having someone like him in your site. Oliver kept telling me how pretty I was, and he never thought he would encounter someone like me. I knew for a fact that he was just saying these words to make me like him, perhaps. He was a guy.

"Oh, thank you, Oliver." I was so fooling myself right now. This was so awkward. He asked me if I wanted some beer to take to the beach or a bottle of wine.

Without blinking, I said, "Yes, wine would be nice." It was not that I was an alcoholic, but who would say no to wine on a first date? So we stopped at the store, and I waited inside the truck while he went inside and chose a bottle of wine. We parked in front of the beach because it was too cold to put a blanket on the sand. We stayed inside the truck. He pulled out a plastic cup and opened the bottle. Before anything else, we toasted for our first meeting but couldn't help but stare at each other still. I said my apologies in advance and started mumbling stories, and we both laughed. I drank more wine to get a little bit of a buzz to help me not think that I was a woman, and I needed to hush my mouth and be gentle so that I'd get some respect. At this current situation, we were in the same mood of excitement and laughter, and I would be myself. When I looked at the time, it was already 11:00 p.m., and we finished the entire bottle. To my surprise, he reached behind the passenger seat and grabbed another bottle of wine. We were both laughing hard.

"Wow, you came prepared," I told him.

As the night passed, we ended up making our very own storybook. Pokeke, our main character, was male and six feet tall with a short skirt like Sailor Moon. Pokeke had high heels and a shirt that only covered his nipples with a tie in the middle. He had missing teeth and was homeless with a grocery cart full of stuff. And every time he was in a rush, he ran real fast with his grocery cart. And because of his short skirt, his granny underwear showed. There was a security guard outside with a flashlight coming toward us. Because it was 2:00 a.m., they were telling everyone to leave the site. I didn't think I was disturbed with our short storytelling, and it didn't seem like Oliver was disturbed either. As we looked for another spot to hang out in, we imagined that Pokeke was somewhere on the street and walking with his cart, so we needed to go slowly as we drove.

It seemed like not one of us wanted to go home yet. I wish I could invite him to the house in the living room, but I was currently renting, and I was not allowed to bring any boys home. I was feeling tired though. It was 4:30 a.m. Before we parted, he asked, "May I kiss you, Amelie?"

I don't think I encountered any guy who asked me if they could kiss me. It was always someone trying to kiss quickly without permission. I thought he was a gentleman. I was speechless for a couple of seconds and said yes. His kiss was so amazing. I felt like I was Cinderella and my time was up and I needed to go, but I didn't want to go. I didn't want him to stop. How I wish I could tell him, "Keep going. If you stop, you die." Wow, I loved it. I thought, *I love him already*.

It was 5:00 a.m. It was time for us to go and get some rest. We both had a horrible baggy eyes, and it was seriously dark and embarrassing. He dropped me off at home and gave me another a kiss of goodbye and see you later. He held my arms and pulled me toward him and hugged me. I waved goodbye as I went upstairs and opened the door. I went straight to the bedroom and removed my pants, put my eye cover, and was knocked out. Good night at 5:30 a.m. I had so much fun. I never wanted the day to end.

CHAPTER 3

I Can't Do This Anymore

It had been two months since I'd been seeing Oliver, and I had not seen where he lived. I didn't know anything about his friends or family. He picked me up at my place around 6:00 p.m. and dropped me back home around 9:00 p.m. to 10:00 p.m. He had been consistent.

After picking me up, we went straight to the park and watched a movie on his iPad. We chatted about how our days went by. I couldn't do this anymore. What was I, a slut? He picked me up at night when the sun went down and dropped me back home. What were we even? There was no label.

I told him straight up, "Oliver, I just want to make myself clear. I apologize for being straightforward, but when I checked your profile, it says that you're looking for a relationship, and I thought that we are in the same boat. But it's been two months since we dated, and we never, not once, eaten out in a restaurant, not even in a burger joint. We never went to a movie theater or even went bowling. I think that this is a huge mistake. I'm not looking for friends with benefits. I'm looking for relationship." *Okay, Amelie, you did it again.* Well, I felt like I was being used for his entertainment, and I was not going to suck it up just because he was handsome, kissed really good, and I felt complete when he hugged me. I didn't want to expect that something would be there and wait. Then later on, he would say, "I'm sorry, but you're mistaken. I'm not looking for relationship."

Here's the problem. I actually told him this in a message. I texted it instead of calling him. I gave him a day for us to communicate before I blocked him. I just completely lost interest in him. He was defensive with his response toward me and said he is interested in me and wanted the same thing as me. "I think we just keep doing what we are doing, and it will come itself. We take our time and not put pressure on it."

Are you kidding me? Go with the flow and continue with what we are doing? He was making me feel like a homeless prostitute. I already went along with his consistency, but he kept me in the car every time we were together. He didn't even bring me anywhere. Obviously, this was not going anywhere at all. That same day, I blocked him. I just didn't want to hear from him again. It was bullshit. I couldn't believe I allowed him to treat me that way. I couldn't blame him entirely. Somehow, it was my fault. I had control of my decisions, and I was the one who put myself in that situation. Ugh. What an experience.

I called and made an appointment for an hour massage in Japantown. Luckily, they had walk-in that day. I took an Uber and checked in at the massage spa. This should help me forget what happened those entire two months with that Oliver guy. I dipped into the hot water after I took my robe off. I couldn't believe he told me to go with the flow because we just met. Ridiculous. I loved myself more than any men I encountered, even if it's Mark Ruffalo. While the Korean lady was massaging me, I was back to my thoughts that I was all alone again here in San Francisco. I thought that when you're in the city, it's easier to find someone to be with. I guess it's not. Perhaps everyone is too busy to be in a relationship. The only consistent thing in my life right now were my clients and agencies, which I was very much thankful for. But the other consistent thing was me being single. I partied all alone, ae in the restaurant alone, and watched my drama with my wine and crying alone because someone died from cancer. And my pimples were being sensitive as well. What's new? So I wouldn't think about Oliver because it was not my loss.

I don't think I was that thrilled to go back to Match.com any time soon. I felt like I'd end up meeting someone with the same mentality. They'd tell me the same thing Oliver said: "It takes time. Go with the flow." My life was too boring. And I didn't want to go with the flow anymore with anyone, because later on, whose lose was it? It was mine, because I would give my everything, my all, and they'd only say, "Amelie, I have decided that it's not working out." Well, to tell you all the truth, it was not working out for me too. My subscription with Match.com ended.

A month had passed, and my life had no activities besides my full-time job. I tried my best to look for something to involve myself in and maybe meet new people and make some friends, but it never happened. I was kind of an introvert but also an extrovert and at the same time a weird person. When I looked at some people and felt like I could read what they were thinking, my anxiety would attack me, and this was why I didn't tag along with groups. I thought about a book club. Oh, how about international travelers who met up in pubs and talked about their experiences? Except that they were all in their early twenties. I was thirty-one years old, and it felt like my life was just starting, that I just finished high school. Wasn't that horrible? I was like a late bloomer, a wild ugly flower in the desert. Was I being too harsh on myself?

Another month went by without me being noticed. Seriously, time nowadays was like a ninja. It went by so fast, and my age did too. I went to POF.com to see if I could start fishing for any man interested on going on a date. Here I go again. I never learn. But how was I going to find myself a date or relationship or a husband if I didn't try going out on dates? No one would ever ask me out from work or public because my face was not that approachable. I sounded so desperate. Well, who wouldn't in my situation and my age? When I turned twenty-five and was single, I got so scared and said, "This is it for me." I was scared to grow old alone. Because of that, I was on a hunt for another adventure with POF.com.

I was home the entire day watching my drama, and I ordered Chinese food. I was craving for orange chicken and chow mien. I left my account open with the online dating site to see who would send a message. There were eight messages in my inbox. Wow, don't you think that's too many? Probably a lot of men were feeling the same way I was feeling. Bored? No doubt. Everyone in the city worked their life away. There was no time to relax so they could pay for their bills. I was so lucky that my rent was so affordable, that I could have a life and have time for myself. I had a sip of my beer and opened the inbox. I looked at each message and waited a minute. Hold on. Oliver? How did he find me here? I mean, why was he on this site? I guess he had the same question as I did. This was insane. After two months of no communication. Wow. My heart did stop. I did miss him tremendously. But I didn't want to go through what I went through with him. I lost respect toward myself. I felt like he disrespected me and that I was a nobody.

I opened his message, and he said, "Hi, Amelie. How are you? Can I speak to you please?" He only sent it like half an hour ago. I ignored the rest of the messages from other men and sent Oliver a response right away. I unblocked him and told him that he could send me messages now. And he called me. I didn't know what to say. I was nervous, but I answered the call. Quickly, when I said hi to him, he apologized and wanted to get things right with me. He asked for a second chance. I felt pressured right now. I didn't want to say no because I liked him a lot. I missed him. But I didn't want to say yes because I'd come out easy. Let me think. I didn't know anything about him. I didn't know where he lived, where he exactly worked, and what kind of job he did, besides him working for the City of San Francisco.

I made a deal with him and gave him a second chance. I mean, what was there to lose, right? So he picked me up, and for the second time, he apologized to me for making me feel that way. He said that he would bring me to where he lived so that I would see. He parked his truck and said that we needed to walk to his house. Wait, his house?

"Here we are." He opened the small gate, and we climbed the stairs, which was seven steps. He unlocked the front door and let me in, and he closed the door and said to me, "Welcome to my house."

Okay, hold on. "Your parents are not here today?"

His parents didn't live in the same roof as him. It was really his house. It was his house? His parents lived next door. Then why was it he never invited me in instead of picking me up from home and hanging out in his truck? And that went on for two months consistently. Now I felt more ill. All this time, I thought that he slept on the couch at his parents' house. I thought that he was an ordinary guy who just worked for the city. But he was not just an ordinary guy. He had a Victorian home, and it was fully paid. He put a bar and blocked the front door. I didn't understand why. I didn't ask him, and I didn't want to know. But I was just waiting to jump and run in case that door popped open. Obviously, he was hiding something, and he was not saying anything. But that would come some other time.

After an hour, he wanted to grab coffee at this café nearby Lands' End before he dropped me off. I was honestly getting suspicious. Why was I still hanging out with him? My body was so stiff. I wanted him to hug me and kiss me. I wanted him bad. But my instinct was telling me that there was something wrong. He ordered two lattes, and we drove to the beach and parked in front. I felt like I was in this scenario before. It was like a dream, or did it happen a couple of months ago with Oliver? It was 11:00 p.m. I didn't saying anything about going home, and I wanted to see how this entire night would go. He said that it was a great night and that he'd drop me home because he started work early the next day.

I was in my bed, tucked in inside my sheets and comforter, staring at the ceiling. I felt numb. I couldn't feel my head and legs, together with my chest. Besides my boobs being small, it felt numb too. Why did I want Oliver so bad? I was so confused and speechless about knowing more of him. Did he want to be just friends with me or just a fling? So he never bothered telling me true information about his life? What was I feeling right now? I just felt bad for myself. Maybe if I went with the flow just like he said a couple of months ago, then maybe emotions would develop. I couldn't overthink this stuff. I put my eye cover on and went to sleep.

CHAPTER 4

The Proposal

On Friday morning, February 13, 2020, Oliver made plans. I didn't know what it was. He never said anything. And after knowing him for a short time, when he had a surprise, it never lasted ten minutes. He ended up telling me because of his excitement before I headed to work Friday night to my client who had brain cancer in Belvedere. Her name was Jane, by the way. She was the sweetest lady I ever met. I loved her so much. She fought for those people she loved and cared for. She was a strong brave woman who was now in heaven. If I could go back to when I was a child and be asked who I wanted to be when I grew up, I would say I wanted to be her.

The plan was made before I headed to work. Oliver would pick me up early that morning. He didn't tell me where we were going. He kept saying that it would be a forty-five-minute drive from where I lived, and he told me to just relax because it was a surprise. I didn't really like surprises. Things got intense, and I got nervous. And he said not to eat. "Save your appetite, Amelie."

Okay. The last guy who told me to save my appetite years ago went bad for me. I didn't eat the entire day because he was going to bring me to this beautiful Japanese restaurant in Fresno. I was so excited and obeyed his order. When the waitress handed us the menu, he said that he would order for the both of us. And I thought that that was the sweetest thing ever. I never had any man order me food. The waitress approached us and had two plates. She slid a plate in front of me. There were four pieces of sushi and nothing else. I pretty much expected a buffet, if he knew what I meant. But I guess he didn't. My starving stomach was in a riot inside me, screaming for justice. The only thing that was on my mind that entire date was how I wish I could run to McDonald's and order five cheeseburgers with fries. But if this ever happened again with this guy I was with right now, I would definitely get mad and demand for a giant plate of pasta, or at least don't pick me up ever. Experiences made you armed. Which was good for you but bad for them. Well, I was only having coffee. He at least allowed me to have that. How about one Madeleine bread? Ugh. What would I wear this time? How would I know what to properly dress in when I had no idea where I was going? That same guy who fed me four pieces of sushi, after our dinner, he opened his trunk and grabbed a badminton racket and set a net for us to play. I thanked the heavens that that night I was wearing my converse and had my pants on. I almost wore high heels because in my head, it was a date. I would have been running around with my heels on, chasing for the birdie. This was insane. As usual, I would wear my polo shirt and jeans. Blue polo shirt, to be exact, with my blue beat Chucks.

    We were on the road. I couldn't contain myself and this nervousness that I was feeling. What if he was actually going to bring me somewhere to murder me? Would this be the end of my life? On a handsome French Creole guy's hand? What if he just stabbed me? That would suck and would be seriously horrible. It would also hurt bad. I never thought about being stabbed. Or what if he raped me after he killed me? At least rape me before you kill me so that I can still feel the pleasure before I bid goodbye to this wonderful earth. I had so many rambling thoughts in my head, but I can't say anything to him because he might think I was weird.

I was being badly skittish that he noticed and said, "Relax, we'll be there soon."

Yes. We will be there soon. Woodside California? What was in here? I never came here in my entire life and never thought this city existed. Or that was because I had been in San Francisco for three years only. I got it. I could see a park. Filoli Gardens? Wow. I was speechless. I looked at him with awe. I was surprised and delighted. Not a word from me. I gave him a small shy smile. He held my hands as we walked the inside the building.

This was a beautiful place. We went through the building then toward the back where the garden was. It had a massive pool and a lot of pretty flowers. I didn't know what Oliver was looking for, but he wanted some privacy in the garden. If he wanted to just get a smooch from me, then I think I'd rather leave now. Besides, I don't think that that is possible as you can see this is a tourist site. But he found a bench that was under an arch with wrapped plants and flowers. We walked toward it and both sat at the same time. The moment my bum hit the bench, he kneeled quickly with a red box on his hands. My mouth was wide open, and I couldn't breathe. I couldn't even speak.

He said, "Amelie, will you marry me?"

Oh my god! At the age of thirty-two, this was it. I was getting married. Of course, it was a *yes*. But how should I say yes to this type of situation? I was already thinking about a wedding dress. Where should I have it done? How about my makeup and hair color? Wait, I needed to say yes first. Here was how I said yes. I covered my face and said yes. I was a complete weirdo. I was so embarrassed, and I didn't know why.

He said, "Amelie, look at me. Will you marry me?"

"Yes. Yes. Yes," I whispered in his ear while he hugged me. He gave me the box and told me to open it. I didn't want to see it. OMG! It was probably a lollipop ring. He was playing games with me. I didn't think he was serious at all. "I can't. I don't want to. Here's my finger. Put it on."

He started laughing and asked me why didn't want to see the ring. Oh well, fake or not, at least it was romantic. He slid the ring on my finger, and I felt the ring. It was thin. Whoa. Hold on. There was one stone on the ring, and it was hard. Most especially, it was not sticky.

I hugged him and I said, "Thank you. I love you." While I was hugging him, I tried to look at the ring on my finger, but the sun's ray was on my eyes. I put my hands closer so I could see it. Oh, wow. He got me a princess cut diamond ring. This was insane. For real, at the age of thirty-two? And all this time, I thought that I would be an old maid. How dare I predict my own life. *I would love to be with you for the rest of my life.* So this was the feeling of being engaged. I wanted to start calling everyone to announce and to celebrate. But I wouldn't do that. Instead, I would take a picture of the ring under the sun, and I would post it on Facebook with the hashtag #FinallyEngaged. What did you expect? This was the twenty-first century. Everything was on social media.

It was a lovely day in the garden, but time is being fast-forwarded, and we needed to leave. He wanted to take me to this seafood restaurant in Halfmoon Bay that was in front of the water. Surprisingly, the restaurant offered some Gumbo. I ordered that, and he got some fish and chips. I was surprised he didn't order for me. Instead, he told me to order whatever I wanted to eat. I asked him if I could order two or three meals, and his response was a yes. The other lady must have been in her thirties. She kept staring at my ring. It felt so good to be stared at, especially if it was a woman. Even Oliver noticed her glancing not just once but twice. I felt so amazing. I had someone to call home, mi amore. This was what I was mainly looking for—someone to eat with, watch movies with, have sex with, rant about problems at work regarding coworkers, etc. Someone to laugh with, to drink coffee with, and to pester when bored. Someone to wrestle and break their bones and say, "*Yes*, I've won, and I claim my title as the strongest person in this household." It felt wonderful.

It was 5:00 p.m. I needed to head to Belvedere for work. It would take us at least forty-five minutes to an hour. While he was driving, I kept taking different pictures of the ring on my finger. We talked. We laughed. Finally, we arrived in Tiburon. We had an extra forty-five minutes. And he pulled over to the side by a tree, where it was.

I looked at him and said, "Thank you. I'm very happy. I don't know what to say." To be honest, I had never experienced this, where a guy proposed to a girl, especially to me. I always thought that there was something wrong with me. I always asked myself, *Why is it that I'm not girlfriend material?* Every guy I encountered would come and go. What was wrong with me? It made me feel like I was nothing. That I was not that pretty. Not worth a guy's time. Good conversationalist, yes. Good company, check. After that, they would all disappear. Now I knew. Like they all said, patience. Everything came at the right time. And I think that we are on the right time right now. He just held my hands and kissed me. And for couple of minutes, we ended up kissing deeply. I couldn't do this anymore. My blood was rushing inside my body, and it was about to explode.

CHAPTER 5

Wedding Planning

After the proposal, I couldn't sit still. I started organizing the kind of wedding I wanted—my dream wedding. It was either a grand wedding where all families would come and celebrate with us or an elopement. I always dreamed of eloping in Italy, in front of an old historic castle, with my beautiful wedding dresses. Only the photographer and the person who would certify us as a married couple, plus me and Oliver, would be there. That was my first choice.

I was a foster child, and I never had a real close family from my foster parents' entire clan besides my brother who was also adopted. But he was in the Philippines with his wife and one-year-old son. He was working as an IT engineer for an American company based in Manila. It would actually be perfect if we did it in Italy because we would have our privacy. And after the wedding, we could rent a vehicle and go on a road trip for our honeymoon. Honeymooning in the same place where you lived was quite ridiculous because you'd be thinking about your work. It was just right there. It would be difficult to relax. But I was not sure where exactly in Italy. All I knew was I wanted it in a castle. Then have some pasta with wine. Bellissima!

The second option was Napa County. I loved the idea of getting married in a vineyard since I was in high school. Oliver and I both loved wine and cheese. We traveled to Tiburon and San Rafael to different stores, hunting for new products of cheese and wine for fun. But with extra time on our hands, we checked in to a hotel in Glen Allen for one night and tried different wine tastings all over Napa. I had so much fun with this person.

    I found the perfect place for our wedding. It was V. Sattui in St. Helena. I loved everything that I saw on the internet, so I made an appointment for a walk through. Oliver couldn't come with me, so I went by myself. It took me at least an hour from San Francisco to the vineyard. I met with the wedding coordinator name Allison, and she made the entire tour less stressful and relaxing. And she even gave me two cards for wine tasting so that Oliver and I could later choose what kind of wine we would want to serve our guests. I loved it. Everything about this place was just wonderful and beautiful. After the meeting, I went straight to the city and showed Oliver the papers I received from V. Sattui. It was a bit pricey, but we would both put money on the table. But having some guests meant we had to do catering. And the cost depended on the number of people coming. Plus the music for entertainment and the giveaways that also cost how much each. And because it was in St. Helena, not a lot might come because it was an hour away or two from our family. We did want the wedding to be memorable and not just throw away money on one day and later on have problem paying bills. Besides, this was the twenty-first century. Everyone went to the court to be married. And they went straight to restaurants for celebration. I was in between, but it was okay. We had two years before we got married. It was perfect. I had two locations to choose, either Italy or Napa County.

Now let me think about the wedding dress. I couldn't believe I was definitely getting married. I was so happy and excited. I was in San Francisco, and I was in a perfect place to hunt for wedding dresses. I called Jin Wang in Union Square and made an appointment. *Yes*. It was booked. I made another one with Winnie Couture, and that was a check. To be honest, I thought my dress would be much more important than anything else in this event. I had to be pretty. This was a one-time big time for me. And the photographer needed to be the best photographer ever so that once I age and hit my fifties, I could go back to the pictures and say that I was young once, with no line and wrinkle on my face.

As a caregiver, I had so many clients I could not count in my fingers that were in their eighties and nineties who were still alert and active. They coached me on how to take care of my skin, which was a great honor to hear from them. It was like a tutorial every time I went to see them to help them. A lot of them only had lines and didn't have any wrinkles because of the consistent care they did. They applied moisturizers and other stuff that helped the skin maintain its youth and tightness. Moving to San Francisco in August 2018 made me change my perspective on how to respect my skin more than the routine I had maintained for myself. I added some serums and youth oil and vitamins with a lot of fruits.

Vintage pink would be a nice color for my wedding day. I didn't want to overdo the color because it would not be pleasant to the eyes. Ugh. Could you imagine a heavy dark pink? The ceremony with all the tables, the flowers, the giveaways, and everything would just be heavy pink, including the bridesmaids. It was awful and sad. I started sending out emails to some photographers and bakeries that made cakes here in the city. I couldn't seem to remember how many businesses I sent inquiries to, but it would be so much fun once they would all respond. My email would be flooded with information.

Oliver and I talked about our budget—$50,000. We both came to terms if the second of the option would be decided, which was Napa with V. Sattui. But if we chose to go with the first option, then it might be less than $10,000, which was more reasonable. But we had two years. Actually, I had two years to finalize my thoughts, and he didn't mind if I took charge of the wedding planning, as long as it was not crappy. Of course. It was either one for him as long as I was happy. Whatever I wanted, according to him. I never met anyone like Oliver. He was very considerate and thoughtful. He always thought about me first before his well-being. He was the type of guy who would jump in front of me when someone tried to stab me just to save me. He was very sweet. And I wouldn't ask for anyone else. I was very happy that I said no and walked out on boys from my past because if not, I wouldn't have had met Oliver. But it was not easy. At the age of thirty-two, I wanted to settle down already. I was hopeless and getting into depression mode. I wanted to be with someone so bad so I could also announce to everyone that I was with someone. Finally!

My high school friends were wondering why I was still single. Did you think that was not embarrassing? It seemed like there was something wrong with me. The day of my appointment for my wedding dress happened, but only with Winnie Couture. Because of COVID-19 this year, a lot of stores had closed. Jin Wang cancelled my appointment because of social distancing. Do you know how much that hurts? My heart was stabbed by Jin Wang. I was so excited and announced that I was doing a dress fitting with them. But they sent me an email and said to reschedule after the lockdown in the city was over. Okay. Deal. At least Winnie Couture was still open for me. I said, "Hallelujah."

Today was the day, and I couldn't hold my smile because of my excitement. Oliver dropped me off at the bridal store and said that he would park somewhere else and wait for me. Parking in San Francisco was horrible. You ended up parking in a spot that maxed to two hours only. When that two hours was over, they gave you a $75 ticket, and you would see them on the white golf cart rides, having fun giving everyone tickets when their parking meters ended. Other spots in the city actually towed your vehicle. It was honestly a crazy place to live. I said no to cars. I'd rather take the public transportation. Besides, it was much more fun. Except for the fact that some people who don't shower hop into the bus you're riding in and sit near you. *Oh*, you'd be out of breath. It was like making a potion in a huge pot. Those witches with tall and pointed hats stirred it more than a gazillion times, and it turned green or purple. I could imagine the big round yucky mole on their nose that seemed like it was glued on their skin. I wondered if they used Elmer's Glue or the Gorilla Strong. And they put all kinds of insane stuff that made it smell horrible. Much worst from the sewage. Or if you wanted a better comparison, it was more ridiculous than a fart of someone who ate red beans. Ugh. How would I know the smell? Oliver made red bean soup. It was so delectable. He was an awesome cook and knew a lot of recipes. Besides the red beans he added some Portuguese linguica, bacon meat chunks, and bay leaf. I devoured it. Well, it was a whole pot. But I filled a bowl and had some brown rice.

Oliver looked at me with no words and just a smile. Later on, he said to me, "I'm glad you liked it."

And I said, "Are you kidding me? I loved it." I got out of control. What did I do? After couple of hours, we were watching a movie. I needed to pass gas, and I thought that it was just an ordinary passing gas. Like excuse, people, I just needed to release it and I'd be on my way. Thank you very much. Because of that thought, I released it. It was the worst decision I ever made in my entire life. I mean, it was one of those reckless decisions in life. It smelled so strong that it was like a bomb in Hiroshima. I wanted to run away from my own mistakes. But Oliver was beside me, and I was so speechless.

I said right away, "I am so sorry I passed gas. I'm dearly sorry."

He said it was fine. But I started fanning it because of my humiliation. Ugh, another wrong judgment. He started laughing and said, "Stop fanning it." He was right because I was making the air blow all over instead of it being in one spot only. Right.

I didn't know why I had to say, "Hey, at least you've smelled Amelie's wrath." Unbelievable. I just said that to him. I was such a mess. It was all those red beans. How could I not think about such a thing? I was pigging out. Here I was. I tried to open the door at the bridal shop, but it was locked. Darn it. And I was so excited. I thought that I had an appointment. Why were they close? I knocked on the glass door, and there was no answer. I called their telephone number, and yes, they acknowledged me. A girl walked toward the door to unlock it. She was smiling and said hi. She welcomed me and said to browse around and pick the ones that I really wanted. Then she would help me try them on.

I found ten wedding dresses that I loved with different styles and designs. It was amazing that the store was lock and it's just me inside with the bridal expert lady. She was fabulous. She made me feel relaxed and didn't pressure me. I had a little chat with her, and she mentioned to me that she was originally from Amsterdam. That was why she was completely different. She was very friendly, and I got no negative feedback from her. And she was pretty and not sloppy. I think *professional* was the word. I remembered when I did my backpacking in Europe back in January 2017. I made sure that I went to Amsterdam in winter because I wanted the water in the canal to freeze so I could go ice-skating. But because money was quite difficult to find when I was not living in San Francisco that time, I planned my travel to a point I would get to see not just one country in one visit. Here was how I did my itinerary—eleven days in five countries. Seemed impossible, right? I bought a round-trip flight from San Francisco to Dublin, Ireland, with a nineteen-hour layover in Toronto, Canada. I took the bus to San Francisco Airport that lasted two hours.

The day of my flight to Ireland, I was so excited that my feet and hands were cold. When I arrived in Toronto, I rented a compact car and drove forty-five minutes from the airport to the hostel I checked in. It was after midnight. Everyone was asleep. Thank God I was bunking with a bunch of females and not men. It was much easier to change clothes without worrying someone was staring at you. Perhaps every person in the room had women's boobs. I parked my car at the parking of the hostel and checked in. I went straight to bed, where I had to climb a ladder just to sleep. Exciting, wasn't it. What was more thrilling was one of the girls sleeping was snoring. Perfect! Could I complain? Perhaps eight women total were in the bedroom. And for the price of CA$40 for a night? Not a word came out from this mouth of mine.

I opened my eyes and saw some sun coming through the window. It was already an awesome day. I went to the bathroom for a shower and for a fresh start. I gathered all my belongings and checked out earlier than the check-out time. I put everything in the vehicle and typed in "coffee shop." I emailed and asked my high school batchmate who was in Toronto if she wanted to meet up. She replied. Mia and I went to different tourist attractions, but because her time was limited, I did myself the honor to tour my own. I think the best part that I loved about my first country was being at St. Lawrence Market. I got some fridge magnets for my souvenir. I loved all the variety of food that was offered, and most of all, people in Canada were obviously different from Americans. They were very pleasant, and they communicated with etiquette and with proper manners. How I wish Americans were the same. I didn't understand why they were not. I wish I could move to Toronto right now.

I made a French friend, and she made pastries as her hobby. At the same time, she sold them when she felt like it. She was so sweet, but I forgot her name and lost contact with her. But I only had one day in Toronto, and I had to leave by the end of the day. My flight to Ireland was at 7:00 p.m. I needed to return the car I rented, so I had to leave right away. I was checking in, and Amelie was going to Europe for the second time around. Six hours and fifty minutes was a quick flight. Here I was, on my second country and on my second day. It was surprising that the airport in Ireland was not packed like San Francisco Airport. I got through the immigration so quick, and now I was in Dublin. Ugh, now what? I saw the green bus in front of me. *Do I ride it?* Yes! It was going downtown. But I needed to wait for half an hour before it started moving. Wow. This was amazing and jaw-dropping. I had to pay €13 to get to town. I saw some Gothic buildings, a castle, and stores with the same names like Casey's Restaurant, Casey's Café, Casey's Auto Shop, and more of Casey's. I wondered who Casey was. Must be a big-time family in Dublin.

I got off the bus and searched my hostel via GPS. I couldn't tell if everyone that I passed by was Irish. It seemed to me that everyone here were all from different cultures. I found it. It was Oliver St. John Gogarty Pub, and behind the pub was the hostel on the second floor. I checked in and received my key. Yes! I opened the room door, and there was this German girl walking around topless without a brassiere. I closed my eyes as I walked in, and everyone started laughing and told the German girl to put something on. I was not used to seeing anyone naked, especially girls. I grew up in the island where everyone wore jeans, shirts, and flip-flops. And it was very conservative.

I stayed in Dublin for a night. I started my journey in the city, but first, something to eat. I was starving and was craving for some rice. I need something cheap. Walking in the inner streets of town was so much fun. There were a lot of adventurers experiencing the Irish culture. This was honestly the best country I had been in. Besides, the Canadian, French, and Irish people were very friendly and sweet.

The entire city was just different. It felt like I was back in the past because of all the buildings. It is incomparable to structural housing designs or just in general. Wait. I thought I would check this out. It was a Taiwanese restaurant, more of a boba store. But their menu said they served chicken and rice and teriyaki. I settled my stomach there with a bowl of teriyaki and rice. The person that made my meal sat at the stool where the register was. We started talking, and he mentioned that he was from the Philippines. He had been a chef in Dublin for years now, and he loved it a lot. He asked me if I had any plans for tonight. I said I didn't besides barhopping. He said that he wanted to join me.

I went around town the entire day and bought souvenirs for my sister-in-law, Ann, and a fridge magnet for myself. I saw Guinness Brewery. It was splendid. I wanted to cry. My love for dark beers was just unexplainable. Dark beers knocked me out after five bottles. Oh well. Around 8:30 p.m., my new friend and I met at the Taiwanese restaurant after his shift ended. We went for a walk to a bar. I loved the pubs in Dublin. People were all dressed up decently compared to the ones in the US. There might be pubs in the US that were decent. I just hadn't seen it. There was some dancing, and bands were singing and playing their instruments lively. And the men were wearing skirts. I was having a blast. Of course, I had some Guinness the entire time but had to drink it slowly. A lot of people were dancing in the middle inside the pub. I was having a blast. This was spectacular. After drinking, my new friend and I went to a small casino. He said, "I have a luck today, so I'm taking you with me."

I told him twice that I had bad luck with gambling. I never played in a casino, not once.

He said, "Nope, I don't believe that." And to his surprise, he lost every game and said that not once did he lose money playing. He always won, even with a small amount. Like I said, I had dark hands when it came to gambling. Why was it that no one ever believed me?

I told him, "It's late, and I need to head back to my hotel. I have a flight to catch tomorrow."

He was another friend added to my social media account. Today was wonderful. I even passed by Temple Bar on my walk back to my hostel, the famous pub, but it was crowded. It would be cool to go in and have a glass of beer, but I was too drowned in all the alcohol I had that night. I didn't want to end up crawling back to my sack.

On the fourth day, I flew to Barcelona, Spain, and my flight was $50 one-way. I took the underground train to get to downtown. I reached my stop, and I jumped out the train and walked the stairs. And there it was. Wow, the perfect stop was in front of Casa Mila, known as the Stone Quarry. It was a modernist building in Barcelona built between 1906 and 1912. My heart was in awe with a huge smile. I was able to see Barcelona with my own savings without asking anyone for help. I felt so courageous, strong, and motivated. I was standing across the famous attraction site with my backpack and luggage. I needed to find my hotel. I looked at my map. It was another ten-minute walk to the hostel. Not bad.

It was astonishing how Spanish citizens were completely different from the Irish and French. They were all unique and peculiar. I found St. Christopher's Inn. People here didn't speak English at all. Thank God for Google Translate. As I walk toward the elevator, I heard group of loud people and a television, so I checked it out before I went to my room. It was a US football game, and you could hear three Americans screaming inside, saying, "Go! Go! Go!" They were surrounded by Spanish people and other cultures. They were all silent and talking to each other with glasses of beer. What was wrong with these three? You come to a different world and you bring your loud and inappropriate behavior and announce that you're American? I didn't understand the logic.

I headed to my room to change and shower. I did not expect that I would be with twenty-four women in a huge bedroom full of bunk beds. And most of them were Koreans. It was not that I felt out of place, but I did feel out of place. Good thing my bed had a curtain you could slide, and no one could see you snore and drool on your pillow. Very cute. Yes!

It was my very first day in Barcelona. I went to the balcony, and the weather was perfect. My excitement made me quickly put my beat-up blue Converse and thick dark green canvas jacket I purchased from Old Navy two years ago. The plan? First off, coffee. I needed to find an authentic Spanish-style café in Barcelona for a latte. I could see a Starbucks in front of me. It was undeniable and very tempting. But nope. I was not going to any Starbucks during my expedition here in Europe.

There were two Spanish guys standing at the corner. I approached them to ask where the La Boqueria Mercado was. And they hardly spoke English but answered me. It was closed because it was Sunday. This was depressing. One of the reasons why I wanted to go to Barcelona was to experience Spanish delicacies and not just entirely explore the nice architecture. Great. Now what? I'd go to La Sagrada Familia, the very popular church that was never finished until today. I took the underground train and did a lot of walking. Wow. The basilica is amazing. I took some snaps on my phone and posted it on my social media account to let my friends know where I was. It was wonderful beyond words. It was marvelous. I found a seat, sat for a moment, enjoyed the view, and saw the different cultures around the cathedral, appreciating the design made by the famous Antoni Gaudi, a Spanish architect.

After an hour at the cathedral, I took the train to go to Park Güell. Ugh, this sucked. I still had to walk for an hour to reach the park. My legs were killing me from all the walking I had been doing. But it was okay. This was all worth it. I continued my journey. And I made it. I could hear someone playing the famous classical Spanish song on a violin. I looked at the architecture. It was fascinating. It was very detailed. The tiles that were used were so colorful and inviting. I didn't know I had to pay at the entrance. I thought that this park was free. But it was very desirable to go in. Worth every penny. No regrets. I was glad I did that. I had so many shots, but it was 5:00 p.m., and it was getting dark. I had to walk for another hour just to get to the train and back to my hostel. Before I left the location, I had to stop by downstairs at the souvenir shop and buy a fridge magnet. It was the third magnet in my third country. And I needed to have my dinner, of course. I ordered a toasted bread that had melted cheese on top with pepperoni and a soda. It was an awesome day. I had so many pictures to share and for me to keep.

Oh no. My feet smelled tremendously awful. I walked too much for a couple of days now, and my feet were very exhausted. That gave me bad odor. What should I do? I was surrounded by female Koreans. I didn't think I wanted to be bullied in Spain at this moment. Besides, I was leaving tomorrow. Or I could care less. That's right, I was leaving tomorrow. I spent two nights in Barcelona. I felt wonderful. I loved my feet and my motivation to see the world. Good night, España. I didn't want to leave, not yet. I was feeling the vibes in this city. It was quite relaxing and exciting. But I couldn't.

I packed all my stuff and went to McDonald's around the corner of the hostel for coffee and a breakfast muffin. I needed to extend the money I had. I still had another two countries to go to. I was at the bus stop, and all of a sudden, I got a charley horse on my right leg. I couldn't move my legs at all. I couldn't even put pressure on it even if I used my left leg. Oh god. What if the bus left me? I needed to get to the airport. I didn't have extra money for this kind of inconveniences. *Lord, please help me.* Oh my. I was palpitating even without caffeine. This was madness. There you go. Whoa. My legs just returned to normal. The tightness was gone, and the bus just arrived. What a coincidence. Praise God. I didn't know anyone in Barcelona, and it would be horrible if I was left behind by the bus and the plane. I was very lucky.

It wasn't boarding yet, and I was the third person in line. When I checked in, the guy said that I was not in the system. I had no flight to Prague. For my fourth country, I was going to Czech Republic. But I showed her my printed sheet of confirmation, and he told me to give him fifteen minutes to make some phone calls to fix it. He also said, "After fifteen minutes, don't get back in line because it's extremely long. Instead, wave at me and come to me straight."

I went to the side and sat down. I gave it twenty minutes. I went back to him. I waved at him, but he was tending another passenger. This young Korean couple looked at me and thought I was trying to sneak my way so I didn't have to get in line. They were blocking me so that the guy wouldn't see me. They were glaring at me, and the girl was rolling her eyes. Unbelievable. I walked toward the guy and passed two Korean couples. And when the guy saw me walking toward him, he waved at me and gave me the sign to come. He had my ticket all printed, and he handed it over to me without any conflict. I would not allow those two to ruin my travel. I had more important things to worry about, like my right leg being in pain. Besides that, my two feet were hurting from walking too much. I didn't have the proper shoes for walking, but I had no interest in changing them either because these shoes travelled so much, and I just had that attachment to it.

I arrived in Prague around 7:00 p.m.. I was in my fourth country. I rode the bus, and I needed to pay. I gave the guy euros, and he said no. I needed different money. He told me to get off the bus. Um, okay? I went back inside the airport and went to the money exchange, and they didn't use euros. Instead, they used Czech koruna. Amazing. I missed the bus.

ARE YOU HAPPY?

Now I had to wait for another half hour. I didn't mind. This was beautiful. It was snowing. It was freezing. Just what I wanted. That's why I booked my travels in winter. One bus ride and one train ride was needed to get to town. Strange. No one wanted to communicate with tourists. No one smiled in this city. No one spoke English. I wondered why. It was dark, and I was scared. I hoped no one approached me and spoke to me. I looked awfully wasted even though I hadn't had any alcohol this entire day yet.

My torn jeans and beat-up blue Converse were giving me the homeless look. I guess I should be happy because no one would be interested to talk to me. And even my luggage looked like it had been to World War II. I walked between the buildings that were Gothic. They were so beautiful. I felt like I was inside a movie from the past, like *Sherlock Holmes*. I was at the Old Town Square. There was the clock tower. Wow. I had no words. I was speechless, I must say. But before I started dreaming and drooling in front of the tower, I forgot that it was actually freezing and snowing. Where was my hostel? I searched it on the map and started to follow the directions while I pulled my beat-up luggage. Thank God the wheels hadn't given up. My phone said I was here, but the only thing I saw was bunch of puppets on strings hung on wall as souvenirs for sale.

I went all the way to the back and asked the guy, and he said it was upstairs. I walked upstairs, and the guy behind me didn't even care to ask me if he could help me with my luggage. How considerate. Or maybe he was thinking that it was my baggage, so it was my problem. I guess he made his point. The person at the reception was nice and welcoming. He was very different. He gave me a key, and the lady with him said, "Do you have any questions?"

Perhaps I did. "Are there ghosts here?"

They started laughing hard and said no. Everything in this town was old and Gothic. Beautiful but frightening. I loved watching horror movies, and I thought this was the best place to scare myself. I just had to make sure I didn't pee on myself. It was just me in the room, and there were eight beds. Did you think some ghosts are on the bed? Oh god. I threw my luggage and backpack on the bed I chose. I kept my passport and money with me and headed back to the astronomical clock tower.

There were a lot of food stalls in the town square. I bought a hot chocolate, and the guy laughed at me and said, "You should be having a shot of vodka at this hour, especially with this type of weather."

"Um, I don't think so. I'll pass." But I did want something to eat, like a long sausage. Mm, delicious. It was the perfect dinner on a snowy evening. I strolled around Old Town Square the entire evening until I was tired. I enjoyed the atmosphere and people passing by. Tomorrow, I would make sure I enjoyed a nice meal with a good beer. Good night, Prague. Was I still alive? So far, I hadn't had any goose bumps in this hostel. No new roommate? Still just me in a huge eight-bed bedroom.

What a morning. Where should I start? Aha, coffee. Days don't start without coffee. I was not a makeup person, but today, for the sake of having the best picture ever, I would put light makeup. I stepped outside the hostel, and yes, the sun and the snow were out and splendid. It was amazing. I didn't know that on my way to Crème de la Crème Coffee Shop, I'd be passing Charles Bridge. Oh my god! Did you know that the construction for Charles Bridge started in 1357 and finished in the fifteenth century? It was incredible how the bridge looked. It was so Gothic, and the statues were just spectacular. How I wish I was wearing a medieval historical dress like the green dress Anne Boleyn was wearing in the movie *The Other Boleyn Girl*. I walked on the bridge and felt like I was Queen Anne. After crossing the bridge, I passed more Gothic buildings and stores. I was in Crème de la Crème. I ordered a latte and a croissant. I sat by the window and watched every person passing by.

This was wonderful. I was taking my time and not rushing. If only I brought a book to read. But that might eat my entire time. I guess it was not a good idea. Oh well. Once I finished my latte, I would head toward the castle. My feet were still hurting, but I'd take things slowly and not worry about my time being limited. I still had my fifth country tomorrow. I could see that there were security guards at a checkpoint before reaching the castle. This was quite scary. Still, I proceeded because I wanted to see it. They checked my bag. They saw my blue American passport, my pads, and a pepper spray. The two security guards asked me what the pepper spray was for.

I said, "It's for me to use in case you do something bad to me." I gave him a huge smile, all teeth out.

They all started laughing at me and said, "Okay, go."

Prague Castle was the largest ancient castle in the world and was built in the ninth century. Was this not insane? And another crazy thing was the St. Vitus Cathedral that was found in the tenth century. It had Gothic design inside and outside. I couldn't believe I was in front of this cathedral. Growing up on the island, I only saw beach. We had cathedrals, but not all were architecturally stylish like here in Europe. They were especially unlikely similar from St. Vitus. I couldn't even compare this cathedral to anything. It was too historical. How I wish I could stay longer and enjoy this beautiful ancient handmade building from the past.

I needed to head back now. There were so many things to see and experience in this country. I was on my way to see John Lennon Wall and the pub dedicated to him. One thing I noticed in Europe was that graffiti was not bad at all but considered as art. And it was very beautiful, especially if it was done correctly by a talented person. The snow was doing a fabulous job making all my pictures perfect. Even my shots at the dancing house were all wonderful. I had never seen a building look like it got squeezed by hands and ended up looking like that. People did have great minds. Imagination was always outside the box.

It was lunchtime, and I found the best spot for steak and beer, U Modré kachničky Restaurant. It was famous for duck meat and is located in a tight street where no one will find unless you were from there or someone mentioned it to you. But because we were in a different era, perhaps things could be found on Google Maps. That was one way of knowing. Smart? I know. I suggest that walking at night in this street for solo female travel would not be safe at all. It was the only business in the alley. Don't get me wrong, it's more fun walking at night. That's a fact. But haven't we seen too many movies with crimes and violence done at night? Or how about some scary ghosts? Besides, I was in a Gothic town, and everything here was from seventy-five years ago. Remember the Prague War from World War II? The city was bombed a couple of times. Obviously, once a place is bombed, someone dies. So if it was bombed a couple of times, there were lots of deaths. There must be a lot of ghosts in this town. I could feel it on my skin. I thought it was coming to get me. I needed to leave now. The duck steak was to die for. It was delicious. But to head back, I needed to pass the Powder Tower. It was a city gate that separated the old town from the new town. I just hope the spirits I felt wouldn't follow me. Wait, I think I was feeling weird because I just paid how much for the food. Darn it. One more country. But it was okay. By God's grace, I would make it.

On my way back, I stopped by some souvenir shops. I wish I could have bought a puppet. They were all handmade and beautiful. But I didn't think it would be good for me too. I'd end up thinking of the movie *Annabelle*, the scary movie? I found a fridge magnet for my fourth country.

My hostel was behind the Old Town Square, and I felt safe because it was surrounded by souvenir shops and restaurants. And there were lots of people walking around the street. A James Bond movie was done here in 2006 with Eva Green. What was this long line in front of a store? They had a dessert like an ice cream cone. I thought I had an extra coin for that sweet dessert. Let me see. Trdelník was a sweet pastry from Slovakia. It was a rolled dough on sugar and walnut and was grilled. Yum. I was patient enough to wait for my turn. This was wonderful. Everything in this city was just splendid. I started heading back to my hostel. I walked slowly on Charles Bridge while devouring my trdelník pastry. I took more photos of the bridge using my dessert as the model. Beautiful. Ugh. Life was so magnificent. I saw an artist sketching the tourists' face. Clever and so artistic. I went straight to the Old Town Square to see the Astronomical Tower. I was leaving tomorrow to my fifth country. How I wish I could stay for a week and enjoy the awesomeness that this city had.

I found a seat and just sat there in the middle where I could see everything. I was freezing. I finished eating my snack. I was wearing the colorful gloves I bought from Old Navy and my brown canvas boots. I had my knee-high socks and doubled another short sock. I couldn't feel my toes any longer because of the coldness. The snow stopped falling, but the cold never disappeared. It was like I was inside the freezer and was being punished for leaving my job for eleven days to explore the world. I got it. I would be back. I just needed some time on my own, away from all the drama and insecurities. I just needed new experiences, and this couldn't be found inside a room.

Ugh, I couldn't take it anymore. I went back to my room. I stayed for two hours to warm myself up, especially my feet. I brushed my teeth before I went back out again. It was getting dark, and I still went out, but only in front of the place I was staying at. I needed some booze. I was quite full, but it was my last night here. I would have a nice meal with a beer. Yay! They gave me a gigantic mug of Prague specialty Bezzer, and I ordered a slow cooked meat. This was amazing. I was drooling on this food but, I needed to keep myself presentable and not crappy in a nice restaurant. Wow. I wish I could marry this slow-cooked beef. Oh my god. I wanted to sleep with it, give it a shower, and make love with it. It was insane. The best food *ever*. I wish I could announce it to the world that this was the best slow cooked meat in the entire existence of humanity. I knew that I would never get over this wonderful experience. Instead, ate it slowly, just how it was cooked. Slow. I had two giant beers, and I needed to act like I was all good to go.

I had to tell myself something, and it was very important: Dear Amelie, thank you for loving yourself. Despite all the worries and dramas you have encountered in your life, you are still standing up and happy inside. Life goes on no matter what happens. Even if the house you're living in burns down. Even if you lose your job. Like the runner trip, you don't look down on yourself and say, "I'm finished."

Why is it that people in their sixties received their bachelor's degree? Never put period on your words, especially your abilities. A person is like a rustic knife, which can be sharpened. We study. Experience life to the fullest. Focus on God's wonderful creation and be thankful for all the great things we see. It's a blessing that we can see things, unlike those who are blind. They are grateful that they hear. Just breathing right now is a great thing to be thankful for.

I didn't want to sleep yet. I didn't want this day to be over. If I kept my eyes open, do you think everything would stop? I prayed that the Astronomical Clock would pause. What if I closed my eyes? What if I moved here for good? I'd just bring one suitcase with me and apply to some restaurants or souvenir shops. I could learn the language too. I didn't think that would be difficult. But where would I stay? It should be like the US. You could find rooms for rent and start life anew. I was falling asleep. I couldn't do this. Good night, Prague.

My flight was not until the afternoon. I went to Captain Candy, which was only a two-minute walk from the Clementinum, and I had to grab some sour worm candy and chocolate. I had to take the underground train back to the airport. I was glad my feet were feeling much better compared to when I was in Barcelona. The snow had stopped pouring since yesterday morning until today. But the city piled snow all over the place, and it was making the entire town beautiful.

There I was in Amsterdam. I wondered how Dutch people were. Base on my research, the country had free will with the use of marijuana. I never tried marijuana. But I smelled it from neighbors or when I was pass by a place and I happened to smell it. Personally, it was not a wonderful smell. It was too strong. The plane just landed. The last country on my list, the fifth country, was Amsterdam. I tried to find the exit. For a moment there, I got lost and had to ask where the exit of the city was. I found some buses that drove to town, and the driver was standing outside happily and said, "Hop on." He had the biggest smile ever at 8:30 p.m. What a great welcome given to a tourist. Hope that every country around the globe would give the same excited spirit. I stared at him the entire time out of curiosity. I wondered if he was high or not. And I was right. His inviting spirit was actually because he under the state of weed. He gladly steered wheel of the bus, perfectly driven straight on the street. I had no idea where I was going and where I needed to get off. I had to approach him and ask for directions. Do you think he would tell me the right destination, or would he tell me something else and start laughing at me? Oh well. I still needed to try. I had no choice. He was a very friendly guy, a good person to drink with. Definitely not a boring dude. He was around his forties. He told me to get off at the next stop and walk. I punched the address on my phone.

It was dark, with some streetlights. A lot of flowers were on a pot by the pavement, and there were quite few bridges. It was honestly a nice street to walk in. Let's see here. I thought I was getting close. My feet were killing me. I was really tired. I needed to cross the street, but the train was blocking. I needed to wait. This one guy with his friends looked at me and saw that I had luggage. He smiled at me and said, "Welcome to Amsterdam."

He looked like he was about to come near me and give me a friendly hug because he was too excited and happy. But like the driver in the bus, this stranger was under the influence of marijuana. This was so fun. So far so good. I felt that I fit in in here compared to the other countries I visited. I crossed the street, and bicycles were coming fast from my right then from my left. They biked where pedestrians walk. I was quite upset because I wanted to get mad, but I couldn't.

A bicycle almost hit me. Now I knew that in Amsterdam, I should be very careful and watchful toward people who biked, not people who might take my money (even though I was broke) or people walking on the street like me.

Yes, finally, the hostel. I needed a good night's rest. My legs were really killing me. I was so tired. I had no idea that this ten-day challenge in five countries would be this draining. It was so worth it, and I wouldn't change a thing. But next time, I'd make sure to stay three nights in each country and not two. I stayed at St. Christopher Hostel. I had no idea this place was also called Winston Nightclub. Was I happy with my decision? No, not at all. There were lots of people outside smoking weed and drinking beer. I guess it was all fine as long as the room was all right. I couldn't wait to get to my room. I went inside the hostel, and I saw people dancing on the floor, and the bar was packed with people ordering liquor. Couples were flirting with each other. A guy touched this girl's behind. Wonderful, wasn't it? The entire hostel smelled of marijuana. Great. I wished to leave, but it wouldn't make sense because Amsterdam was a country of marijuana, so everywhere I went, it would smell.

I got my key and went to my room. *No.* I wanted to scream. I would be here for two nights, and my roommates were all different cultures, which I was very excited about, but they all smoked, and they all looked dirty. They were all backpackers with no time to shower, I guess. But there was a bathroom right there. Oh my. On the other hand, their smiles and friendly attitude changed my perspective. Was I too judgmental? I might need a hit on the head. But the smell of the plant was not strong in the room. I could tolerate it. And they had new sheets and a pillowcase. All I wanted was to close my eyes and rest my legs. I went outside to the bar and bought a bottle of Heineken to help me fall asleep.

I brought it back to my room. I showered and brushed my teeth. I browsed my phone while sipping on my booze. Now I was about to knock out. To my amusement, all my roommates were honestly quiet and considerate about others. My night was wonderful.

Breakfast was splendid. I went to Pancake Amsterdam. It was delicious. I had pancakes, of course, and a cup of coffee. I didn't know they only accepted cash, and I only had my debit card with me. I ran out of euros. I didn't go to the ATM. I was inside the restaurant for more than half an hour, explaining to the waitress that I didn't have cash besides my US dollars, and she accepted it. I thought that she'd hold me captive inside for the entire day. I explained that I would be leaving the city tomorrow to Dublin for my final flight to the US, where I lived. Yes, I was out. Worst thing that could happen was a cop taking me in to the police station. Please, not in Europe. But on the other hand, being taken would be nice too. I would end up staying longer, and it was an honor.

First stop? Ice-skating. It was a beautiful sunny day. It was freezing, but walking might lessen the coldness. I saw the beautiful canal with bikers here and there. But the water was flowing, and I thought that it froze because it was January. It was heartbreaking. This hurts me more than knowing I was single for years now. I walked toward Rijksmuseum at the Museum Square. Because God heard my cry, he surprised me with an ice-skating rink. It was a big round one, and there was a bridge on top it. It was not packed. It had the right amount of people skating early in the morning. I put the skating shoes on my feet, got up, and walked toward the ice.

This was wonderful. I couldn't explain the joy I was feeling right now. I skated for an hour. I hoped people didn't think I was weird because I was smiling the entire time I was skating. But who cared, right? No one knew me in Amsterdam. Even if I picked on my nose and flicked it. Oh my. I remembered someone I knew from the past where when we spoke in person and her nose was bothering her, she poked it with her finger and really dug inside. And when she pulled it out, the booger sat at the point of her index finger. She'd stare at it for a second then round it up using her thumb then flick it. How talented could she be? A woman conversing while flicking her nasal mucus. No elegance for a lady. And as to the famous signage of the word *Amsterdam* where everyone took picture and selfie, I couldn't leave without my very own picture too.

Next stop, Heineken Company. One thing I forgot to go see was the Van Gogh Museum. Darn it. I was to focused on ice-skating and Heineken. It's okay. It gave me reason to come back. Besides, I was leaving tomorrow back to Dublin. Why was it that everything had an entrance fee? It's okay. At least the souvenir shop was open. How I wish I could go on the tour inside. But my budget didn't permit me. I bought a fridge magnet and a bottle opener with the sign of Heineken. I was content. I took loads of picture outside with the huge sign of the company.

Bloemenmarkt, here I come. Lovely. I had no words but *beauty*. All the Dutch tulips were amazing. I wish my apartment was just outside this store so I could buy these pretty flowers every week to put on my dining table. I guess I could only take so many photos to bring back with me. I purchased a canvas bag for only €3. It had a drawing of the bicycle and the city name *Amsterdam*. There were so many Dutch shoes. Most stores asked tourists to not take any pictures of the merchandise. I will not lie, but I was one of those people who would still take a snap if I could do it without getting caught, but not all the time. Just on a reasonable matter.

Next was the red-light district. The sites I visited were very limited. There was so much more to see in this city. But in my one day here, I thought I was happy. My hostel was near the red-light district, so I went back and lay down for a bit. My feet were strained, and I was not going to ask why. After an hour, I went back out.

I was hungry. I saw a pizza house and ordered myself a slice and a beer. This guy asked for my ID. In Europe? I was never carded when purchasing liquor here in Europe. This was very strange. I wanted to ask him, "Are you an American?" I did ask him if he was joking, and he said *no*. Great. Should I walk away? But the pizza was so affordable, and I was hungry. I only had pancakes this morning. Okay, White boy. I wouldn't argue with you because somehow, you were handsome.

"Here is my ID, sir."

He put my pizza in the oven and gave it to me. After one bite, he said to me that he was just messing with me. Amsterdam didn't really card people with alcohol. Right. He did look different. Guess what, he was another person I encountered who was under the influence of marijuana. I loved it. Everything was so fun here.

I left the pizza store and walked toward the red-light district. Wow. This was real. Girls dancing in the mirror? And men just chose who they wanted, and the girl would go to them. People tried to take pictures, but the girls were so alert that they hid their faces, and they turned their backs away when they noticed someone taking pictures of them. It was amazing how plenty of people were there at this area of the canal. It was quite late, but I was glad my hostel was on the other side of this street. I needed to use the bathroom. The beer was doing me bad. I couldn't hold it anymore. It was another ten-minute walk. I went inside a pub and asked where the toilet was, and they said it was downstairs. I was so embarrassed that I came in just to use the toilet and I didn't even buy anything. At least one beer. Okay. I went back upstairs and walked straight to the bar and sat at the stool and said, "One pint of Heineken."

After I ordered, I looked at my surroundings and had no idea it was all men in here, and it was just me alone, a woman drinking a pint of beer. This was insane. The guy on my left turned to me and smiled. He was a Dutch guy in his late twenties. He was six feet tall, skinny, and blond. Handsome? Definitely. He asked me, "What are you doing alone drinking, surrounded by Dutch men?"

I said that I used the toilet and felt obliged to purchase something for my gratefulness.

He replied, "Are you sure? Or are you trying to hitch some Dutch man?"

Was he crazy? Of course not. He asked me another question: "Do you think Dutch men are handsome?"

Hold on. Let's be smart here. If I started laughing and said no, he might punch me in the face or might embarrass me inside the bar or probably say that I was the one who had bad looks, not them. Or he might even stab me with a fork or a knife. No. He had a spoon. He might stab me with the spoon he was holding.

Of course, I said, "Yes, you are all handsome. You see, I don't want to die here in Amsterdam, here in this wonderful bar. I still want to go back to my country. So I say yes. You all are cute and handsome."

I thought I was only talking to him, yet I heard everyone on the bar laughing, including the bartender. I returned his question and asked him what he was celebrating with his boyfriends. He said that they lost the game. They were professional football players. But they were all figuring out what they did wrong so next time, they could better themselves. And I thought my day here was done with wonderful stuff. The guys on my left were all tall and couldn't be reached unless I stood on the chair. I wanted to say that this Dutch guy on my left was hitting on me, or maybe I was just overreacting. Perhaps. I was a woman. Women did overreact to a lot of things. I finished my beer, and the bartender gave me another pint. I said, "I haven't ordered yet."

He didn't say a thing and smiled at me. He looked at the guy sitting on my right side and nodded toward him. I looked toward the guy on my right and said, "Thank you. How are you?"

He cracked a bit laugh and said that he was good and asked me where I was from. I told him that I was backpacking, and so far, everything in this city was wonderful, and I was having a blast. Except that I was leaving tomorrow.

"Why not stay another day?" he asked me. One day would not allow me to see everything. He was right.

I asked him what he was doing in the bar alone. He said that he was the owner of the bar, and he was looking for drinkers that might cause a mess in his business. At least when he was there, he could call the cops. Life kept getting better and better, don't you think? I was surrounded by cute Dutch men. It was every girl's dream to feel young and beautiful. Oh my god, the bar was about to close. My phone was drained. I looked at my watch, and it was 1:50 a.m. I got up and said good night and goodbye to everyone.

The football guy on my left asked where I was going, and he said that it was too early for me to go to sleep. I laughed at him and said good night and goodbye. I thanked the bar owner for the pint he gave me for free and walked quickly toward the door. I couldn't believe it was already two in the morning. I went straight back to the hostel and to the bed. I set my alarm for 5:00 a.m. A few hours of sleep wouldn't do. What had I done?

What was with the loud noises? I heard someone taking a shower. Another one was putting her makeup on. A guy was having coffee. The rest were asleep. I checked my phone, but it was dead. I asked my roommate, and she said that it was 6:45 a.m. Oh my god! My flight was at 9:25 a.m. I rushed and didn't bother washing up and brushing my teeth. I still had to walk toward the underground train. I thought that I was going to miss my flight. I took one train ride tow the airport? Why was it I did not do that when I got here the other day instead of taking the bus? I made it. I was so scared. Good thing I was not left behind.

Hello, Dublin. I'm back. My friend Sydney emailed me through social media and said that he saw my travels, and if I was in Dublin, I should hit him back so we could get some beer and catch up with each other. I sent him a reply: "Tonight at 7:00 p.m. at Temple Bar?"

He said, "At 9:00 p.m. That's too late." He didn't get off work until 7:00 p.m. Really? He was an IT guy, a Brazilian friend I met in Paris back in April 2016 l. Now that was a different story, a different expedition. The biggest fun of them all? I was staying at the same hostel I stayed at nine days ago—Oliver St. John Gogarty Hostel and pub.

I was leaving for the US tomorrow. At least there were no German girls walking around naked like the first time I was here. I needed sleep. I felt so rested. Three to four hours of sleep helped me a lot. Before anything else, a shower was a must and a toothbrush. This felt great. I didn't have to rush anything. I had seen all the countries on my list. Five countries in ten days. My favorite was Prague. The slow cooked meat was fabulous and delicious. The Gothic buildings and cathedrals were just spectacular. The entire flight and hostels

I stayed in all countries cost me $995. My pocket money was $500. The total was $1,495. Splendid. Goal achieved. The very first time I went to Europe, I spent $7,000. That was ridiculous. I never thought that with the right itinerary and budgeting, everything was possible. Except I was still not able to buy those expensive stuff I wanted, but thinking of it, I didn't really need them. It would just be added to the stuff I was hoarding.

In January 2017, I lived in the care home where I worked as a caregiver. I couldn't have too many things because I had no place to put them. I was getting much better in doing an itinerary and with budgeting. I remember my foster mom told me to open my own travel business. And I loved the idea, except that a lot of people were doing it, and it was quite scary because of the demands of people. If they were not satisfied with the service, they could just go off on you. Maybe another business? I loved freedom. A business might be quite difficult, especially with all the drama and problems it could bring.

I put pants on with my black knee-high boots with heels. I flat ironed my blond hair. I put some mascara and pinkish blush on. Tonight, I would be all sexy and pretty not for my friend but for pictures because it was my last day in Europe. I didn't know when I would have another opportunity to visit. Sydney texted and wanted to pick me up at the hostel. I said no. I would meet him at the pub. I was so embarrassed. I didn't know why. It had been exactly a year since we had seen each other in Paris. I remember him inviting me to go dancing in a club. We both ordered beers and chatted. When the DJ turned the music on, he stood up and started to dance with some chick. I stayed in our table while I finished my beer. I looked at him and smiled. I tried to hold my laugh, but he had seen it. After one song, he came back to the table and was all embarrassed. He told me to go back to the hostel.

"Excuse me, you invited me to come here. I am enjoying myself watching you make a fool of yourself."

He begged me and said please a couple of times. He wanted to enjoy and really go deep into it. And he said to me that I had no idea about the word *dancing*. He was Brazilian, and their dancing was very different. I would find it too sexy. I wouldn't appreciate it, according to him. Fine. Good night. I walked toward the pub. We gave each other a hug as friends. I didn't have any horrible thoughts. I thought, *Another drink? I'm getting sick of it. But if it's my last night, why not?* Oh god. I just hoped I wouldn't end up in the hospital. When I'd get back to California, I would go see my primary physician and ask for all the tests regarding drinking. What if I needed surgery for drinking too much? I had a Guinness, and so did he. He had been living in Dublin as an IT specialist for almost three years now. He was renting a bedroom in a house with a bunch of housemates. Syd was a tall guy, maybe five-eleven? Handsome, yes, he was. He was a great friend and fun to be around with. He was always laughing. He wouldn't leave Ireland, he said. His heart was here in this country. I was very happy for him. He found what he really wanted in life and where he wanted to put his roots down. His girlfriend broke up with him when we were in Paris. That's how I met him. But he never shared his relationship story to me. He was somehow a private person.

A little chat here and there killed the entire night. I was tired and ready to be on bed. "Good night, my friend. It was very nice to see you again. I hope that there will be a next time."

It was fun catching up with an old friend. We both walked back to our own destination. I went to the left, and he went to the right. All I wanted to do was remove my shoes and set my two feet free. Today was just a relaxing day. Nothing extravagant. I brushed my teeth and washed that powder I put on my face. I hated pimples. Worst thing that could ever happen to you is have that little round red thing on your face. It was early, but the sun was gone. It rested earlier than everyone else. Perhaps it was early to go to work tomorrow. I browsed my phone with all the pictures I had taken in all the countries, and I just wanted to cry with a thankful heart. This trip was a story to be told. And as I was fitting on the dresses that I picked, I was conversing with the Dutch girl.

I asked her what she thought about San Francisco. Perhaps it was different from Amsterdam. And she said that it was different from her country. I had made my decision. I had my eyes on this wedding dress, which was the Averil style. It was a lace drop waist with deep a plunging neckline, and the back was dramatically open. I loved the fact that it was open in the back where all my freckles could be seen. It was so beautiful. I asked her to take a picture of me wearing it. I wanted to show it to Oliver. I was so excited. But wait. There was a saying that a bride should not show herself wearing a wedding dress to the future groom because the wedding might not happen. I definitely wanted the wedding to happen, so I would listen to the old saying. It took me two hours to fit all the wedding dresses. I couldn't believe she didn't say anything to me. As far as I knew, I only had an hour with her because she had another person, a future bride like me, to help with fitting wedding dresses. But she allowed me to enjoy. She was amazing. I called Oliver and said that I was done.

He drove in front of the bridal store and said, "Did you have fun?"

I replied, "OMG! Yes, I did. I found the one that I really like." I felt really bad that he waited in his truck for two hours.

"Can I see it? The pictures?"

Are you kidding me? Of course, I wanted to show him, but I would not jinx this wedding. "*No.* Don't ever ask again or I'll beat you up."

CHAPTER 6

DNA Ancestry

That was it. He was being too much. It had been three months now, and he wouldn't leave me alone. I told him that I was adopted and that my foster parents said I was Filipino, Japanese, and White. They were not specific with the word White but generalized it as White. Oliver insisted that I do a DNA test with this famous website called Ancestry. He did it years ago, and he said that it was very accurate.

I was honestly worried if I was not who I thought I was. Then that would change my thoughts toward myself. How would I handle that anyway? He ordered me a DNA kit online, and when we received it, Oliver instantly stuck something inside my mouth and told me to put more saliva on the stick. Um, okay? He wrapped it all up and put it in the box, and right at that moment, we went to the post office and sent it.

I tried my best not to think about it, but it wouldn't give me peace. I was hoping that somehow, that White part of mine, even if it was 5 percent, would be Irish or French. That would be so cool. It took a month for the result to come out. Part of me didn't want to know, but part of me did want to know. What if my foster parents were wrong? But I doubt that they were. I was born in a small clinic in

Zambales, Philippines, on April 22, 1988. I was left in that clinic by my real mother, who got pregnant by an American soldier that was stationed in Clark Air Force Base. By May 2, 1988, an old lady name Margaretta took me in her home because her older daughter could not bear a child. She was a dressmaker, a seamstress. She owned a bunch of fish ponds. Grandma Margaretta lost her husband from the time General McArthur was in the Philippines, and they had the opportunity for their family to go to United States. I was with my grandma from three weeks old until seven years of age. Then her daughter retired from the US Air Force when she was in her forties. She could not bring me to the States because the government wouldn't allow them. So they decided to move to Manila for good.

Mr. and Mrs. Smith retired from the US military to do missions. And growing up with them was a great blessing from above. Being accepted by a couple as their very own daughter was the greatest gift someone could ever have in this lifetime. I was flooded with beautiful dolls, and I even had my own bookshelves for it. I had my very own bedroom. I got to eat three times a day with a snack. I went to a private school called Sacred Heart of Jesus High School. I was able to wear beautiful and wonderful clothes. I was able to explore the world. Their hearts were just as fat as an obese person that had no hope because of eating five burgers in one sitting.

One month later, DNA results came in. I received an email from the Ancestry website. I called Oliver before I opened the site to check. I was so nervous. Should I open it or not. "Hello?"

The first thing he said to me was "The DNA results are back."

I was so scared and didn't know what to expect. He sounded so excited and wanted to log in to the site right away. He could not control his emotions. This was insane. Okay, I was logging in right now. Let's see. Oh my god! I was speechless. My heart stopped beating. I didn't know what to say. I left Oliver hanging. He kept babbling and asking what the result was, and the only thing I could say was "Oh my god. What my parents said wasn't all true, except the fact that I was 50 percent Filipina. The Japanese culture is not here. But the White ethnicity…"

Oliver asked me again, "Amelie, come on, tell me everything on the profile."

Um, well, okay. "It says that I'm 50 percent Filipino, 25 percent English, and 25 percent Scottish."

He was blown away and was also speechless. What was more amazing was that Oliver could not accept the fact that I was not part Japanese because I looked like one according to him and to my foster parents. He wanted me to do another test with another company. I was not doing that. It was already too much for me to handle this surprising fact in my life. Wow. I couldn't believe I was half English and Scottish. Was that why my two front teeth were so big like a rabbit's? Was this why I was a bit of a weird person? Was this why I would rather talk and write? I never liked to listen to anyone except my own voice. Or maybe that was just my personality, a disorder? Okay, I was overthinking this surprising news.

I called my foster parents, and we had a video chat. "Hi, Mom and Dad. I have something I wanted to share to you."

They were both astonished that I came out of the blue with this news. I reminded them about how they told me that I was part Japanese and part White, besides being Filipino. And they said, "Yes?"

I spit it out and revealed what I found. And I screenshotted the results and sent it to them as evidence. My father's eyes went wide, and he was shocked.

My mother said, "Wait, hold on. Say that again."

It wouldn't sink in to anybody. I couldn't blame them. It wouldn't sink in to my skull either. I was 50 percent English and Scottish, and guess what? I was related to Queen Elizabeth. I bet that I was part of royalty. Right. I was dreaming. Guess what? America is a free country. No one was ruining my imagination on being royalty. What was I going to do now? Growing up, I told everyone, even at work, that I was Filipino Japanese. I actually never acknowledged my Caucasian part. And now I was actually Caucasian and Asian. If anyone found out, they might say that I was a con artist. Should I say, "You're right. I'm an artist, but not a con." That would be great. Splendid. I thought that this was madness. I was getting all these mixed feelings of happiness but also regret that I did the test. I should have stuck with the information my foster parents gave me. But on the other hand, I was figuring out who I am slowly. I was getting to know who I was. And I was excited.

England, in 2016, was the third country I visited when I first did my expedition in Europe. From San Francisco, I bought a one-way ticket to Manila to visit my parents and brother for a month. It was a great time, mostly shared in eating out at restaurants, having beer with my brother, talking shit about everything, and laughing until four in the morning. After a month with my family, my next trip was to Tokyo. Fourteen days in Japan would be so much fun. I couldn't believe I stayed that long in a country. I was not familiar with the language and the roads.

The next day, my mother threw a going-away party and invited the neighborhood. She made some Mexican food. That was her specialty, by the way. She made a bunch of tacos on the table for everyone and other stuff that I never paid attention to, so I had no idea. A lot of people came. It was a fun night. Except for those who were doing the dishes. Which was actually *me*.

Early morning, I got an Uber to pick me up. We spent forty-five-plus minutes in traffic just to get to the airport. Lucky me, I got a nice driver who was an entertainer. I said goodbye to my mom and dad and to my brother and his wife. I'm not going to lie. I was excited to get into that taxi and fly to Tokyo. The international airport in Manila was always packed. It was always crowded with people. The system was just difficult compared to other international airports. They checked your luggage in the scanning machine outside, and you had to remove your shoes. And when you were inside, you checked in to your airline and leave your luggage or bags and take your boarding pass. Then another line to get inside the main gate. You had to remove your shoes again and go through the scanner and put your purse in a different scanning machine. It was insane. I couldn't believe a lot of travelers loved going to the Philippines when everything here was hectic. Yes. Finally, I was inside. Now I was putting my shoes back on. I gathered all my stuff. Now which gate do I go to? Gate 12, I think.

Tokyo, Japan. It was my first backpacking experience in my entire life. I was afraid but excited. What if I got killed? Or maybe not. It was okay. They'd understand me. I spoke English. Right? My cousin on my mother's side was picking me up. She married a Japanese guy and had two teenage boys. They went to a private school and were involved in baseball. She had been living in Japan for more than fifteen years now. I was so glad her family moved to Tokyo from another town of Japan. Now I had someone with me in the city in case I got lost.

I actually booked a hostel in Akihabara for fifteen days and fourteen nights. Behind it was the mall, and the train station was a walking distance. There were a bunch of ramen shops out on the street. Okay, hold on. The plane just landed. I was trying my best to hold my tears of joy. Please, Amelie, don't make a mess here. They might think you're going through depression. Where was Akane? Oh my god, I was in Japan. There she was and her husband, Hiroki. They lived thirteen minutes away from Haneda Airport. This was so embarrassing. I told her so many times that I'd take the train to my hostel. I had a place to stay, and she didn't have to worry, but she insisted that I didn't know Tokyo. Okay, she won. I didn't have any Japanese money, so before we left, I went to the money exchange. I was looking at the both of them with a huge smile and amused that the language was completely different already around me.

I went to the right side of the vehicle to open the sliding door of the van. I thought that there was something wrong with the vehicle. I had no idea everything was the opposite. They started laughing at me. The Philippines and the United States were all on right side. I would not debate because I didn't want them to leave me in the cold weather outside of Tokyo. I was not feeling well. I was coughing bad, and my head was feeling light. I wish to just be on a bed. We arrived at their condo unit with three bedrooms and one bathroom. It was on the fifth floor. The hallways in the building looked exactly like the hallways in the movie where there was a white lady that came out and scared you, and after, it would kill you. This was awesome. It was my first night. They opened the door, and it was so tight. We all had to remove our shoes and kept our socks on or wore slipper.

Akane showed me my room, and I told her it was just for one night. I didn't want to waste my money on the hostel. I believed in karma and not just ghosts. I put all my stuff in the bedroom, and she said that I was the only one with the bed. All of them slept on the floor, including my two nephews who were in their teens. But the difficult thing was that the walls were sliding doors and paper. Paper walls? Really? I just hoped I wouldn't hear my cousin and her husband doing something strange tonight. I didn't mind, and it was not my business. But the words *awkward* and *weird*, in addition of *what the fuck*? I wish I could have gone straight to my hostel so I could do whatever I wanted without anyone having their eyes on me. Did you think it was easy to move in a house where there were other people? Definitely not.

    I asked Akane if we could go to the grocery store. I knew that it was already midnight, but everything didn't close until 2:00 a.m. I couldn't wait to explore the city. She said it was fine. We took the bicycle. She drove, and I was behind her. It was funny because she was five feet tall and forty kilograms while I was five-seven with the weight of I won't tell. Do you know how hard it is for a woman to tell her weight, most especially when they gain it on and off? It was ridiculous. We parked the bicycle outside the store called Family Mart. At the right side of the store inside was a manga rack. Mostly *One Piece*. This was really cool. As a huge collector of manga, this was really jaw-dropping. I went around the store and took pictures. Akane and I grabbed some coffee. Funny, wasn't it? Coffee at midnight. I hoped the cashier wouldn't find me weird. Akane said that it was very late, and we needed to get back. But she needed two minutes. She took a pack of her cigarette and smoked a stick. She was wearing black heels and a black coat with a pink lipstick. She had long beautiful hair, and I had never seen her wear flat shoes or sandals. She was always wearing high heels and booty shorts.

    We went back to her condo, and they all went to sleep while I stayed up. I couldn't sleep. I tried my best to close my eyes, but it wouldn't work. I thought I was too excited to be here. How I wish Mr. Sun was outside right now so I could go for a walk. It was April 3, and all the cherry blossom trees were in bloom. I loved pink too much that I wish I was pink. Not to be weird, but could I say I'm a girl, so could I be excused with my stupid dreams and wishes? I tried to drink Sapporo in the kitchen and just looked around the entire condo unit. How different was this place compare to the Philippines and the States? It was fascinating.

Akane came out and joined me. I was about to finish my second can of beer, and she was only starting and already getting buzzed. She started to complain why I was not getting hit while drinking, and she was about to fall asleep with one drink. Well, guess how much you weigh? She went to sleep, so I went to bed as well. I wish it was already 7:00 a.m. I couldn't open my eyes. There was something stuck. Ugh, nasty. Where was I, anyway? I had a good sleep. I did not feel any pressure and stress from anywhere. No bad karma. Thank God. Where was my phone? Oh god, I was in Japan. Holy cow. What time was it? What? It was already 10:00 a.m. I opened the sliding door and saw Akane watching television while putting on her makeup and having tea.

"Why didn't you wake me up?" I asked her. I was so disappointed with myself. I could not waste time sleeping instead of touring around. But today was my first day; plus I was not feeling well. Hiroki, Akane's husband, wanted to bring me to the hospital because of my extreme coughing. But I only had insurance in the States and not anywhere else. I insisted for him to ignore me and that I would go to the pharmacy and buy cough medicine. I just needed some rest because I was exhausted from too much swimming back in Manila. I was in the beach the entire day with my family. I would take things slow for today. Perhaps fourteen days in Tokyo would give me enough time to see every place I wanted to see.

I brought coffee just in case I couldn't find any coffee shop in places I'd go to, and I had no idea what kind of coffee they offered. I boiled hot water and tore the bag of coffee and put it in the mug. I sipped on it for a while and took a shower. I loved the bathroom here. The tub sang after it was filled with water. It was so cute. Ugh, so tight. I had to sit. Japanese people were small, and for my size as an Asian and Caucasian, I felt that I was quite big and tall. But I could not live life without showering. All the shampoo and conditioners, including the liquid soap, were in Japanese. How would I know that I was not putting soap on my hair and conditioner on my body? I needed to ask Akane.

It was already 12:00 p.m., and Akane was still putting her makeup on. I was not into makeup that much, but I loved a good amount of moisturizer on my face. If I had an obsession, it was with moisturizers. I hadn't eaten anything yet. I was starving, and I needed to eat something. I needed ramen.

"I'll be back. You don't eat ramen. I'll use my map to reach some ramen stores. Don't worry and just stay here." She hadn't even dressed yet. So I found this old-school traditional ramen store. It only had six stools on a bar. I had to copy the other customers so they wouldn't think I was an alien. I put my coat on the hook by the wall on the side. I sat at one of the stools. The Japanese guy gave me a menu and said something. I had no idea what he just told me, but I nodded. I looked at the variety of noodles and made my decision. I looked at the Japanese guy and pointed at the menu, and he approached me. I pointed at the ramen with an egg and nodded again. Should I say *arigato*? What if he just laughed at me? Then he would realize I was an outsider. At least by not saying a word, he could think that I was mute. I'd rather have it like that.

Finally, he came with my ramen. Oh my god! This was madness. I couldn't eat all of this. This was a gigantic bowl. This was crazy. Crazy fun. I was so excited I had to take a picture of this ramen. I mean, every angle of this bowl was amazing, and would look good on my social media account. I picked up the chopstick at the cup and broke it apart. I smelled my lunch and sipped on the broth with a soup spoon that was on my left hand. Wow. This was delicious. This was wonderful. I could live with ramen for the rest of my life. I started digging in, and I couldn't stop smiling while eating. I was worried because the Japanese guy was looking at me like I was insane. He had no idea that I was in heaven. Wait. They had no soda. Days were not complete without coffee and a soda. I guess I had to stick with water. Wait, they just gave me tea. This was so exciting. I tried to take pictures when the employee turned around. It was embarrassing. I didn't think you were allowed to take pictures of the food. It was disrespectful. I guess it was okay if I said I was a foreigner. Or they'd think I was full of shit. Right. I would shut my mouth.

I was done with my meal. Now what? How would I pay them when they didn't understand me? I felt like I would burp the food out. I tried my best to eat all of it because the other customers finished their bowls. This was crazy. My stomach was harder than a guy's balls. I looked at the menu again and check the price. It was ¥1,300. Okay, how much was that in US dollars? Did I just spend my entire pocket money? I gave her ¥2,000, and she gave me change. I headed back. Good thing I was walking back. It would help digest the food I just had. This was crazy.

I wanted to go to my hostel in Akihabara. Akane called my dad and said I was staying with her my entire vacation in Tokyo with her and husband. Now I thought that she was not being fair to me. Ugh, I needed my freedom. But finally, she was ready to go out, and it was already 2:30 p.m. What a waste of time. Okay. So we finally got out. First thing I wanted to go see was Shibuya. I had a list of things I wanted to do in that spot. I wanted to see Hachiko the dog. I had a picture with it, and it was brilliant. We went to the Shibuya Crossing ten to twenty times. We just went back and forth. It was so much fun.

Akane said, "What is wrong with you? This is just a crossing."

"For you, it is, Akane," I told her. "Not for me. This is not just the Shibuya Crossing. It's the most famous crossing of all time."

After that, we went to the Pokémon store, and I purchased three small Pikachu plushies. I stayed for at least thirty minutes. It wouldn't sink in to my head how I got there. This was so amazing. A bunch of nerdy Americans were there at the store. I needed to pretend I was not into anime and stuff, but obviously I had been in the store for thirty minutes now. I was being obvious. Akane kept asking me to move to the other go-to place. Darn it. I wish I went alone. But if I did go alone, then I would end up being at the store for hours just staring at the stuff. We went to the One Piece store, which was on a different building. We couldn't find it. We had to ask different people, including the security guards and police. There it was, the statue of the great Luffy outside the store. As I was walking toward it, there were bunch of cute stores on both my right and left sides. It felt like I was walking toward the man I loved, but this time I was walking toward my favorite store. I went to each item they had in the store, and I was there for at least forty-five minutes. Akane was getting so bored and would rather go to the clubs. I didn't do clubbing, Akane. Okay? I'm sorry. This was my trip. This was my time. I would go to all the anime stores here in Tokyo. I couldn't contain my smile. I actually wanted to tear up, but Akane would be more irritated at me for being weird.

I grabbed a *One Piece* pillow to buy and a keychain, and that was it. I was backpacking. I couldn't have too much stuff with me, or else it would be difficult. My next trip would be in Italy. We went to Starbucks, and I ordered a small hot macchiato and a strawberry cake. It was late and dark. It was 7:00 p.m., dinnertime.

"What do you want to eat?" she asked me.

What else should I say? Of course, ramen! She looked at me in, disgusted. Hey, it was my vacation time. I wanted to eat ramen every single day for fourteen days. She started laughing at me and told her husband what I said. But she didn't have a choice. We did go to a ramen store. Yum! That was satisfaction. She told me to be careful of eating noodles every day. I might gain weight. I didn't think I would want to gain weight, as you can see it's very difficult to lose weight once all those tasty meals are inside your flabby body. But it was okay. This happened once in a lifetime. I couldn't believe the ramen store didn't sell beer and soda. We decided to head back to her apartment because it was already 9:00 p.m. Not yet though. I saw this cat café. And that was on my list too. So while we were in Shibuya, I would love to go pet a cat, even though I was allergic. It's not like I was going to sleep with it. So it was totally fine, I thought. We have to pay an entrance fee, and we washed our hands and left our shoes by the door. I never experienced a cat café. This was awesome. All the cats here were healthy, and their hair was so elegant and well taken care of. They even served tea and coffee for customers. Akane seemed to be so bored, but it was okay. I only needed half an hour. Just to experience this in Tokyo was wonderful.

We walked back to the train station and had to cross the Shibuya Crossing the thirtieth time. I was so speechless. At this hour, the station was packed, and we were shoved inside the train so that it would close. The most fascinating thing here right now was that the train was packed like a sardine can, but I couldn't hear one person. I didn't hear any music. Anyone still breathing? I saw bunch of grandpas reading manga the entire time they were standing. I saw a high school student in a skirt that reaches her knees, but she raised it so her panty could almost be seen. A lot of men now started staring. Ugh. I was glad her mother was not me. But Akane and I just reached our stop, and we were walking toward the parking lot to get her bicycle. It was 11:30 p.m. I didn't want to go home yet. And she didn't want to bring me to my hostel at all. She was keeping me hostage in her apartment. I decided that at this hour, I would like to go to karaoke. And Akane was extremely excited and agreed that we should go. So we biked toward this karaoke place near her place and parked the bicycle at the side. We did an hour of singing, and I ordered sake, a Japanese rice wine. This was the very first time I was trying this, and I heard that it was really good and strong, according to my cousin. While she sang, I put on a school girl outfit and had some of the rice wine to boost my confidence before I started to open my mouth and sing. What would I sing? Would I survive? I didn't have to worry about anyone hearing my voice because it was just me and Akane. I could just make a mess. Okay, here we go. I had to order another sake because it was very light. The Japanese guy and my cousin thought I was an alcoholic because I drank hard. I think that with the size of my body, it was very tolerable, and it was an easy drink compared to soju. Well, soju, I think, is impossible and strong. I just couldn't drink that alcohol.

It was 2:00 a.m. We had to go. I wanted to wake up early and explore early the next day. I paid the Japanese guy, and we tried to head back to the apartment. On our way back, we were pulled over by police, who was also biking and was holding a flashlight. He didn't speak English at all, so my cousin spoke to him and mentioned that I was an American. Akane showed him my US passport and said that I was just visiting and was lazy to walk. I didn't know that only one person could be on a bicycle in Japan, and I didn't even realize that every bicycle had a plate number. Akane was so small, and instead of me driving, she would rather drive because she insisted that I didn't know how to bike. It was totally fine with me. I had my GoPro wobbling all over the place. I was taking picture of every scenery. This skinny Japanese police guy was staring at me like he was about to beat me up.

Akane turned around and said, "Don't say anything and try to be serious." She said she made up some stuff and that was fun, according to her. Fun? He could have put me in jail if he wanted to. But because I was an American, he didn't want to deal with me because he didn't speak English.

Wow, today was really fun. I took off my pants and my brassiere. I went inside the blanket without washing my face and brushing my teeth. I was so exhausted, and I wanted to ignore it. Good night, Tokyo. I love you. That's it. I really wanted to go to my hostel and be on my own. I wanted to walk around and get lost alone and not wait. It was already 1:00 p.m., and I was still inside Akane's apartment. I wasted half the day because of her putting makeup on the entire morning. I wanted to go to the Sanrio Puroland. That's where we went. We had to take a train, and it took us an hour from where we were. I was so excited. My legs were tired from walking all over the place. How I wish we could rent a vehicle, but my cousin didn't trust me and kept insisting I didn't know Japan. Fine. We were there. You're kidding me. Sanrio Puroland was closed. With the distance we traveled and the cost of the ticket, now they said they were closed. I felt like a giant ball just dropped from heaven and crushed me. I couldn't breathe. Perhaps there would be no next time on this trip. I couldn't just waste time and money coming all the way here, hoping for this place to be open. My cousin didn't do her assignment. I couldn't do it. I didn't understand the language. I wanted to cry. My tears were about to drop. Akane thought I was a goofball and being a childish. She didn't understand a thing because she lived here. I just lost a million dollars in a casino.

"Maybe we can grab something to eat here before we take the train back to Tokyo?" I asked my cousin. I had a bento box with tempura and teriyaki chicken with rice. My heart was aching right now. I was really trying my best to be an adult, but that childlike mind of mine was like an anime face with huge eyes that wanted to burst out and scream. We tried to go to the Odaiba Oedo-Onsen Monogatari in Koto City. We approached the building. Oh no. I saw a sign that said No Tattoo Allowed. My inch tattoo on my wrist could be hidden. It was totally fine. Wait. Okay, I didn't think they would let me in. The tattoo at the side of my ribs was very long with dark ink. This was madness. Sanrio Puroland was closed. The *onsen* wouldn't let me in because they thought I was a yakuza. Should I act scary so they'd let me in? They might throw me in prison. I guess I'd shower in the bathroom. It was not worth going crazy. Today was the worst day. We can't have it all. Not everything we want in life will be given to us. I had been punished from above by tattooing my wrist and my ribs. Well, I thought it was sexy. Akane and I took the bus to go back to Otaku, where she lived. We went to the mall instead, and I bought *uwabaki* as a souvenir. I also got some cute—they call it *kawaii*—pens and chopsticks. I found a Rilakkuma teddy. I wish I could get the biggest one, but there was no way I could bring that with me back to the US. Especially because I had other three countries to go to.

It was late and dark. We grabbed Akane's bicycle and rode back to the apartment. We passed by these shopping stores which were mainly ramen stores. There were a bunch of freshmen students from college hanging out like gangsters in one spot. One boy looked at me while Akane paddled the bicycle, and I was sitting behind her. He yelled something to me in Japanese, and I didn't understand what he said. I wonder what that was. Did he say he was going to beat me up? I had blond hair at the moment, and perhaps he probably hated it.

I asked my cousin what he said, and she said he wanted to go out me. Wow. At the age of twenty-seven? And he was eighteen or nineteen. That was like child abuse, wasn't it? Or did I just feel like I was an old fart? Kid, I don't date boys younger than me. You're still a baby. I had no plan on speaking back to him. As a matter of fact, Akane was actually biking so fast that we were so far away. I couldn't even glance back at that boy. When we got home, Akane told her husband, Hiroki, that they didn't let us in the onsen because of my tattoo. She was laughing at me.

Hiroki asked Akane if I was sick. Because I was backpacking like I was about to die, and that my last wish was to see the world. I didn't think I needed to be sick to explore the world but because I was still strong and I wanted to see my dream countries and get some ideas, new habits, to have an eye-opening experience, to be moved and have a change of heart. I didn't think Hiroki understood me. He was a very serious guy. He was focused on his career and making sure that he provided for his family. I admired him as a father, husband, and as a son. He could be a serious stubborn person, but he did have a good heart and cared for people. Status was important for him though. I think to everyone, it is. I tried to stay away from him and not converse. I didn't want him asking me about my education. At this moment, I just didn't want to think. I wanted to live life to the fullest while I was capable.

I asked Akane for some beer, and she told me to open the small cabinet close to my room. I drank it right away without putting it in the fridge. They both looked at me like I was crazy. I thought what was crazier was when I drank all the bottles in the cabinet. It was embarrassing, but I guess I didn't care at all. Sometimes rudeness just can't be controlled with every human being in this world. I was making excuses for my insanity. I didn't want to sleep yet, but today's experience was not that wonderful. The two things on my list were not fulfilled because of my personal decisions in life. When I got back to the US, I needed to make an appointment with a dermatologist and have my tattoo removed. It made everything in life difficult.

My nephew gave me a paper with his drawing. A dragon ball? I love the *Dragon Ball* anime. Very smart kid. His older brother told me that he was only fourteen years old, and he's got girlfriend already. He was popular in school for being cute and being on the baseball team called Giants. What surprised me was that baseball teams in Tokyo were all named based on the baseball teams in the US. I was excited and hoping that it would be something in Japanese and it would be a cool team. That just killed my excitement. I hope I didn't show him too many emotions of mine. Instead, they both showed me their bedroom. They both had their own table to study, and on both sides, they had their own bookshelves of anime and anime figures on their tables. They slept on the floor on a mat with their pillow and blanket. After they gave me a tour, they kicked me out and closed the door. Wonderful tour, I must say. They were too focused on their studies because of their father demanding them to have the best grades. That would definitely help the both of them get to the best school in Japan. But the father wanted to send the both of them to New York after high school. I thought I was very fortunate that I was free and doing what I wanted. I did not have my foster father hold a stick in front of me and demand me to study and have straight As in class. I might have ended up in the psych ward.

My nephew came out to give me a *Dragon Ball* action figure because he said he was going to throw it out. Was I not happy to stay here instead of going to my hostel in Akihabara? I changed my clothes and washed my face and put some moisturizer. My facial routine only lasted five to ten minutes. On the other hand, Akane had been on her face for an hour or two. She was now putting water gel and moisturizer. I had never seen a woman like my cousin so intense when it came to the word *beauty*. At least she was loving herself, right? That was the important thing. I didn't want to go to sleep yet. But I guess I had no choice. I was glad that I was sleepy and tired. I didn't want to wait until 2:00 a.m. to close my eyes again like last night. I was getting comfortable here in Tokyo. I feel like I didn't want to leave. Good night, second day.

It was my third day. Rise and shine, my little pork buns. Ugh, I needed some coffee. But first, I showered to wake myself up. My two nephews were gone and left for school early for an exam. Akane was in front of the mirror and putting makeup on. Surprisingly, she was all showered, except she was running around the apartment in her bra and underwear. I didn't know sometimes if I hated her or I just wanted to choke her. The bathtub just started singing in Japanese. It meant it was done filling water. I sat on the small chair on the floor, and I rinsed myself before I got into the tub. Today, the plan was to just relax until lunchtime and wait for Hiroki. He would drive us to Mount Fuji. It was so embarrassing because he called in his work just to give me and Akane a tour of Mount Fuji. Akane and I went to a ramen shop. She was getting sick of ramen, she said. I thought I wanted to marry the Japanese ramen for the rest of my life. It was so delicious and irresistible. As far as I knew, only Japanese people I have encountered eat without looking elsewhere, and they leave when they are finished. But other cultures I have experienced, they browse around while eating and look at other people who are putting spoonfuls in their mouth and chewing. It was a stupid habit, but what could I say? I was one of those population that stared at others while they devoured their meal. And right now, I could see bunch of Japanese men in black suits eating noodles and not even speaking to each other. More action and less talk. That was one big thing that's hard to adapt and practice. My mouth was just full of nonsense, and it has practiced talking meaningless things since I was born.

I was kind of jealous with Akane that she lived in Japan. But to think of it, I lived in America. Should I feel jealous? Both had its positives and negatives. We walked back to the apartment and waited for Hiroki. I turned on the television, and I just regretted touching it. Everything was in Japanese. And according to Akane, the stations here in Tokyo didn't put violence on television because the country wanted the citizens to live life peacefully and not be scared or worried. How I wish the US and Philippines would do the same thing.

That's why the economy was getting worst because of what they put on the show, and they thought that it was normal. They all imitated what they saw, most especially teenagers and kids. Ugh, television was upsetting; I turned it off.

    Hiroki was finally here. About two hours was the estimated time before we reached the beautiful Mount Fuji. We were just chatting the entire time and stopped by the gasoline station and grabbed something to eat because Hiroki was hungry and didn't get his lunch yet. After an hour and a half, we went to this cafeteria by the gasoline station where the giant *Evangelion* statue was. Akane said that it was Hiroki's dream to take a picture with the statue, but he never had the chance to go because he was busy and didn't have any good reason to go out this way. He was so funny. He wanted his own picture without her. I ordered some tempura and rice with it and tea. I went to the vending machine to grab a soda, but I didn't see any. I guess I'd stick with the pink lemonade. Our driver was now full, and we went back inside the van.

    There it was. I could see the tip of Mount Fuji. This was unbelievable. As usual, my yesterday just continued until today. Mount Fuji was close. They put a barricade so no one could go. It was snowing, and it was not safe. I wondered who was jinxing me. This was too much. What did I do wrong that everything was not available to me? We stayed at the bottom of the mountain where we found a parking lot. We parked the van and got out and did our best to take pictures. There were a lot of tourists here besides us. Because it took two hours to get back to Otaku, we needed to start heading back. Hiroki mentioned that traffic could be horrible, like entering to San Francisco City and going through the Bay Bridge. That bridge was the worst thing ever, especially early in the morning. Heading to work sucked. Might as well rent a sofa at someone's house in the city if you know anyone and take the bus to work instead of traveling from somewhere, and driving that far with the rush hour was just impossible. But that was what we were in right now. The rush hour to Tokyo. I was trying my best to not fall asleep, and I entertained myself with my phone. It was embarrassing to nap when Hiroki and Akani were awake and driving.

    I loved all the pictures I had taken. I sent some of my photos to my dad in the Philippines, and he was thrilled to know that I was in the famous mountain in Japan. When we parked the vehicle, I just feel like crashing and sleeping. I was so tired from this trip. I couldn't change my clothes and brush my teeth. I didn't care anymore, but I was knocked out. Where was my eye cover? That was all I needed. Surprisingly, I didn't even need a beer tonight to put me to sleep.

    It was the fourth day, and what was the plan is? I had no idea. So I would just go anywhere the wind blew me. And first thing to do for me was to have a coffee and get that caffeine in my system. Because after I changed my clothes, I would be heading toward the ramen shop. I didn't think I would even bother brushing my teeth. I didn't come to Tokyo to make my teeth yellow, but brushing my teeth before I eat would ruin my sense of taste. I would rather have stinky breath and enjoy the delicious taste of ramen. Yum.

    So far, everything was great. Akane, as usual, was in front of the mirror on the dining table, putting her makeup on. She worked in the department store and sold makeup and women's perfume. I wish I had her patience on fixing my own face. But my interests were just completely different. I didn't like tight clothes and colorful ones. I loved plain beige color in everything. I love canvas bags inside of those expensive bags that cost $2,000. My canvas bag was only $15. With $2,000.00, a flight to Tokyo and a hotel for a week is booked. I asked Akane to teach me how to cook. She promised that she would, but she never did. Fourteen days of my stay here and I didn't even learn how to make any sushi and ramen. It was very sad. It was on my list. This was honestly ridiculous. Everything that was on my list wasn't done at all. I thought I should disregard it and just go with the flow. But the problem was waiting for Akane every day. We ended up leaving the apartment at 11:00 a.m. to 12:00 p.m. She never went outside the house without a makeup. Ugh.

This was my first time traveling by myself, and it did scare me to go explore the city alone. And that was why I always waited for Akane. I didn't know what I was going to do once I got to Europe in a week. Today, we were going to Shinjuku and just get lost. My cousin and I went to the ramen restaurant together. I was just thankful that she didn't go work while I was there. I didn't honestly know how to thank her. She entertained me since day 1. I couldn't have done it without her.

While walking toward the second train station, we passed by stairs. Akane wanted me to go with her. I didn't want to go up there. I wanted to go straight to Shinjuku. Oh, come on. While whining to her, I still walked the stairs. To my surprise, I saw cherry blossoms all over the place and a lot of people under it with their picnic blankets. They were drinking sake and having laughs. This was so beautiful. I was so amazed. It was so beautiful. I didn't have to go to Shinjuku. I asked Akane if we could go grab a blanket at home and come back here and just be with the rest of strangers. This was so much fun.

Ten minutes later, I started sneezing, and my eyes were getting red and itchy. Oh no! My allergy was triggered because of the flowers. This was horrible. I couldn't even be here. I was so embarrassed my pictures wouldn't end up good. I needed to go now. We went to the wrestling arena where sumo fought. They were closed. But it was worth the travel, and I saw a huge picture of sumo. And I was able to buy a sumo key chain. Just being outside made me excited. Our walks were taking our entire time, and it was getting dark already. I hated the fact that we left so late at lunchtime instead of 7:00 a.m. To complete this day, karaoke would be fun. So we went to a karaoke place, and I ordered beer instead of sake this time. Wine rice just didn't do anything to my body. Some nineties music would be great for this night. Backstreet Boys were always safe to sing in a karaoke, especially when your voice was not really good like Celine Dion's. I never experienced living life in a different country without any pressure. I took my time to get to know a place that I loved. And seeing it for the first time and living like one of them? It was wonderful.

My parents' friends from their Bible school were here in Tokyo and invited me for a dinner. They were from the Philippines and had been living in Japan for years now. They served a Baptist church and continued life in this country. But I didn't get to see them because of my laziness and lack of communication. How I wish I could have seen them. Not because I was getting free ramen but to show respect on behalf of my parents. I was not feeling well too. I was sick the entire time. I was coughing and was having an allergic reaction because of the cherry blossom trees. Good thing I brought Zyrtec. I always carried this allergy medicine in my bag. It was so useful, especially in my situation. Even if I went to the pharmacy, I wouldn't understand a single medicine they had at the store because of the language. And even if I asked them, I'd be wasting my time because they would not understand me. So I sent them a message saying that I couldn't go meet them. I was not feeling well, and transportation was difficult, especially because Akane didn't have the time to go with me. Perhaps another time.

Today, the plan was to go out with Hiroki. He wanted to bring me and Akane to the Tokyo Tower for an experience. But before we went there, we had to go to another place, which I requested. It was a small and tight alley with loads of restaurants and good places for alcohol and food. They had fresh seafood in boxes soaked in water at the side of the alley. It was so amazing how clean Tokyo was, and the people were so civilized and respectful toward one another and to their surroundings. I had not seen anyone litter on the street. Hiroki found this spot and said it was where we'd sit and drink and order some oysters. Yum. This was so much fun. Our table was too long. On the other side, there was a cute White guy sitting across from me on my left. He was sitting on the same bench as Hiroki. I had too much to drink. I ended up staring at him. He was about six feet tall and had blond hair. Because of my current status, being Buzz Lightyear, the only thing I could say was that he was very handsome. He noticed me staring at him, and he stared back and smiled.

After a couple of minutes, a White girl came and sat across him. He looked at her, and I looked at Hiroki right away because Akane was sitting beside me. I saw the White guy glance at me again, but nope, I was not looking back at him anymore unless I wanted to be slapped on the face by the girl. I would eat my oyster until I was satisfied. Hiroki and Akane were laughing at me so bad that I wanted to cry. Do you know the feeling of not being in any relationship? No boyfriend. No husband. And this was the reason why I was in Tokyo, in case someone discovered me and wanted to take me home for good. But so far, I had no luck with anything. I wanted to say life sucked, but being in Tokyo right now, I felt fortunate. So I would forget about the word *boys* because I didn't need that right now. I thought the three of us were seriously buzzed. We were still aware of things but tipsy. While walking toward Tokyo Tower, Hiroki and Akane were arguing. Then they started laughing and hugged the post with a map on the street. I didn't think this was acceptable in the Japanese culture at all. But what could I say? We were having a great night. We passed this Buddhist temple that had no light. It was kind of creepy. We went inside the building and took the elevator all the way to the top. I couldn't remember what floor it was. Oh, right, it had fifteen floors.

Hiroki treated us big time tonight. He ordered us some beer. We just sat in the lounge and chatted. It was a gorgeous view. Everything was just beautiful. It was a wonderful experience. I was glad I was not alone to do all these things. It was always fun doing things with people. We couldn't walk back to the train station. We ended up taking the taxi. This was so funny. The driver was on the right side. I was trying to hold my laughter, and my drunkenness was not helping at all. Good night, my fellow alcoholic friends. I would be knocking out. How I wish I could cancel the hostel I booked for fifteen days and fourteen nights. Good thing I only paid $350. That wasted money could have went to six Olay moisturizers or more probably, and it could last me for months. It was sad.

I didn't think I tried any fresh sushi yet. I would try my best to go to Tsukiji Market alone. I was a big girl, and I could do this. I had my cellphone with me. I could use Google Translate if ever I encountered a Japanese person, and I could use Google Maps. Bon voyage, Amelie. I grabbed my backpack and made sure I had my GoPro, my DSLR camera, and my charger in case my phone died. Goodbye, Akane and Hiroki. I would see you later in the afternoon. I searched for the train station through my phone, and it showed me

I needed to walk for thirty to forty-five minutes just to get there. Okay. I was not happy about this. But I would suck it up and be the man. I was already getting lazy just thinking about the walk. I did find Tsukiji Market, and it was packed. A lot of tourists were eating salmon while standing out on the street. Street restaurants were packed, and I needed to push myself in there to get some fish in my mouth.

A Japanese lady in her small restaurant was stirring the giant pot filled with soup. And her husband was cutting the fish and serving it to the customers. I went inside an alley and saw huge salmon. Oh my god, this was so amazing. I tried to take a picture from my camera, but I saw the sign said No Photograph. Now I didn't want the Japanese people to be upset with me. So I put my camera back in my backpack and took my phone out and used it to take the picture. Was I the only one who was committing crime in here? I didn't think so. I needed to make my final decision how and where I should settle down and eat. I walked around the market for an hour. I browsed different stuff they were selling, from kitchen items to kimono. A Japanese girl just passed me and was wearing a beautiful pink kimono. I turned around to follow her with my stare, and to my surprise, I saw a temple. Wow. And it was surrounded by pretty cherry blossom trees. Now I didn't see any signs that I was not allowed to take a picture. When I took a picture of the temple, the girl in the kimono turned around and smiled. She was so sweet for making my picture the best.

I said, "Arigato." There was a well in front of the temple. I thought you'd drop some money there and make your wish. What if I made my own well somewhere in US and put a Wishing Well sign? Then after a month, I would take all the money. What kind of a crook could I be? The best one.

I guess I was full of shit. Hey, that could be travel money or pocket money.

I found spot for my first meal of the day. I could see one stool left in one of the restaurants in the street. Good thing they had a menu, or else I was history. I pointed at the one I wanted. I wanted some salmon. Yum. But I didn't think this was enough for my stomach's satisfaction. I ordered ramen. Oh god, I couldn't get up. I couldn't walk. My belly was as hard as a rock. I wanted to sleep. This was not good. How was I going back to the apartment? I was so far away. I had a lot of walking to do. I guess it would help the food go down. My back was wet from walking the entire day. I wish I had a bicycle.

My next stop was Ginza, a fourteen-minute walk. I was so close. Thank God. I was worried that I might get lost on my way to Ginza just by riding the train. I felt so out of place here. Women here were obviously well off. They were wearing nice and expensive clothes and purses, while I was in my blue Converse and jeans that were all cut off in front. It made me look like a homeless person. It was all shopping malls in there and department stores. I walked around for almost two hours, and my legs were hurting. I needed to sit down. What did I expect? I was on my second country. One month in the Philippines was crazy. There was too much walking and swimming. It was fun, and I had a blast, except that it was exhausting. Huh. I found a sophisticated coffee shop in Ginza called Tsubakiya Coffee. I needed a regular coffee with cream and sugar. My main purpose on coming in here? To sit and rest my legs that were about to cramp. This shop was so cute. The coffee mugs were so elegant with French designs, and the waitresses were wearing cool outfits with headbands. They all matched and very polite. How I wish I could live here and adapt their culture by not always getting upset. Americans and Filipinos were always on top of their lungs when they were talking. Yet they were not even mad. It was just a normal and regular day for them. I could sit longer inside the coffee shop. I ordered a piece of vanilla cake with frosting on top and a cherry. I felt like I could go to heaven. I was so content with life and everything right now.

I was forty minutes away from Otaku. I headed back before it got dark. I did a good job, I thought, for being brave and going all alone without the help of my cousin. I got back to the apartment and saw Akane still in front of the mirror, putting water gel on her face and a moisturizer. Oh god.

"Oh, hey, Amelie. You're still alive. Surprising." Was I really an idiot that everyone thought I am incapable of taking care of myself?

As my days went on here in Tokyo, every day was quite the same. Staying with Akane or not, I had a paid place. I guess the main thing I spent on was mostly the ramen that I had been eating every single day of my life. Second was the karaoke that almost happened every night. That was quite expensive, and the rest was the souvenirs I bought. I needed to go to the post office the next day so I could mail it to US. I couldn't believe I accumulated a lot of stuff here in Tokyo, but I would definitely have a lot of interesting things to go through once I got back. How I wish I didn't have to leave this place. My very first country I went to by myself without my parents was Japan. And why did I even come here? Because for thirty-one years of my existence, I thought I was 25 percent Japanese. My foster parents thought I was part Japanese. So Japan was the first country on my list.

Akane came with me to Narita Airport because I had no idea how to get there. We had to take the bullet train for an hour, if I remembered that right. When I was checking in my luggage, this Japanese girl was asking me detailed questions, which I found weird. She asked what my next destination was. Then after that, where was I going? Then what was my final destination, and where was the place I called home? I didn't think I was obligated to answer her about the other countries I was going to. But she was having an attitude, and Akane was telling me in a whisper to just answer all her questions unless I wanted to be grabbed by the police and be interrogated. But this was ridiculous. Wasn't this nonsense? I was all red and angry but tried my best to stay calm. It was my last moment in Tokyo, and this was how it ended? I actually wanted to get out of there. But everything went well, thank God.

Next thing I knew, I was inside the plane heading to Italy. Benvenuto! The plane landed safely, and I was in Venice Marco Polo International Airport. I didn't think I knew exactly what I was doing there, but all I knew was that I wanted to eat real spaghetti and pizza, and this was where I would get them. I grabbed my luggage and went straight to the information desk. They told me that I had to take a bus by land and the water-bus. Okay, hold on. Water-bus? I thought that was the one I saw on the internet when I was doing my research. I was so excited. I would spend seven days and six nights in Venice. New adventure, here I come.

The bus didn't seem to excite me. I only saw small houses or buildings and mainly empty land. The bus finally stopped in front of a terminal. Wow. I saw the water-bus, a bridge to the other island. A beautiful canal. But it was raining, and I didn't have an umbrella. It was okay. I risked it and ran to catch the other bus. The conductor of the water-bus didn't speak English at all. She asked me where I was going. I told her to the Generator Hostel, and she replied to me, "Generatrice Ostelo."

I didn't understand what she said so, I said three times where I wanted to go. She kept repeating what she was saying to me. So I just said, "Si!"

She smiled at me. I had no idea where I would end up, but screw it. I had the entire day to get lost in this beautiful place. This was amazing. I was standing in the boat with my luggage, and it was packed with tourists. The conductor told me to put my backpack in front of me and to be careful of shoplifters. How did she tell me? Sign language. But hey, I got that right. She gave me a thumbs up when I put my backpack in front of me. I was so impressed with Venice. My jaw dropped the entire time, but at the same time, my camera kept clicking. I never thought that seeing something in a picture could really be experienced if you really wanted it to. My parents had their honeymoon in Venice. So when I was in third year high school, I wanted to experience Italy. After ten years, I really did.

The water-bus was approaching another island, and there it was, the Generator Hostel on the second island. Next stop was me. I was thrilled. I felt all dirty and nasty. The first thing I did when I got to my room was shower and rest. Four guys just came out from the hostel, and this one Asian guy gave me a token and said it was for a free breakfast. He was leaving late this afternoon, and he had an extra token for tomorrow. Splendid.

"Grazie!" I told him. Lucky, was I not? I didn't purchase any breakfast tokens because I only drank coffee in the morning. Usually, I ate lunch and dinner. I checked in and received my room key. I would be rooming with five other girls. I had no idea who they were. But my bed had a locker for my luggage, and it was good. I felt safe. The entire atmosphere was great and very neat and clean. My bed was by the window. It was a huge old-school window. When you peeked, you would see clothes hanging in a string with clothing pin. It was awesome exactly the same as the pictures I saw on the internet. Just what I expected. I showered and tried my best to sleep. I needed to remove those dark circles around my eyes from exhaustion. Sleeping too late in Japan didn't help me with my cough. But I should be fine here.

Outside the hostel was a mini pizza place. I ordered one slice of pepperoni pizza just to try it. She put the pizza in the big cave oven. She looked and waited for a couple of minutes before she gave it to me. I sat at a stool facing outside with an open window where I could see the canal and the water. The water taxi and water-bus were just marvelous. Before I took a bite of this wonderful creation, first I smelled it. It was really good, and I took a picture of it like it was Gigi Hadid, the supermodel. Mmm. Yum. It tasted *so* good. It was unexplainable. The flavor, taste, smell. This pizza was so perfect, just like Chris Hemsworth's abs. It was so fine. Every bite was mouthwatering. I ordered my second slice of pizza.

This was what I wanted to eat before I left this earth. I stepped out of the mini restaurant stuffed and belly all sticking out. I hopped onto the water-bus to go to the main island to look for a souvenir shop. I needed to walk around for my stomach to go down a bit. I saw Doge's Palace as the water-bus approached the main island. I didn't attempt to go inside. I only took pictures from the outside.

The biggest regret I had was not going inside St. Mark's Basilica. Even though I stayed seven days in Venice, the line at the Basilica never disappeared. It was always long. And I had no patience in getting in line. So I walked around the floating city and took a lot of lovely pictures as my souvenir. I found this souvenir shop with masks where the owner of the store was the one carving everything he was selling. It was gorgeous. I took a stroll into a small alley where a bunch of Italian restaurants were. It was so crowded with tourists, so I went to a different route toward St. Mark's Square. It was still crowded, and people were overflowing everywhere. I had to take the water-bus just to get to the square. This was madness. I went back to the hostel. I hoped that first thing in the morning, the city would be empty if I tried to go out early. I stayed at the lobby. It was too early to be in my room. I ordered a pint of Guinness beer and scrolled the photos in my phone.

I never thought I would be in Italy. It was just a dream ten years ago. I didn't know what triggered this motivation in me that I just bought the ticket six months ago. Sometimes my compulsiveness did me good in life. But a lot of times, it put me in danger and bad decisions. Wasn't life all about good and bad? About making the right and wrong decisions and learning from it? The only thing I prayed to God was that I didn't die in the countries I went to. I was so scared of everyone I encountered, but according to what I read before I left San Francisco, I had to be calm and try my best to blend in with the citizen of the country. Don't look like you're scared, and don't look like you're a tourist. Okay. So that's what I had been trying. I guess people just knew exactly who the real residents of the city were. I would not spend another dime and just go to bed and rest. Perhaps my first day was enough for me, and rest is much needed.

It was the next day. Good morning, sunshine. Thank goodness my bed was by the window. I opened my phone, and I received a message from my mother's sister who was stationed in Vicenza with her husband in the US Army. I opened her message, and she invited me to stay with them. They had a penthouse condo unit in Vicenza. That was a very generous offer, Auntie, but I had a bed in a hostel paid. I wouldn't want to do what I did back in Tokyo. I replied to her and decided that we would meet in a cathedral across the train station and attend the mass. And guess what, that was actually in two hours because it was Sunday. I wished I could be alone. Ugh. I rushed and got changed and headed to the cathedral. Perhaps I needed to take the water-bus.

I sat at the steps of the train station, waiting for my uncle and auntie. A lady in her early twenties approached me and asked if she could use my phone to call. She looked very suspicious. I remembered what I read from my research before I started traveling that people in Europe stole your information from your phone, so you had to be careful. I told her that my phone was not working. I only used it for taking pictures. But she didn't believe me, and I told her, "Sorry, no English" with an accent. Then she left me alone.

Finally, they were here. We went inside the church after we crossed the bridge. I felt like I was in an exorcist movie when the church started singing their hymn. Oh my god, the demons started to come out and possess each person inside the church. Should I walk out? I was frightened. No, I couldn't. My uncle would be mad at me. I thought happy thoughts. I thought about SpongeBob the entire time I was inside the church, how SpongeBob irritated Squidward in every episode and how stupid Patrick could be. I tried not to laugh. I was going crazy. Outside the door, an old man with his handsome grandson approached my uncle and asked for help to get down the stairs. Good job, uncle dear. That was a good deed. How would I sneak myself away from both of them? I couldn't because I was always beside them. Fabulous. They asked me where I wanted to go and what I wanted to see. Besides seeing the city of Venice, I always wanted to go to Verona where Romeo and Juliet were. So they said yes. And Uncle bought three one-way tickets from Venezia to Verona for an hour and thirty minutes.

ARE YOU HAPPY?

During the train ride, my uncle asked me why I was traveling alone instead of being in a relationship with someone. At my age, most girls were married and settled. How do I tell him that I desperately wanted to settle down with a man, except that I had not found my match? I was a difficult breed to calm, and men in this generation were afraid of women like me. If I didn't like something and it was forced toward me by a man, I might end up wrestling this person and break his bones. But I just told my uncle that I was not ready yet. I wanted to be all over the place alone. And he gave me the look like I needed to be tied down in one place because I was ruining the family's reputation. Ugh. Right now, I did not focus on his face and thought about Romeo's hands on Juliet's breast. That was more exciting.

When we reached Verona train station, the goal was for us to go straight to Juliet's house. So my uncle and auntie figured out how to get there. And there it was, the wall with all the love letters to Juliet. It was beautiful. Juliet's statue was splendid. I was in awe. I couldn't believe I was in front of this statue. But the biggest question was, how was I going to take a picture with it if it was crowded with tourists? We went inside for a tour and saw the bed, the clothes they wore, and a bunch of computers where you can type your letter about love. I went to the balcony, and my uncle was outside to take my picture. It was spectacular. Auntie and I went back outside. Because of my desperation to have a picture with Juliet, I cut everyone in line. I asked my aunt right away to take a picture of me. One decent one and another with my left hand touching her boobs. Everyone started laughing at me. Oh well. The only people who know me was my two family members with me.

I was so happy and content with life. Then we walked toward Verona Arena. It was built in the first century. It was wonderful. We went inside, and I climbed the stairs to see the entirety of Verona. I could see everyone from downstairs. Splendid. I even took a picture with two Italian guys wearing costumes like they were from the past. The most surprising part was that outside the arena were bunch of food stalls. We tried the paella, and yum. It was beautiful. You will get tired of me saying beautiful every single time. But everything was just beautiful.

We took a train ride from Verona to Vicenza, where Uncle and Auntie lived for two years in their penthouse. But first, they took me inside the Del Din Military base where I was introduced to my uncle's coworkers. They all said hi to me, and I just waved and smiled back to them. But my uncle was not happy with my response. He looked at me in the eye, and I never had seen him look pissed. I didn't want him to beat me up in public. He told me to say hello out loud.

I said, "Hello." Out loud. I shouldn't have met them here. It was supposed to be Amelie time. Just me and no one else, except in Japan because it was difficult to roam that city. I hated it. We went to a building where all the soldiers dined in, including my uncle. I couldn't believe this was our lunch. Soldiers' meal? I was thrilled with the paella earlier in Verona, but I guess the entire time I was with them, they would decide my life. I couldn't just bum around just as I wanted to. All I wanted was to eat some Italian spaghetti every single day. I had a mashed potato, some green beans and broccoli, and a small piece of meat. It was filling, but an American meal? Come on, I had been here for less than a week, and you guys had been here for two years now. This entire time, I battled with my own mind, sparring with it like a samurai. But none of us were winning.

We passed by this female and male at the corner. Guess what? They were friends of my uncle. Again, I was introduced, and the lady said, "Lei e molto bella."

My uncle looked at me again and said with a tone, "Say thank you."

I felt like a robot. Did I even own my life or what? We left and went straight to their condo unit by foot. It took us thirty to forty-five minutes to walk there. We rode an elevator all the way up. They had a double door, and when they opened it, my jaw just dropped. The entire wall where the living room and dining area was were huge clear windows. You could see a castle from the living room. It was so beautiful. This was amazing. Auntie said I could stay with them during my stay in Italy. But within a second, I responded, "I can't. I paid hostel. But thank you so much for the offer."

Heck no. I was not staying with an uncle and auntie during my escapade here in Italy. I stayed for one night and borrowed my auntie's nightgown. And the next day, my aunt and her girlfriend and I took the train back to Venezia to see Murano and Burano. One thing I regret not doing was riding the gondola. It was quite expensive. Even though my auntie was offering, it was embarrassing. She did give me couple hundred dollars. I exchanged it for pounds. So I had money once I reached London. I was so thankful. I was running low with cash. When we were at the water-bus toward Murano, we passed by buildings and houses that I hadn't seen. It was just splendid. Everything was wonderful. How I wish I could stay there for another week and just pretend that I lived there to satisfy my imagination.

We crossed different bridges that connected to another island. Houses here were just marvelous. But they made me think why they were so colorful. I wonder what made them think to paint it with bright colors. It was so eye-catching.

They did not seem to look like homes but a museum. There were lots of glass stores where they made it in front of you using fire. It was amazing. The guy made a cat, and I told him I wanted it. I had to wait for a little while before I could take it because it was hot. It was the best gift for myself. I got my mom a Murano vase. I had it wrapped with two papers so it wouldn't get broken. I had to put it in between my clothes when I packed it, and I put it in my backpack instead of the luggage. This could not break. We found a pizza house and ordered spaghetti and a huge pizza. Yum. I couldn't even order a beer or red wine because I didn't want my aunt to look at me like I had no manners or something. It was so difficult. I was trying so hard to please my family. Who can relate? I couldn't even fart comfortably.

    I remember when I did a mission trip in Cambodia back in high school. I was with a group of missionaries, and we went to the Tuol Sleng Genocide Museum. I was sitting on my own feet on the ground, and a girl was beside me. A guy was standing on my left side a few feet away from me. I was trying so hard not to pass gas because I knew this would be silent but deadly. Oh god. I held on to it so bad, but it still came out from me. Boom. The guy smelled it and asked who passed gas, and little girl just said it straight, "It's her. It's Amelie."

    Why would she put me on the spot? Did I have to understand her? Or maybe I could put a TNT bomb on top of her head so she'd explode for talking nonsense. Like *Crash Bandicoot*. That was my favorite video game in PlayStation 4. I had to raise my voice and deny it.

    I said, "That was not me. That was you. Why are you pointing fingers at me?" My god. I was such a horrible adult.

    Before the day was over, my aunt asked for us to meet again, and I said I that I had other agendas. I needed to cut my tied with her and my uncle. I bid her farewell, and when I turned around toward the water-bus, I wanted to celebrate my freedom. I couldn't be so much happier to be back at my hostel. I ordered a beer when I got in and went straight to my room. I needed to plan next day's escapade. I woke up early as usual. I did not wait for lunchtime to get out of the hostel and to experience this beautiful city. The tourists were just crazy, like ants. I took the water-bus to Burano.

I did not wait for lunchtime to get out of the hostel and to experience this beautiful city. The tourists were just crazy, like ants. I took the water-bus to Burano. I found a chair and just sat there for half an hour in the cold weather. I threw some bread on the ground, and the birds started flocking in front of me. Okay, now I was frightened. They were aggressive birds, like hyenas. Burano was quite similar to Murano island.

Another pizza meal for today? I couldn't get enough. My cousin from Tokyo just facetimed me. I answered it, and when the video opened, there she was in her bra and underwear. These two Italian guys behind me were waving at her. How pleasant was that? Should I be in my underwear too, just to be noticed by men? I was an old soul. I liked vintage clothes that had buttons up to my neck and a full-length skirt. But I guess men wanted someone that showed skin? Well, screw them. Exactly what they were saying back to me. Screw me. These Italian guys asked me where Akane was right now. I said in Japan. And they got excited but disappointed at the same time because they couldn't see her. What for? Sex, of course. Well, I was out of here. Ugh, men. Why was it they didn't like descent women?

My friend from Australia just called and wanted to converse. Edward was his name. We went to the same high school, but he was four years higher level from me. I could say he was a big brother. But not really because we were flirting back and forth. Ridiculous, wasn't it?

I wish I could stay longer in Italy. I didn't even get the chance to go to Rome. My biggest regret was leaving Rome out of my itinerary. I was about to leave Venezia. How could life be so cruel? I experienced Tokyo and Venice wonderfully, then I had to leave? I wonder if I could be a citizen. I bet most women wanted to be Italian citizens. The wine and spaghetti. Yum. My favorite country. I was content and satisfied. After days of being here, my cough that came with me all the way from Manila disappeared. Now I was ready for Paris. I had to wake up super early to go to the airport. Yet there was no bus toward San Marco International Airport. I was at the corner of the building on the ground, sitting with my luggage and waiting for the bus for an hour. I finally asked this taxi guy, and he asked me for €80. I only paid €15 for the bus. But I would be late. And I didn't want to miss my flight. This was crazy. I would not wait for another hour.

I didn't know how Paris would be like, but I was excited and at the same time scared. It would definitely be a new experience. Okay. Nobody spoke English here. At all. I didn't speak French. I should have studied the language, at least the basic French. I tried my best to find my way to get to my hostel by train. I did not understand how the transit worked. I asked two White Frenchmen, and they shook their heads, saying, "No English."

I saw a Black woman. Okay, I bet she spoke English. Oh my lord. She only spoke French. I flagged a taxicab and just gave the driver the address of my destination. He pressed the meter after he tried to communicate with me in French. This was already getting difficult. But I would stay calm and enjoy this country without saying a word. But here I was in Generator Hostel in Colonel Fabien. I wondered why there was a security guy more than six feet tall outside the door. I wondered if there were crimes going on here. While checking in, there was a Brazilian guy who checked in at my left side. He was six feet tall with a beard. He was wearing a brown canvas jacket and blue jeans with a backpack.

I received my key card and went toward the elevator. I took the right elevator, and the Brazilian guy took the left elevator. I pressed 2. *Ting*. Here was my floor, and here was that Brazilian guy again. Aha. I went toward the right door, and he went the opposite. He couldn't open his side door, so he asked me. How do I say yes in a friendly way? He was kind of cute. Should I bend and snap? I approached him and opened his door for him. He said, "Thank you!"

I just gave him a smile and went back to my luggage and opened my side door. There was another hallway with room numbers. I thought this was it. I looked for my room. I turned left, and there it was. I found it. And there was a guy trying to open the door and couldn't open it. I asked him if he needed help, and when he turned around, it was the Brazilian guy again. We started laughing so hard. We were going to the same room and had no idea. We were played by the receptionist. It was so hilarious. And we both got a bunk bed. He asked me about my plans for today, and I said I didn't know yet. He was going to the rooftop if I wanted to join him. I was never going to say no, but I said this in a simple way. "Sure." Like, whatever. Did I sound like I was not that interested? Geez. I didn't want to be like those women who throw themselves to men.

We looked at the view. It was beautiful. Just wow. Amazing. But I was amazingly bored, so I left him alone and started my tour. I wanted to see the Eiffel Tower, but it was quite far by foot from the hostel, and asking people here would be difficult because of the language. Louvre Museum was much closer, and there was a park where I could sit. That was a good plan. This place was really pretty. I had not seen one big girl. The stores were cool, and so were the coffee shops. I started my walk from the hostel to the Eiffel Tower, and by golly, it took me two to three hours by foot. I did a lot of stops like the Lock Bridge. It was so funny. I thought that I was the only one currently doing solo travel at the moment, but this guy set his camera alarm and ran to take his own picture. I only realized it because I was setting my own alarm, and when I was walked toward the edge where the locks were, he just finished doing it.

Could you believe the construction of the buildings in this city? It was gorgeous. One thing that upset me was that I had forgotten to go see the Shakespeare and Company bookstore, and it was quite popular for readers. But I did just pass Hotel de Ville, and it was beautiful. I wondered if it was open for public. If anyone could just check-in, that would be cool. There was a merry-go-round in front of it, except it was closed. I was in my late twenties, and I did not think that there was something wrong riding the kids' rides. Then there was the Petit Palais that was situated at 8th Arrondissement, a beautiful museum that was built in 1900 that held dazzling fine arts. Sad, but I never went inside any museums during my backpacking. I was on a tight budget, and I didn't know what life would bring me once I reached London after five days. I only had how much left in my pocket, and I was panicking deep inside my veins. I had not even had any coffee today, and it felt like there was caffeine in my system, and it was kicking in big time. I had to watch my every expense, or else I would go on days without eating. Being homeless, me? In Europe? That was insanity.

I bought my train ticket from Paris to London, assuming that it will only cost me some €50. But I was wrong.

I spent £190. British money. "I thought it was less than a hundred? According to my research, that's what the internet said," I told the lady somewhere in her fifties.

She looked at me in a weird way, like, "Hey, if you can't afford the price for the bullet train, you can start walking your way to England. Perhaps you have a long way to go, my child." I got it. I gave her the money because my luggage was super heavy, and I didn't know how much they charged me for the excessive baggage at the check-in. So I had to take the train. The entire time I was in Paris, I never took the train. Everything was all by foot. My concern now was that I would be in London for ten days. I would need to stay put for a while at my hostel before I could tour around because my two feet were hurting badly. There I could see the Eiffel Tower, but I was nowhere near it, and I was starving. I only had a packet of three-in-one coffee that had sugar and cream. And the Chinese restaurant was open, yes. I ordered rice and an orange chicken.

There was this couple who just got married and were on their honeymoon in the city. The woman was friendly, and she ended up asking me if I could take their picture under the Eiffel Tower today or in two days because it was just the two of them. They came from the States. I was trying my best not to choke when she said that. I chewed the chicken slowly and just nodded. But her husband said, "Baby, no. She is also traveling like us. We are not taking her time in touring the city to take our picture. We can do it ourselves or hire a professional from here. We apologize."

Well, I guess he could read people. I didn't mind at all, but I wouldn't have time for myself. I would end up following them around the city like a rat chasing cheese. They left first and finished their meal quicker than I did. I was taking my time. I was on vacation. I had leftovers. It was good for my dinner tonight.

I started my walk again, and finally, I was there after another hour of walking. I sat at the cement bench surrounded by trees and grass together with other tourists that were from around the world. I was in awe. I never thought I would like Paris this much. I didn't like things that everyone liked and wanted. I always wanted to be different and unique, but Paris was definitely in my top bucket list at this moment.

It was my birthday today. I mean, my real birthday, the day I was born. There was an ice cream stand across the street beside the carousel where there were lots of children. I ate the ice cream cone under the tree as I stared at the Eiffel Tower. I sang myself "Happy Birthday" in my head. This was the best birthday gift I ever gave myself. I did not ask anyone for money and did not take out any loans either. I worked hard to come to this country, and it was just amazing. I saw the ice cream guy looking at me and smiling. I widened my eyes and opened my phone and started taking pictures. Okay, he was coming my way. I got up and started walking. He was cute, but I didn't think so. No one was ruining my day with my ice cream cone, at the Eiffel Tower, just because he looked like he was up for something. You know Frenchmen when it came to sex. I read too much about it. For sure, they did love their sex here and there. But sayonara, Mufasa.

My feet were hurting. I couldn't walk properly anymore. I was going super slow. A bicycle tour guy approached me and asked me if I wanted a ride. I laughed at him and said, "Oh, thank you, Mr. French guy, but my beat-up shoes will bring me to where I want to go."

He insisted, "But my bicycle is much comfortable. You can just sit, and I can take you wherever you want to go."

No kidding, man. Seriously. That was very sweet of him, but the fact was I didn't really have money. But I did not tell him that. I was firm with my words and continued, "No, thank you." He did give up. He probably needed money like me. How about if I did the biking for him and looked for tourist around to earn money so he could get a break? I doubt he would say yes to me. But I did good today. I saw a lot of famous sites, the ones I always saw on social media. Today was the best.

I headed back to the hostel, and there was this Middle Eastern guy who came out from a restaurant. He said something to me, but I didn't quite understand because he spoke French. I looked at him and did not say anything. I did not stop. I continued walking. I was panting. I was scared for my life. I watched too many of the terrorist movies where they snatched the girl and used them for sex trafficking. But because he did not pursue me, it was either he was afraid of me because my body built was somewhat sporty, or he did not pursue me because I was not really that attractive. That's right. He would just lose his business. Look for someone else, dude. Praise the Lord.

When I reached the hostel, I was breathing heavily, and the bouncer outside asked me, "Are you okay?" That was nice of him.

"Why, yes. Thank you. I appreciate it."

He was a tall handsome African guy. He looked more like a basketball player to me than a bouncer. I saw Sid bumming on his bed when I opened the door.

"Hey, where have you been?" He was laughing and smiled at me when he asked me this question.

"I went around the city. I went to the Eiffel Tower. I don't know, I got lost. I just walked."

The Argentinian girl looked at me with her eyes wide open and said, "You walked all the way to the Eiffel Tower? Why did you not take the subway?"

I wish I could say I did not have the money anymore and I still had another country to go to. I was trying my best to conserve whatever I had left. But I did spill it out, "Well, it's expensive. I don't have millions of dollars to spend, so I walk."

They started laughing at me. "Amelie, it's only €1 to €2 for one way." They almost cried laughing at me.

That was good. I was glad I could make them laugh. How about that? Way to go. I took my shoes off and put everything on the bunk bed. Ugh. My feet were hurting. How was I going out tomorrow? How I wish I could borrow a bicycle, but I had to pay and put down a deposit. I didn't have a credit card. Whatever cash I had was all I had until I returned to California. What have you done for yourself? Have you traveled outside your country for your birthday? What is your way of healing yourself when you are upset? I love traveling. It helps me cope with all the negative things I am dealing with life, especially being broke. Life is just difficult to not enjoy, but at the same time, life is too beautiful to be ignored.

I couldn't believe I was on the top of the bunk bed, and I couldn't sleep well. It was two in the morning, and these two German girls just came in. It seemed like they just hit their twenties. They turned on the light switch, and guess what? The light bulb of the entire room was on my face. I covered my face with the blanket. It was okay. I could ignore it, but the thing that I could not brush off was their giggles early this morning. Why not be considerate toward others?

I yelled under my blankets, "*Hoy*, what the fuck!"

They turned off the light and jumped onto their bed. I heard the Brazilian guy and the girl from Argentina laughing quietly in their own beds. I couldn't take it. Thank God they were quiet. But what if they actually got mad at me and attacked me? What if they grabbed me and pulled me down from the bunk bed and started beating me up? Oh my god. That would be embarrassing. The bouncer of this place was all the way downstairs at the front desk. I didn't think he would hear me at all if ever I ended up screaming. I didn't think that Brazilian guy would stop the fight if ever it happened. I could imagine him being a referee and having fun watching a catfight. He invited me to go dancing. I looked at him and said, "Sure." I laughed mockingly.

It was 8:00 p.m. There was this bar and restaurant one block away from the hostel. I didn't bring a dress, so I was in my ripped jeans I bought from the secondhand store and a regular T-shirt with a sweatshirt, and I was wearing my beat-up blue Converse. I did put some makeup. I didn't want to look all ugly with what I was wearing and look all bland. People started coming in. Oh god, I did feel old for dancing and drinking. The Brazilian got us a drink, and we ordered a fry for our dinner. I was thrilled to know that I was not the only one broke here. But we split the cost to make sure we would still survive the next day. He got up when the music got loud, and everyone was on the dance floor.

He looked at me and said, "I will dance."

I smiled at him and tried my best not to laugh. "Well, go ahead. I will be here drinking."

He went to the dance floor and started dancing with this lady. He looked at me again, and I gave him a thumbs up. He started laughing. After the first song, he came to our table where I was sitting and he told me I had to leave. He wanted me to go back to the hostel. Wait, what?

"I can't dance properly. Brazilian dancing is sexy dancing. Are you aware of it, Amelie?" Well, yeah.

"Then go dance. I am not stopping you," I told him.

"Well, that's the problem. Every time I see you, I am embarrassed, and I feel like laughing all the time. So you need to go back to the hostel so I can dance properly."

What a crap. I was having fun making fun of him. He invited me here, and now he was uninviting me? Thanks anyway. "Okay. I get it. Goodbye and enjoy grinding that ground with that flabby lady."

He started laughing, and the guy beside him stood. Well, what could I say? Her boobs were both looking the opposite ways, and her stomach was not tucked in properly in her dress. And where were her collar and button-up shirt? I got it. I was an old-school person. I went back to the hostel and lay on my bed, staring at my phone with all the pictures I took. Unbelievable. Ugh. Next day? What did I do today again? Oh, right, I went to the most expensive mall I had ever been to in my entire life called Printemps Haussmann, located in Boulevard Haussmann. Every stuff I laid my eye on was unbelievable. The prices were all out of reach. It was definitely a high-class mall. I found the Ladurée and got a small box of macaroons. At least that was affordable. Still, it was almost €30. But that was on the main bucket list. When I got to Paris, I had to eat macaroons. And oh yeah, I was in Cathédrale Notre-Dame de Paris. Growing up in the island, I only saw this church from *The Hunchback of Notre Dame*. I never imagined seeing it in real life.

The entire time I was in Paris, it was like I was eating the best meal in my entire life. I was just content and happy. Better yet, when you are starving and just want to put something in your tummy before you pass out, and after that, you turn out to be a couch potato and just hang out in the couch and do nothing, except imagine that gigantic burger you just had, worrying about how it will digest. But this time, my only concern was finance. I was honestly broke.

It was time to say goodbye and say hello to a new world. England, here I come. This time, I took the train to the main train station. I stopped at the newspaper stand and browsed for an Eiffel Tower key chain. All of a sudden, there was a guy running really fast, and in the blink of an eye, a cop on a bicycle was like Flash. I felt the wind and him just zoom by. He was trying to catch this guy. I didn't understand why he needed to run from a cop instead of just talking to them. I wonder what he did for him to be chased like that. Why was it that I was not being chased by police? What should I do to be chased? I felt like I was too innocent. Here comes my train. I thought it would take me at least six hours, but it was only two hours and twenty minutes. Amazing. The train was packed with English people.

So far, I was loving it. It was fascinating. The people here spoke completely differently compared to Parisians. I felt like I belonged here more than any other country I had been to. They spoke English. Obviously, it was England. People were nice. When I say nice, it's with all capital letters—Nice. I was with my luggage, and there was no elevator, not even an escalator. A young man who is in high school years, and was a six-foot-tall boy, helped me carry my suitcase all the way to the top where the taxi and buses were.

"Do you need some help?" he asked with an accent.

"Yes, please," I replied. And when I reached the top, I told him right away, "Thank you."

When he left and turned to his right, that's when I let my breath out. Jesus Christ, I think I climbed three floors. I could walk in a straight path for hours with no problem, but

I didn't run, and I didn't climb. I was panting and sat at the edge of the ground with my luggage.

A lady behind me approached me and asked me, "Hi, are you okay? Do you need any help?"

You see what I meant with the word *nice*? "Yes, I am just out of shape. The stairs are overwhelming," I said to her.

She replied, "Okay." And she headed out.

Good thing my phone was working in Europe, or else I wouldn't know what I was going to do with directions. I typed my hostel address, and by God's grace, it was only eighteen minutes away. My suitcase had gotten heavier because of all the souvenirs I accumulated from the other four countries I went to. I was just glad that I was in my last country. Ten days, and I would be home.

I was at the address. I didn't think I was in the right place. I went inside the bar and asked where it was, and the Englishman said, "This is the building. You are here."

Wait, what? Where?

He said, "It's upstairs, and down here is the pub. Upstairs is the hostel. You go through the salon. Then you have to carry your luggage upstairs because there is no elevator here."

I happily said, "It is fine." I even gave him a smile. I pushed the salon door, and the stairs were steep. My suitcase was unbelievably heavy, and I was incredibly exhausted, especially my feet. The guy gave me a key to the room, but it was a card key. It was cool. And what was cooler was when I opened the room door, there were seven bunk beds, and each bunk bed had three single beds. Three people could sleep in one tall bunk bed. Wasn't that insane? Good thing I was all the way at the bottom. But the concern was, what if it just collapsed? Then I wouldn't be saying great anymore, because I would be crushed down here. Good luck to me.

ARE YOU HAPPY?

  The person on my right side was an Australian guy who just received his degree and flew all the way to London to hunt for a job. That was exciting, and I thought he just gave me lots of ideas on how to leave my current situation, which was my job and the home I was living in. Fantastic. I desperately wanted to go out for a walk, but my feet didn't want too. So today, I was taking a day off from walking. I could go downstairs for lunch or dinner. They served hamburgers. I watched comedy movies the entire day and played with my phone.
  The next day, I could still feel my two feet. I had my first coffee early in the morning in the pub. Good thing it was free. Here I go. It felt like I was Dora the Explorer with my backpack. The only thing I didn't have was the monkey.
  I went to the Buckingham Palace. Wow, this was amazing. I was outside an English palace. They were close though. It was only seven in the morning. I woke up very early today. I didn't know if that was good here or not. I always got up before the chickens started yelling. Because of that, I was all alone walking the streets of London. It felt like it was a Zombieland. It was okay. I could always come back. I had nine days left here in England.
  I took so many pictures. From the palace, I went to Big Ben and the London Eye. The only thing that was open so far was a 7-Eleven by Big Ben. The line was super long because everyone was buying their coffee to start their morning. What if I moved here to this country? Why not? I felt like I was from here. Could you imagine that?
  I went to England and felt like I belonged. It felt like I used to live here, that I was from here. And that was because I was 50 percent English. Thanks to Oliver, I was able to find my true identity. He was amazing, I was very grateful to have him in my life.

Have you ever seen that giant sushi shaped like a triangle and wrapped with the black seaweed? It was thick and filled with rice with different vegetables inside. It was so affordable, and in the past nine days, that was the main food I had been eating until I left the country! I went toward Tower Bridge and sat on one of the benches. I stayed in one spot for hours, just contemplating about my life. The birds started flocking by my feet. The crumbs of my chocolate were very tasty, I believe. It was just birdie and me, sharing my bar of candy. I had no energy at all to walk around. I felt wasted and beat up. Next time, I would make sure I would not travel five countries for three months again. I thought that was too long for a vacation.

I heard a lot of criticism about English people on the internet. That they were frosty toward tourists, most especially Americans. Or maybe that was just whispers. Because based on political view, the United States and United Kingdom did have a good relationship. So I wondered what really was the truth. Politics could be very suspicious. I felt like I was lost in life, with no direction. I was told by my foster family that I needed a husband and start my own family. But how would I do that when men were more complicated than I was?

I did see some travelers that were with their partners, and I got sad most of the time and wished I was with someone too. But my personality was just inexplicable. After a few days, there were newer tourists in the hostel, and another Brazilian guy happened to be very friendly. It was his first time to travel outside his country, and he was super thrilled to make new friends. His name is Atila. He was exactly the same age as me, and because it was his first day and did not know anything about London and I had been there for more than a week now, he and I went to the Beatles crosswalk. We passed Big Ben, and then we went to the Harry Potter attraction site. The line was long just to take a picture with the cart that was attached to the wall. My heel was bleeding.

When Atila and I took the red bus to the Beatles crosswalk, the bus driver just closed the door without informing us that we needed to move, and so the door closed behind me, and my feet got caught. The skin peeled badly, and the blood was all over my beat-up Converse. I tried my best to ignore my feet because I didn't want to stop walking around with Atila. I was having fun though. I needed to go to the pharmacy and buy Band-Aids. This wouldn't do. The bleeding wouldn't stop. I had to sit down. I told Atila that I would just sit down at the sushi café and have a cup of coffee. He could continue with whatever he wanted to do. But before that, we went inside the Harry Potter shop after we took a picture at the station cart. I found a shirt and a key chain for a souvenir. My suitcase would have more stuff. I would never be able to leave this country. I wouldn't have money to pay the check-in counter for the suitcase. Maybe a carry-on would do?

We went back to the hostel and thought that our day was over. Two French guys came in, and Atila tried to be friends with both of them, except they didn't speak English. I pulled out my cellphone and type in the translator and asked Atila's questions for them. I played it, and both Francois and Dimitri had their eyes wide open with surprise. They jumped from the bunk bed and looked at my phone. Atila was so surprises and got closer to look at the phone too. Now there were four of us. We all went downstairs and hung out in front of the hostel. We bought two beer cans each, and another two Italian guys who were staying in the hostel joined us too. There was this girl from Iceland that was sitting alone behind us. The two Italian guys with us tried to speak to her, but she only answered their questions and left. She hung out with us, but she had forgotten about her own personal agenda. Now there were two girls in the group. The group was getting bigger, and it was more fun.

It was getting dark, and our group was still together. The Italian guy said that he had a friend who was getting off school soon. We could meet him in a park. We brought some beer and just celebrated each other and the word *travel*. To my surprise, we ended up in a cemetery. We took the underground train and walked miles and miles. I was getting really sleepy, but I was at the borderline of me saying goodbye to all of them. So enjoyed myself and partied with them. They were all great people. None of them smoked. They just drank for fun. And not one of them said a curse word. There were eight of us in the group. It was amazing.

We headed back because it was around one in the morning. We stayed in the lobby and played Jenga. There were five of us left trying to fight our exhaustion and sleepiness. But it did not prevail, so we went back upstairs to our bunks and slept. How I wish that day never ended. I would always treasure this day. I hated the fact that today was my last day here Europe, and tomorrow, I was flying back to San Francisco. I was grateful for social media. It had been five years now, and I still had contact with all of them. Fascinating.

So I did see England. Experiencing it felt like I lived there at some point in my life. And knowing that I was actually half English with Scottish blood was more compelling. How I wish I knew before I went there. Everyone was asking me what my ethnic background was because I didn't look 100 percent Filipino. Well, I said it, with my few freckles that were on my face. Was I happy? Yes! I was very happy to know that I was part English.

CHAPTER 7

The Ex-Evil Witch

It was March 2020, at my client's house somewhere in Marin County. We were watching *Start Trek* in the TV room when my phone rang. I didn't understand when things were smooth and at peace, it always got poked by evilness and at least weird stuff. I answered my phone. "Hello?"

Boom! It was like an explosion. It was the ex. Not just the ex-girlfriend but ex-wife. She was going off on me, ranting, screaming in my ears, and calling me names. I was an Asian bitch, according to her. (Wait. Asian bitch? I was 50 percent Scottish.) I asked her who she was, and she said, "Agatha, the evil witch." And she said it out loud.

I had to walk outside because it did not sound good. I tried to talk to her, but she wouldn't calm down. She told me that Oliver was currently married to her, that Oliver was cheating because he was currently married. It was impossible because he showed me papers that they were legally separated for more than four years now. They were not divorced because this evil witch, Agatha, wouldn't sign the papers.

She screamed at me again and said, "You're sleeping on my bed, in my house. You need to stay out of my house. You're a f—— bitch."

If that was her house, then why were none of her belongings there? I guess I had to play along. I just told her, "I need to go back to my job."

She said, "Goodbye." How ruthless could she be toward me yet she was able to say goodbye? Amazing lady. Now what? I didn't know what to say. My chest was palpitating, faster than the run of the action hero Flash. I was attacked, obviously. So who was telling me the truth? Oliver or that evil freaking witch? I felt her wrath. She had a vengeful spirit and must have had a voodoo doll made just for me. I wondered what she looked like. I never met her. At least I could have introduced myself as her husband's woman. Wait, was this for real? Was I really a mistress?

Everything just stopped. Even the mosquito stopped flying. The breeze of the wind had completely ended. I wanted to burst into tears, but not right now. Not at this moment, where I was at work. I needed to stay professional and hold everything in. I went back to the TV room where my client was, and he asked me if I was fine. He looked me in the eye and saw my sorrow from deep inside. I said, "Yes! Thank you so much for asking." I smiled at him and pretended that everything was good.

I texted Oliver and mentioned that his wife just called me and introduced herself in a super friendly way, which confused him. He said that he was not married but legally separated. And he told me this before too. During my conversation with the witch Agatha, the reason why I stepped outside was to put her on a speakerphone so I could record her. I sent that voice record to Oliver. Surprisingly, he did have a lawyer and was continuously filing for divorce and trying to fight this witch with all his might. She was trying to take his Victorian house. Can you imagine that there are just people in this world with thick faces? She never put not one penny on the house and never cleaned during her stay, yet he sent her to school and paid her tuition entirely. She was trying to ruin his life after she walked out on him four years ago. Now she came back because she found out he was with someone else. And she was all over the place, unhappy, screaming that I was committing adultery, and so was Oliver. Splendid, I must say.

Before going to bed, I needed a time for some deep breathing sessions alone and ask myself, "Why are you in this situation, Amelie? What are you going to do?" After a week of staying with my client who needed companionship because of dementia, Oliver picked me up, and we headed back to his house in San Francisco. Petrified I was, but he said to not worry because he had not been with that woman for years.

On our way home, we stopped by Sprout Market to grab some breakfast meals and some groceries good for a couple of days. We walked toward the house, and the gate was open. I told Oliver that I had a bad feeling about this. He told me that everything was fine. It was probably the mailman just dropping the letters. But my heart was telling me it was not the mail man. It was something else, which I didn't know what.

We went upstairs, and he opened the front door. We both stepped inside and closed the door, and there she was. She was inside Oliver's house. This was very weird.

"Oliver, do you want me to step outside?"

He said, "*No.*"

Agatha, the wicked witch, started talking down on me. She called me names and was taking my picture (how I wish I could have posed for her). She was screaming and telling me that this was her house and her bed. She was very disgusted because I slept with her husband on the bed where she slept with him. Oliver grabbed my arms and pulled me toward the master bedroom. I sat at the edge of the bed and stared at her, and she stopped talking down on me. She looked at me with no words. If ever she came at me, well, I would defend myself. But that did not happen. I stayed put, and I told Oliver calmly to call the police because she was not stopping, and she was causing a scene in the entire neighborhood.

I really did not expect him to call the cops, but they did come. He closed the bedroom door, and I stayed inside. He stepped outside with two cops, explaining to them exactly the situation with the wife and his relationship with me. Honestly, this was awful and embarrassing. I never thought I would be in this position. Another two cops came in. I could hear them walking toward the kitchen with Agatha. The tone of her voice went down. It was soft and calm. One cop from outside came in and stood at the hallway in front of the bedroom where I was in. I could hear him converse with his superior. He confirmed that he was taking her outside the house. Okay. I thought that I was being picked up by the cops and be thrown outside. I was still waiting for them to open the door. I didn't move from my spot. I was still at the edge of the bed. But I heard that cop go toward the kitchen and told Agatha that she needed to step outside, that she was actually not allowed to be inside Oliver's house. Trespassing, harassment, verbal abuse, and a lot more heavy stuff could be filed against her.

Wow. Must I tell her boohoo and smile at her like I beat her ass like how Ryu kicked Ken's butt on *Street Fighter*? KO! Oliver came back inside the house and closed the door. He looked at me with a smile and said, "It's all good."

Right, he thought that was all good? I didn't feel good. We were attacked and ambushed by a wicked witch from his past.

And his house seemed haunted because Agatha left her vengeful spirit. I would not say that my day was ruined. Perhaps a very memorable involvement in my existence that could be contributed to interesting tales for life's maturity. I went to the kitchen and put all the groceries away after that awesome entertainment. I started drinking a bottle of Heineken. Something inside me was trying to say that I was nothing, and I deserved to be in that situation. Agatha was a skinny lady in her fifties. She stood below my ears. She was that short. But she did have horrible skin. I was not a skin expert, but I did hydrate myself for the sake of my complexion. And I put some on moisturizer and saw my dermatologist at Market St. here and there. Great, now I was comparing myself to her. Why would I do that when Oliver chose me over her? That's right, Ms. Ego of mine that's inside me. Stop with the nonsense because I'm stronger than you think.

I was on my second beer and on the bed with Oliver, talking about everything that happened that day. He wanted me to be comfortable in his Victorian house. Was he serious? After what just happened inside his home, he asked for me to be cozy? I couldn't. Unless maybe if he allowed me to rearrange stuff in his house, then it might help me be at ease. He agreed and said, "Mi casa is your casa. Do as you please."

I looked at him and smiled. I told him first thing in the bedroom, "I want that closet out and this huge dresser too. And this sunflower comforter is honestly awful. I want everything inside this bedroom out because that wicked witch used to be in here, and I don't feel comfortable."

I expected him to say, "No, not everything in this room." After a week of being at my client's residence, when I came back to Oliver in San Francisco, the closet was gone. Wow! Look at that space. All the clutter was no longer present. We both took the dresser down to the garage and even the sunflower comforter. We ordered a new mattress and a bedframe. We even painted the bedroom with my choice of color, which was beige. He was actually frightened that I'd pick a strong bright pink, which was hilarious. I liked making things suspenseful and making him think. It was always fun for me when I made him worried because he looked at my face for a long time without breathing, if it was true what I was telling him. Then we started laughing hard.

There were no days that we never bullied each other. I hated it when he did it to me. He loved doing it a lot, especially when I screamed at him and started stomping my legs super hard. Then I'd give him an emoji look and say, "You're dead meat."

Oliver was very sweet, and I felt that he really loved me. Defending me from that wicked witch was a huge thing, and he allowed me to rearrange furniture and stuff in the house. I was having so much fun. I always wanted to do interior designing, and this was an opportunity for me to apply what I knew. We ordered an antique bedframe, a small dresser, and a right size closet, all in varnished wood brown. It all came after a month. We also changed the flooring in the master bedroom.

"How do you feel? Are you happy?" he asked me.

"Yes, I am happy. Very happy. I feel a lot more comfortable." I cleared out the living room too. I removed the sofa and everything in the dining area. Everything that was not needed was thrown away. Other stuff was donated. I was not trying to control everything in his house, but everything was cluttered, and it was in a serious mess. He was a guy and was very busy with his work. That was probably why this was the perfect time for me to have met him. He needed a lot of help in the house, like cleaning, folding clothes, and making some dishes for him. I was glad that I loved doing all of that.

I would point fingers and to tell you this: Agatha not once cleaned. She never touched the broom. I couldn't imagine a woman not having the word *clean* saved in her vocabulary. Meeting her last week was unexpected. I thought that she would be somewhat into fashion, elegant with nice skin and some blush on, and a have a beautiful dress on some nice luxury branded heels. But I made a mistake. She looked sick. The dark circles around her eyes were bigger than the ¢25 coin. She was wearing jeans that seemed already worn many times, and she hadn't washed it. Her bag looked like it came from a thrift store. Don't get me wrong. I loved my tote canvas bags, especially when I went for a walk in the city with my book inside it and go to my favorite coffee shop. I'd order a latte and stay there for hours until I at least read fifty pages. My goal was to read fifty pages of a book in a day. I got so thrilled when I exceed to seventy-five pages. But somehow, and I don't know why, I never reached a hundred pages. I had this dilemma with my attention span. My butt couldn't be still and needed to roam around or at least do something different besides reading, like cleaning or doing the laundry.

I had a question for Agatha. After more than four years of leaving your husband, why are you now back? For what? I could not understand. What's strange was that she worked for a hospital. So she must be well with life. She must have a good job and settled. But why are you attacking someone you don't know? You never met her in your entire life, yet you cursed that person? Intriguing. But what's more amazing was that no matter what I did with Oliver's house—rearranging it, buying new furniture, and changing some of the knick-knacks—I could still feel the hateful spirit of Agatha. It was clinging to the house. I mentioned it to Oliver, and he said that he could sell the house. I said no. He bought his house when he was twenty-one with the help of his parents and put all his effort in this house. It would be very sad to see him sell it just because that wicked witch wouldn't sign the contract and tried to harass the both of us. But he had decided.

"We will never have peace in this house." He was right. In every room, I could feel something heavy. I thought at first that there might be an indoor camera inside. So while I was dusting, I looked very carefully if there were cameras, but there weren't any. At least the witch was not here with us, except the presence of her spirit that she left was very strong.

After a couple of days, Oliver and I were having wine and watching horror movies when my phone rang. I called it back, and it was a pizza place. I figured to ask the guy, "Was it a petite woman in her fifties that called?" He didn't want to answer me. He was laughing, saying other things, and I said, "You're fine. Just wondering because if it's that person, well, she has a restraining order from me because of harassment and trespassing."

He said, "Yes, it's her."

Wow. Did I do something in this life or in my previous life to be in this kind of conflict with someone I had no connection with? Oliver didn't want to be with her, and she walked out on him four years ago. Why was she back? To seek vengeance, of course. But why? How I wish I had a fairy godmother who could help me. Instead of turning the pumpkin into a carriage, she'd turn this witch into a rat. Or that was probably a bad idea. Now what? She was harassing me. She wouldn't leave me alone.

Oliver emailed his lawyer everything that happened. We sent her the video I recorded from when she called me and called me names. It was terrifying. I wanted to say that this night had been ruined, but I would not allow that wicked witch to demolish our happiness and fun. Life continued no matter what. As long as I knew that I was not stepping over someone's life, then I continued with life.

When the police would come in, if ever they grabbed me and said that I needed to leave because I was actually a mistress, then something was wrong with me for still being with him and fighting for something that was not mine, and it was not right. But the police and the lawyer confirmed that I was good. My relationship with Oliver was normal and acceptable by law.

It was the next day. Consistency, I must say. Agatha was hired. She texted Oliver a long message that had no period, but she kept going on and on. That was how evil witches were, right? They had no time to waste. Instead, they were aggressive and consistent with their annoyance with people. If I could build her a monument myself, then I definitely would. Salute!

Oliver ignored the messages, yet he screenshotted it and sent it to his lawyer for evidence of harassment in addition to her other violations. She probably did want to go to jail. But if she ended up in jail, how would she see how happy Oliver was with me in my arms? I hope she wouldn't end up in jail. That would be sad for me. Despite all these feelings I had been hiding, I couldn't keep my grip on it anymore. I had an breakdown when Oliver went to the kitchen to grab us a soda. I started crying out loud. My tears were uncontrollable. I called my sister-in-law in the Philippines and told her everything about it while crying. I told her that I just needed to open up and talk to a girl who would understand me.

Her response was "I can't believe you didn't bitch slap that witch." She was right. Knowing me, I would MMA that wicked witch's dumb face for even coming in front of me. No one talked down on Amelie. I was Amelie, the Amelie. At least that's what I thought. I was making a fool of myself. I just needed this time to release everything I had been holding inside.

Oliver heard me and ran to back to the bedroom. He comforted me and was sorry for putting me in this situation. It was never his fault. He didn't put me in this position. He was not even aware that his past would come back just to ruin his life with the new person he was with. After today, I should be okay. Usually, I just needed a one-time big cry and a good night's sleep. Then I'd be fine. Tonight, I would make sure I'd have six bottles of beer. We went to the store and purchased twenty-four bottles of beer. This should help me.

CHAPTER 8

Confused

It was 7:30 a.m. on a Friday. How I wish I didn't have to get out of bed. I dreamed of calling in sick for work. But if I didn't put those hours in, I wouldn't have any money for next week. Ugh. I got up and put my slippers on. I turned the portable heater. This house was super cold, and it was insane. I didn't want to turn the main heater in the house because I was trying to save. Oliver did. Well, it was his house, his rules. I moaned while walking toward the kitchen. I didn't understand that every morning, it was always difficult to get up. If I slept on the floor every night, things might be different. I would want to get up right away, just like those soldiers in the military.

I turned on the kitchen television to Fox News and filled the kettle with water. While I waited for it to boil, I used the bathroom and changed my clothes. I tried my best to pack two bags for this weekend client of mine and not more than that. It was too hard to carry bunch of bags to a client's home. And after three days, I always dragged it all out to the car. I couldn't even leave anything at the client's house because what if they canceled me, and my agency might tell me that that was actually my last day. How was I going back to grab my things? The kettle boiled. I put the ground coffee on the Chemex and ran the hot water slowly. The smell of the coffee was just amazing. It made my morning complete. I put all my clothes and shampoos in the first canvas bag, and the other bag contained food and coffee, of course.

Now that the bags were ready to go, I made breakfast before I left. The news was horrible in every station. Oliver just called to say hi. Every day, when I woke up, we spoke on the phone just to accompany each other and see if we both needed something, and each of us could take it to whoever was in need. And the conversation just lasted for forty-five minutes. I had to hang up on him so I could start heading out and drive myself all the way to San Jose. It had been more than a month of me driving to my client's home, and I still needed to type his address in my map. One thing that made me so uncomfortable being in this beautiful Victorian house was that Oliver's parents lived beside this house. I had never seen them, but they had seen me so many times from their window. How unfair could that be? And Oliver, just last month, told me that his divorce was rescheduled again from March to July 9. Wow. So this was now the third court hearing that was never done but always scheduled.

What could I say? What was I feeling the moment he said it to me? I felt like the people walking in the street of San Francisco just stopped. I felt that my heart stopped pumping. I didn't know what to say. I had no feelings anymore. The dogs in Duboce Park were all in slow motion with their master. I had no words to give to him as a response to what he said that moment. I did ask myself, Can I still do this? Why am I in this situation? What in the world is that woman thinking? Oliver paid for her education. He gave her a roof when he got her pregnant and even married her. People's selfishness was just amazing and couldn't be explained. I was feeling weird. Feeling that I was a mistress never disappeared from my mind. Perhaps I was one. By papers, by law, he was still married, and by the law of the church, he was still a married man. Who was I? Why was I still here? On a snap, he could change his mind and say, "Amelie, I am sorry, but this isn't working out for me, and you need to move out from my house."

I'd be screwed. That was like a horse pooping on your feet, and it was a giant one. It would be difficult to remove and would smell so bad. Then my phone rang. It was Oliver. My one-hour drive to my client was not that bad, except the conversation Oliver and I had was very much stressful. How I wish I could pull my hair, but I needed my hands on the wheels. We ended up arguing, and I couldn't take it anymore. My headache was starting again. I threw my cell phone on the passenger seat. I didn't want to hear what he had to say.

The tension and bad energy never ended. It had been more than a year now, and we were like this every single week. One thing that made it worst on my side was that the wicked witch kept ordering catalog from different companies and had them sent to Oliver's home. I ended up receiving them. Her harassment never ended. I read my horoscope and his if it matched or somehow maybe we could compromise for the sake of this relationship. Was I missing something? Was I doing something that was actually making us dig our own hole and want to walk out on each other?

I stopped by a coffee shop to grab a latte. It was five minutes away from my client's home here in San Jose. I tried to relax. And what just happened to Oliver and I with our recent conversation, I will brush it off. As far as I knew, I did my best. Around 6:00 p.m., Oliver called me to converse. I could tell he was trying his best not to put any tension in this conversation. He was calm and lying down on the sofa at home while I sat in the recliner at my client's house, talking to him. Seriously, we started talking about the things that must be said and not be said during his court hearing for his divorce. We talked about the lawyer and other stuff that were in regards of this matter, until the wicked witch was mentioned, and so he talked about her hate and anger and trying to ruin his life badly, about her trying her best to take half of his home. I thought I'd listen because I was his girlfriend, his new partner, perhaps his fiancée.

He talked the entire time, and I agreed. I looked at my phone to see what time it was, and I noticed that we had been talking for fifty-two minutes. He had been talking about his wife for fifty-two minutes now. Okay, hold on. I stopped him and asked him why we were talking about his wife. I asked him why he was talking about his ex-partner to me. Why were we even giving her a minute to be discussed in this relationship? I felt so stupid for even listening. Why did I even bother listening to what he had to say about that woman? I mean, I understood that he was telling me how he felt, but it had been more than a year now since she harassed me.

That woman called me names. I put her in a prejudiced and racist category. He told me to stop, because he would not speak of her name again. But how could I just forget about this? Fifty-two minutes of conversation about his ex-wife? Was he still feeling something for her? Why would he dare speak of such a thing? I was honestly hurt, and most of all, I was speechless. I didn't want to hear from him again. I just didn't want to talk to him again. I hung up the phone and didn't have any plans on answering it for the rest of my life. He sent me ten messages that night, and the only thing I said was "Oliver, you talked about your ex-partner to me for an hour. What do you think I will feel? Please do not message me. Please leave me alone."

Saturday passed by. I did not answer any of his phone calls and text messages. I was able to calm myself and relax. I downloaded this app called Calm on my phone and started listening to it when I felt stressed out. It was a huge help. My headache disappeared like a snap. I had a peaceful sleep that night. It was Sunday morning. I looked at my phone, and I saw a hundred messages from him. Wow. Was this even normal? He called, and I finally answered. He sounded irritated. He said that he was accommodating me and giving me everything he could, and this was what I repaid him. I was in a relationship with him, yet I treated him like he was not my partner. And he said that I was a big liar. Okay, hold. This was not good at all. This was my door out of this relationship. I didn't want to be with him if this was how he talked to me.

A liar? I told him, "First of all, accommodating? I gave up my two-bedroom and two-bathroom apartment because you have been asking me to move in with you for almost a year. So you have no right to say such a thing to me. Now the word *lies*. What did I lie about, Oliver? Please tell me, because I don't really know." He kept talking here and there. I just couldn't do this anymore. "You know what, I can't honestly do this anymore. Please, it's been every month since last year that I've been trying to break up with you. Just let me go. Please leave me alone. You never brought peace into my life. Everything is a mess. I love you, but I love myself more. I already ignored the fact that I was harassed by the wicked witch and that you're still in the process of divorce for two years now. The only negative energy that I should be experiencing is the longing of you being set free from that woman. But no, you are just difficult. Extremely hectic to dealt with. I am at the point where I want to hurt myself bad. I want to stab myself and crash the car whenever I am driving. My anxiety level every time I see your message on my phone is unbelievable. I think a relationship should not make me feel this way. I can't do this anymore, Oliver. I am leaving, and I need time to put money on the side so I can hire a moving company to take all my furniture out from your house. Good luck with life." I hung up.

I turned off the volume on my phone and put it in my purse. I completely shut myself from him. I didn't care anymore. Today was Easter Sunday, and my client was being picked up by his kids. I had to go home. But I didn't want to go home. So I checked in to a hotel in downtown San Jose. I just needed to get away so bad. I wanted this relationship. I wanted Oliver. But this relationship was just ridiculous. I shouldn't be feeling what I felt toward him. And it seemed like he didn't care about my current health and what I was currently feeling. Did he think I was overreacting? Women usually overreacted and exaggerated, but at this point, was I really? My emotions at this moment were scattered.

I was so confused. I didn't know what to do. I wanted to leave him. I wanted to get my own apartment again. I needed that peace of mind and clarity with life. But how was I going to do that? I practically just moved in with him five months ago. I was like a fly that moved around so much that I didn't even have a permanent address. I couldn't be tracked that by whoever. I guessed this was actually good? I was so tired of moving around. I accumulated furniture throughout last year. And so it would not be easy to just move. I had at least twenty boxes of stuff, including my clothes and a dining set with chairs, a kitchen table with four chairs, and two queen-size bedframes and mattresses. And how about my nine-inch sofa? My two giant rugs that I got from West Elm were not cheap. I would forget all this stuff and walk away to make my life easier. Well, what was I going to do when I got a new apartment? Purchase new stuff? I called a moving company to inquire and was told that it all depended on the location.

And if I was moving nearby, it would be between $1,500 to $2,000. All my stuff was worth more than that. I thought that it was worth taking with me, except the fact that I had to see Oliver again.

I would take my time and really think about what I wanted to do with my life. I was turning thirty-three in a couple of weeks, and I didn't know what to do with my life. I thought that I was cursed in this lifetime because I had been a bad daughter to my foster parents. Was that even right when I was not actually related to them by blood? Or maybe my real blood family had something to do with my decisions in life. I booked a two-night stay at Westin Hotel in downtown San Jose, just until Tuesday, 5:00 a.m. I needed to clock in at my other client around 6:00 a.m. on a Tuesday.

What should I do today to destress myself? How about a Thai massage? Yes. I googled some massage places nearby and called them. Hopefully, they would take walk-in customers. And by luck, yes, they did. I was outside parking the truck and putting my mask on because it was mandated because of the pandemic. The Thai lady opened the door for me. She asked me to sit down, and she took my temperature to make sure I didn't have the coronavirus. I filled a paper form with my information, and there was a drawing of a body, and she asked me to circle the parts I wanted the therapist to focus on. I asked for the Thai herbal massage, which I honestly regretted. I wish I could have sticked to the Thai massage.

The therapist put a cold white linen over me and massaged my back with this cute round white thing with herbs inside. It was all sophisticated and nice, good for a social media post, except that it was cool. I was getting chicken skin the entire time I was being massaged. How I wish I could have stopped her and said, "I'm done with this type of massage and please just apply massage oil in my back."

But I didn't want her to think I had an attitude and that I was making it difficult for her. So I ended up sucking the entire massage session for ninety minutes. I didn't think I was pleased at all. Ugh. I gave her a $10 tip, and the two ladies at the reception looked at me like I gave her a dollar bill. Well, how much should a tip be, $20? Wasn't that too much, or was I being a cheapskate? I would not look back, and I gave my thanks to them. "It was wonderful. Thank you so much." And I was out.

I didn't think that actually did anything to me, except for the coolness it gave my body. Good thing it was not that cold outside on a spring season in the Bay Area. It was still too early to check in to the hotel. What was next? My phone kept beeping, and Oliver had sent me fifty messages already. I didn't understand. I asked him nicely to give me space, but he wouldn't. I couldn't breathe. I felt like I was choked extremely. Because of that, I went to the store and shopped around. I went to Target. I got a book called "The Yellow Bird Sings" by Jennifer Rosner, pajamas, new underwear, socks, and a bunch of chocolate bars.

I called the hotel and asked if I could check in earlier than the regular check-in time. I guess I was one lucky chicken. They said to come now because the room had been cleaned and was ready for me. I could feel my stomach growling. I hadn't eaten anything since I got up this morning. I couldn't believe I felt like a single person today. I shouldn't feel bad because I was trying to destress. I was just too polluted by toxic emotions and thoughts. I deserved this day. I stopped by the Italian restaurant on my way to the hotel, and the waiter said that they were not accepting any orders at the moment and to call around 6:00 p.m. I didn't think so. I saw Wienerschnitzel and got two hot dogs and parked the truck on the side and devoured it with a large soda. This was the reason why I wanted to be alone, so I could pig out. You couldn't really eat well when you were with a guy, even if it was your partner. \

I reserved a room with a full or queen-size mattress, but this Filipino lady gave me a king-size bed. How cool was that? Surprisingly, there was an Italian restaurant at the first floor of the hotel. And before I went upstairs to my room, I got a Cabernet Sauvignon. The waiter was quite nice and pleasant. I hoped every restaurant had him. I guess he could split his body apart? I hit the number 5 button inside the elevator with my right hand, making sure I didn't spill the wine that was in my left hand. I opened my bedroom door, and the smell of fresh linen, freshly cleaned room, and newly renovated bathroom was just what I needed.

I changed into my pajamas and dimmed the lights and slid myself inside the blanket. This was wonderful. I turned the television on and found the *Friends* series, and at this moment, I was very pleased, sipping on my wine. I didn't want to think about anything right now, most especially because my phone kept beeping with calls and text messages from Oliver. I ignored it all. How dare he call me, and what was with all the text messages? After everything that he said to me?

It was Monday morning. I made a cup of coffee inside my room and took a shower. I opened the curtain and turned on the CNN news. While browsing for an apartment through my phone, Oliver sent me a hundred messages. Was I the only one getting stressed out by this? I appreciated the concern, if you could call that concern. Wait. If someone was concerned, why would they even say the words *liar* and *accommodating*? I loved him, and I didn't want to lose him, but how about me? I would understand if I was doing him wrong, but I was just working so I wouldn't rely on him and ask him for money. Do you even know how embarrassing that is? Unless I was in a wheelchair and incapable. Yet people in wheelchairs were still active and still did work and earned a living. I continued to ignore him. Perhaps today would be a long day for me.

I called a Korean lady who did hair and asked her if she could color my hair gray. She said to come right away. To be honest, she did an awesome job on my hair, except that my head feet numb. I thought it was because of the bleach that she used. Totally not her fault. It was one of the requirements. I was so satisfied and extremely happy with my new look, even though it took seven hours to finish. My butt was hurting from not moving. Every time I tried to stand and do a little stretch, she looked at me with her eyeballs all wide and clear and said, "Sit down."

I followed her instructions right away because I didn't want her to leave my hair hanging. My day was consumed by my hair appointment, which was great. I went back to the hotel and ordered lasagna for dinner. And finally, I was in the mood to answer Oliver's phone call, just right in time as I got in to the elevator.

"Yes! Can I help you?"

Right away, he asked me not to hang up on him, that he was sorry for everything he said to me and that he only said those words because he was trying to hurt me. He wouldn't do it again ever in his entire lifetime. How could a person do that to someone they loved? Say hurtful words to hurt them for no reason? Was it for his own entertainment, or maybe manipulation and control? It'd been exactly a year now that noticed him telling white lies, which accumulated. I felt that this time, they were not just small little lies. I could sense that he was hiding something from me, but I never thought I'd ask him. I wanted to trust him. I wanted this relationship, honesty. But it was not just white lies. Here was one thing I found funny about him. For exactly a year now, he had been telling me that he would put my name in his life insurance. I didn't really care, seriously. What I cared was that he had been saying it for a year, making me feel like I was asking. I never asked him to put me in his life insurance. I had my very own. And he never actually did it. He was just saying it. I didn't understand what it was for. To make me believe what? A lie? He walked inside the house with his work shoes, and I walked around barefooted. I mean, wasn't that disgusting and dirty? And he told me that he never did it not once, but I had seen it so many times. He did it in front of me. I caught him doing it, and he got defensive and denied it. Another thing was, when he told me that he did it, he called the place and that he paid for it, yet he did not. I caught him doing it after he just said he'd done it days or weeks ago. Then he would tell me how much he loved me, that I was his everything and it would be nonstop courting with flowers and chocolates. What else?

Now that I thought about it, it felt like it was kind of a manipulation. What I didn't understand was that this relationship lasted a year with bad energy. What should I do? I loved him. I never wanted to lose him. I was not trying to change him, but I needed him to stop choking me. Perhaps our ages had something to do with it. But insecurities wouldn't help at all. If I showed a bit of kindness, I was worried that he might take advantage of me again and go back to how things were. I missed him so much, but I was also ready to move out. What should I do? I was so confused. I felt like going out of the country and dissociate myself from everything for at least a year. But isolation was not the solution for my current mental state. Perhaps some girlfriends to talk to? But I had none because the word *isolation* happened to be my number one favorite word in my dictionary. Was I ignoring my importance by forgiving him every single time?

I asked him, "Maybe a therapist or counselor will help us with this relationship we are in. Would you be open to something like that?" Okay, what did I just do? My two feet were out the door already. This was the chance for me to be single again and party like a rock star without conflict. I thought that he got into my head and manipulated it without me being aware. I just couldn't get enough of him despite all the conflict. He was like a drug that I looked for all the time. But the cycle? It had been exactly a year with consistency. Okay, I actually did not hang up and ended up speaking to him. He asked me how I was doing. I can't believe I was excited to tell him about my new feature. The entire conversation was filled with apologies and sincerity of love and longing. We both agreed to meet with a counselor or therapist for them to intervene and give us both clarification as to what it was we lacked in supporting each other. Based on what I was hearing, he sounded very calm and different. He had a tone of patience and was not that eager as usual and greedy for attention.

"I will work for the entire week, and I don't really feel like going back home. I just need to disengage from the negativity."

To my surprise, he actually said, "Okay, please take your time, Amelie. I will just be here waiting for you until you are ready."

I completely fell for his spell. On a snap, I said, "Okay, thank you for understanding me." I went to work around 6:00 a.m. on Tuesday, and so far, I didn't feel any pressure from Oliver. By Thursday, I texted Oliver and asked him if he could go with me for two weeks somewhere. Okay. I didn't really know where I wanted to go, except the fact that

I wanted to disappear really bad from work and family. I wanted to go far away where no one knew me.

He said, "Amelie, anywhere you want to go, I'll go with you."

With that said, I bought two tickets from San Francisco to Marrakech, Morocco. It was a two-week trip. It was not completely a vacation, but it was to clear our minds of everything. I found a yoga spot that was ten minutes away, walking distance from the Riad Medina Art Suite and Heated Pool. I knew that I could meditate anywhere here in San Francisco, anywhere in the US, but I didn't know where to start and how to start. I told Oliver that in less than two months, we would need to get our COVID vaccine and that once we got to the airport, we would have to do a COVID testing swab.

"You can take luggage that is fifty pounds and a carry-on or backpack."

He asked, "Where are we going? May I please know? But if you don't want to tell me, it's okay."

I replied, "Africa. We are going to Morocco." It would be his very first international travel. I couldn't imagine that his ex-wife had been to Europe, and she didn't even bring him. Yet she wanted half of the worth of his house? Unbelievable. I never encountered greedy people in my entire life. Oliver was surprised and had no words to say to me, except a thank you. "We need this to clear our heads."

I couldn't wait for the trip to happen. My butt was getting itchy. How I wish I could leave tomorrow, but there were no last-minute flights. The only thing I wanted to do for two weeks in Morocco was meditate and do some yoga. I wanted to go to cooking classes and bring a book to read and relax by the pool with the famous mint tea. I prayed that Oliver would be at peace and wouldn't bring stress with us once we got there. Except the stress that his anxiety brought because of his excitement for this escapade.

I was so happy and excited. I didn't know if I would be able to sleep this entire week. But I was glad that everything with me and Oliver was back to normal and that he was trying his best to change for the good of this relationship. Perhaps, I'd choose to forgive him. And that's what you called love. Wasn't it? But the next time he tried to swing back to that route, I swear to my neighbor's grave that I would acupuncture his entire face, just like what Chinese people did. After that, he wouldn't be able to call me baby again.

I had a dream last night. I was surrounded by some people, and there was a white casket in the same room I was in. Someone was holding my hands and said, "Everything will be fine. You want this, remember, Amelie? You've been wanting this for a long time now."

In my dream, I agreed and said, "Yes, I do."

A lady in a white outfit had a super long syringe. I was in a chair facing the windows. I could hear her walking toward me from behind. She said, "This will be very quick. You need to say your goodbyes now. Say as much as you can say, everything you want to say."

My heart started racing when I heard her say that, but this person on my right side was comforting me the entire time.

"Okay, don't move. Take a deep breath."

She was standing behind me and poked me with the syringe on my left shoulder. It took couple of seconds for her to finish. The needle went all the way in, and I started to feel by legs both numb.

The lady said, "It's all done. You're all good."

Besides my legs being numb, my entire body went numb too. And I couldn't move my body, not even my hands. The only thing I could see was the white casket and the person beside me smiling at me the entire time.

"I'm very happy and proud of you." What did that mean? But why?

I asked the lady in white dress, "What's happening to me? What did you do to me?"

She said to me, "Oh, sweetie, you're dead. That's why I told you to say your goodbyes earlier. Actually, you've been dead for an hour now. I don't know why you're still talking."

I could feel my entire body slowly declining. I woke up. I noticed both my hands were holding my face on both sides. I grabbed my phone under my pillow to see what time it was, and it was 4:05 a.m. I went to the search engine immediately to ask a question about my dream. What did it mean when you dreamed about seeing a white coffin?

I imagined that I would die any time soon or someone close to me dearly might pass away. Wasn't this the interpretation of this dream? The search engine said that it was actually an ending of something in my life, or changing for worse. It could also mean for me to move ahead with life and leave the things that did not suit me in my current living. It meant leaving the toxic life that I shouldn't even be carrying with me. A close casket represented something that would make me move on in life. Whatever it was, I felt like a snake that removed its dead skin to be renewed.

I thought about Oliver's freedom from his ex-wife. Was this what my dream was talking about? This was like a huge thorn of a rose that had been in my chest for at least a year now. Since I was a young girl, most of my dreams happened. I didn't know if I could call myself a psychic or a complete psycho. I questioned the search engine about being numb entirely and what it meant. It said that I was suffering from emotional hardships. It meant that something might be missing in my life right now. And most especially, I was not happy or pleased in my current situation. That was definitely true.

I was honestly not happy. I felt lonely, but I couldn't complain because it was my decision to stay in this relationship even though I was being attacked. A year ago, I dreamed of a yellow snake, and I shared this to my friend. I was told that I needed to leave Oliver because my relationship with him would not do me any good. And for exactly a year, our relationship was not just cats and dogs. I don't think I could even describe it as a roller coaster. Every week, I felt like I got hit by a bus, and the grim reaper was right there at the corner, smiling and excited to take me. How could he not be thrilled? It was like a commission to them, to bring a soul back down there. But I guess everything had its time.

CHAPTER 9

My Mirror Image

My alarm went off at five thirty in the morning. I needed to put everything away. The other caregiver was coming in half an hour. My other shift didn't start until 10:00 a.m. How I wish I could sleep a couple more hours. Ugh. When I got out of the bathroom, Sophie had settled all her things and clocked in for her shift. She didn't mind whenever I stayed until I headed toward my other client.

The banana bread that I made yesterday was a sellable. I mixed granola with it. Sophie and I warmed it up, and we were having it with our dark coffee while we were talking. I asked her about the dream that I had last night and if she knew how to interpret or if she somehow understood dreams.

She asked me what it was, and I said, "I was standing in front of my mom with another woman beside her. They were both in the sofa watching television. I approached them, and I said there is something in my neck sticking out. She asked me what it was, and I said I don't know. So I pulled that thing out of my neck, and it was a long dirty white stick, as long as my spine. Then in my dream, my mother looked at me with her eyes wide open. I said, 'Hold on, there is more.' This time, I kept pulling and pulling, and it did not come out until I reached the dead end. It got stuck inside my neck, so I pushed it all back inside my neck. Then I woke up."

Sophie said that she got premonitions and dreams like this, but what was worse was it happened when she was awake. She got dark visions and saw dark shadows when someone passed her by. There were times that she got scared because after a while, or even on the same day, they'd die. She discovered this dream of hers when she was eight years old. While she was talking, I was thinking that I had seen this situation in a movie.

I asked her, "Are you telling me a story from a movie or drama?" I was getting goose bumps. She asked about my horoscope sign, and I said Taurus. She said that she was a Taurus too. What a coincidence. Then she said that her birthday was last week, April 26. I got excited and said that my birthday was just last week too, on April 22. She looked at me like I was crazy. I asked her, "Why? What's wrong?"

"This is the reason why you get dreams like mine, Amelie. The only difference is that mine is stronger," she said.

"So I'm a psychic or that person in horror movies who gets feelings if there are spirits in the house? In conclusion, I'm a witch. Yup. Wow."

Sophie started cracking up and laughing and said, "No, we are not witches, but it's a gift that was given to us."

I thought she was honestly insane. But she told me about her current situation with her boyfriend who was ten years older than her. When she met him, the guy made it clear that he was still married, and he lived with his wife in the same roof. But they were not together anymore. They had too many properties, and lots of money was involved. Instead of filing a divorce and splitting the entire thing, they would rather help each other. The problem was, her boyfriend and his wife still messed with each other, which was very strange.

She had her own bedroom. The wife had her own, too, and Sophie's boyfriend was also in a different room. Should they not share the same room if they were both in the relationship? Or was the guy trying not to hurt his wife's emotions and so that they could still sleep with each other?

I asked her how she could tolerate living with him in the same house where the wife was. I knew I couldn't do that. I'd go insane. I was already going mentally ill with my situation with Oliver and being harassed by his wife who was legally separated with him for at least five years now. But she had been with him for fourteen years now in Alameda. He bought her a car. Now I was jealous of her. Two years of being with Oliver, and he didn't buy me a car or a house. I bought furniture for his house. What a lucky bastard, and I was the mistress.

Sophie was very happy with the situation she was in right now. I guess she wouldn't last fourteen years with him if she was not happy. Hey, that was not my concern anymore, and besides, I was not living her life. She was the one dealing with it. So I told her about my situation, and she said that I needed to get out of this relationship. According to her, he was using me. But how could that be, when he was actually providing me a roof over my head? And he didn't even ask me for monthly rent. I did groceries here and there, but other than that? He even lent me his truck so I could get to work without spending $50 on an Uber, and that was only for a one-way trip. It was honestly expensive.

She said, "Amelie, you are too young. Don't waste your life. He has too much baggage. You are an easygoing person, and experiencing this kind of life is just unfair. You will meet more guys out there who are more suitable for you and baggage-free."

I asked her where she was originally from, and she said Olongapo City. I felt my heart jump. I told her that I was born in Olongapo City. My birth mother was from Olongapo City, and she met my birth father there. He was stationed in Clark Air Force Base back in 1987. Then she had me in April 1988 in a small clinic in the village, where she actually left me. I was found by an old lady looking for an infant for her eldest daughter who couldn't conceive a child. And that was on May 2, 1988, after two weeks. How could they be so lucky to find me? A cute little baby? My head was a bit big and full of crap. I never found my real parents, except for that DNA testing. They might have their own families now, and I didn't want to ruin it. Besides, they might think that I might just wanted money from them.

I did feel very empty inside, especially when my foster parents brought me to the US after high school. After six months, they flew back to the Philippines and left me in San Antonio, Texas, after enrolling me in a community college. They put me with one of the members of the church that they had known for years. They were friends already before I was born. So they all had a good relationship. But that did not work out for me. I ran away and tried to look for my own life. I tried to look for someone or anyone who would be beside me and hug me, someone who would comfort me. I was desperate to be with someone.

Growing up with my foster parents, I didn't know if it was normal or not, but they always left me and my brother in the house, and they'd travel four hours to the city because they said that there was a seminar and that it was important. I would never forget what my foster mother told me: "My ministry with the Lord in the mountain and with the native pastors is much more important than you and your brother. You two are just second on the list." I heard that so many times growing up. I didn't understand. Why was I adopted? Why did I have to hear that I was not that important compared to those people who didn't wear pants and had no slippers? Their women had no tops on and lived in huts. They had to walk a couple of miles down just to get a bucket of water to bring back to where they lived.

I was never prejudiced toward these people. I even printed coloring stuff and brought cookies for them when I was nine years old. I read them stories from the Bible while my foster parents built a church with the native people. But I was compared by the parents I knew to those kids that I was exactly the same as them, and there was no difference between me and them. I felt so broken emotionally and mentally. Kyle, my friend, said to me that I had attachment issues. I thought so too. I mean, who wouldn't? I was left by real mother in a clinic, then I was adopted and brought to a different country. And after six months, she left me too. Seriously, I thought I was actually mentally screwed up. Plus with my current situation right now? Seriously, it seemed like my life got better as I aged.

What if Sophie was actually my blood relative? I mean, the earth was too small. Even criminals could be found if you really searched good. I was able to find my gay ex-boyfriend who wore my dresses back in 2012. It was so funny. I had no idea he was a crossdresser. That's why I wondered why when I washed my clothes, the underarms were all stretched out. It was really odd. One time, he was at work, and I stayed home and was bored. I went through his pictures on his laptop and found a file of him wearing my dresses, makeup, and earrings. He had too many selfies that he even had some where he was pouting with his red lipstick. I mean, my red lipstick that was in his lips.

I just remembered my foster dad's message to me: "Amelie, Jacob sent me a message saying that you broke up with him." How dare him.

"Dad, I can't be with a guy who's prettier than me," I said in front of my parents. They were speechless. There were no words from either one of them. I thought they would ask me more questions about what happened to our relationship, and I would not know how to explain things to them besides the fact he was a crossdresser. And oh, wait, he also cheated on me many times.

CHAPTER 10

Fixing This Relationship

After a month of booking our trip, I thought about Morocco. I read too many frightening stories about it, and even Oliver questioned my interest about the country a gazillion times. He wanted to go somewhere he would fit in. For his first international travel, he wanted to feel at ease. And so I called the airline and cancelled the trip. Besides, it was not for another month of waiting. I changed our route, and it was cheaper. It was a country I hadn't to been yet—Lisbon, Portugal. I had been intrigued about the country since 2017. I just didn't have the time to go back to Europe after I moved to San Francisco. Actually, the month I moved to San Francisco, I had a ticket to Paris for eleven days and ten nights. Except I had to make my choice. Should I fly to Paris, enjoy that cappuccino, sit on the grass in front of the Eiffel Tower, or should I stay and keep my client, my work? If I left, I'd spend more money out of my pocket. I just moved to the city, and my workdays would stop.

I decided to stay. It was kind of sad because Paris's borders were closed because of the pandemic. He was thrilled about the change because it was Portugal, and he loved seafood.

"I will definitely fit in. Thank you, Amelie."

I didn't even finish what I was telling him, and he cut me off because of his excitement. I waited for a minute, and I said that there was more.

"What is it?" he asked.

Well, here it goes. "We leave next week."

The *what* word was loud in my ear. I told him over the phone because I was at work. Okay, to be honest, another month of waiting was ridiculous. I couldn't do this anymore. I needed to go somewhere away from San Francisco or the States. It was all my fault. I was used to traveling every year internationally.

"What happened?" he asked.

"I took your word in consideration, and, myself am uncomfortable about the idea of Marrakech, so I decided for us to fly to Lisbon without consulting you. I sincerely apologize for taking control over this."

He didn't mind at all, but he made a suggestion. He asked about Amsterdam like three times, so I questioned him if he wanted to see the country. "It is definitely possible, and it's only a three-hour flight from Lisbon to Amsterdam. If you want to go there, it's not a problem. I can do my research and see if our budget permits us to go to a second country."

I got us an apartment in Amsterdam for five days and four nights for only $370. I thought that it was a good deal. We got the entire apartment to ourselves without the owner. In the email, she said, "No Parties." For two years now, Oliver and I never partied, not once. Maybe we were done and experienced it in our younger years. Or maybe we were just both party poopers. That's why he and I clicked. Our apartment in Lisbon was also booked and fully paid. I like everything organize. I can't go anywhere without being prepared.

It was our last night in San Francisco. I couldn't wait. On Thursday, I woke up at 8:00 a.m. and checked my email through my phone. The airline company just sent an email saying that the return flight was cancelled, and it was an involuntary thing. They suggested instead of coming back on the nineteenth, they put us on the eighteenth of May. I didn't really want to go back earlier than the set date. That would suck. I actually hoped I didn't have to come back to the States. I wanted to start a new life in Europe. I called the airline and asked them to put us on the twenty-second. Perhaps it was an involuntary flight change? And they approved it.

I just needed to send an email to the owner of the apartment we were staying in and let them know that our flight got cancelled until the twenty-second. Hopefully, they'd reply right away. Oliver and I went to get his haircut this morning and to the bank and bought some euros. It was sad that the bank could only give us €1,000 maximum. We had to go to the exchange store at the airport. The teller said that they had to save some for others who would need it. I guess that was understandable. But my greediness was telling me it was not acceptable. I couldn't tell her this though. She might not give me the euros.

Oliver dropped me back home. He went to see his friend Phil for an hour and a half, then he picked me back up to go to the bakery. We needed some ham sandwiches to bring with us to the airport and plane. Food in the plane was triple the price. We didn't want to go broke. In the afternoon, we finished all the errands. I cleaned my nails and put on new beige nail polish while Oliver did his laundry and threw the garbage. And then I heard him talking to himself for ten to fifteen minutes. He was cursing and saying how much he hated his family on the other side. I tried my best to ignore him, but after a while, I realized that today was our last day, and I didn't I want to hear any drama, stress, or bullshit cursing.

I said something to him, and to my surprise, he actually told me to stop it, like I did something. Wait a minute. He just said, "Amelie, it's done. I am done. I was ranting and talking to myself for just a couple of minutes."

"Don't you think it's weird that I am hearing my boyfriend talk to himself and curse and rant?" He said that he just needed that sometimes. I said, "It's completely fine if you do that. Just let me leave the house because I don't want to be in the safe roof with my partner talking to himself and cursing for half an hour." Didn't you think that was weird? What did you think that was? I felt weird, to be honest. I grabbed my beer and headed to the bedroom. I was playing on my phone.

Oliver came and said, "You don't know what it feels or how it feels like. You have no idea how much I am losing here."

Was I not trying my best all this time to help? I just paid all his parking tickets and toll tickets that was about $500. I didn't think I even had any extra money now for our trip, but I didn't say that to him. I was trying, and I had been trying my best. This was unfair. Was I wrong?

"What did I ever do to you, Oliver? Is it my fault that you are losing your house? I thought that it's been five years now since you and your wife separated. Why is it my fault?"

He paced back and forth in the bedroom and the living room, saying things I didn't understand. He told me, "I'm worried that when we go to Portugal, you might walk out on me because you get upset or pissed at me." He was sincerely afraid for his first international flight and with our rocky relationship. I could understand him.

I assured him that I had his back and would never let anything happen, as far as I was concerned. Even if I got so irritated with him, I wouldn't just walk away from him, most especially because I had never been to Portugal. I would never leave him hanging. I guaranteed him. Hey, I did have an attitude, but when it came to inviting someone to a different place, I wouldn't just leave them there. That was a different story.

I was so scared that our argument was being triggered again. I didn't want to leave tomorrow with my burden, feeling all this confusion, this pain I had. The reason for this trip was to destress and fix us, fix our relationship. On our last day, you do this, really? How fun, Oliver.

At that moment, I was on my second beer. How I wish I was drowning in alcohol. Was it even possible to skip this day, or was that only possible in movies? I wanted to fast forward a day or time that was horrible and sad. I doubt if I closed my eyes and opened it, everything would be calm. It would be back to me and Oliver hugging each other in the couch. That would be a lie. I wanted to cry deep inside. I felt like stabbing myself because I wanted everything to stop. I didn't want to hear anything that painful or anything hurtful. I was a carefree person, and I was trying to help Oliver with what he was going through and what he was feeling, but it was not working at all.

He sat beside me on the bed and put a horror movie on. He tried to be silent the entire night. He couldn't bother me. He did try his best. But after an hour, he said, "Amelie, let's just have a good last night today. We are leaving tomorrow. Just give me a break. Just chill, okay?" He grabbed my hands and chest. "You need a good fucking."

I moved his hands away from me, and he got upset with me. Was I in the right place right now? I felt disrespected. I felt like my feelings were ignored. He brought his cat inside the house after all this, and yesterday, the cat scratched my $950 rug from this nice expensive store in Emeryville. I just bought the rug for the dining area a couple of months ago. It hadn't gone a year yet. Was I overreacting? Should I allow his cat to ruin my beautiful rug? Should I let him just shut my mouth whenever he wanted to rant, scream, and curse about his family next door? Was it normal for your boyfriend to raise his voice and curse for half a house every other month just because he wanted to release all the pain he was feeling?

He walked out and went to the living room to watch a movie by himself. He left me in the bedroom. I wanted to cry badly. Was I losing it? Or had I lost it already? Was I asking too much? Was I the one being unfair toward him? Yet I had been thinking he was the one being too much on me. I never wanted to leave him. I loved Oliver, but I thought this was unfair. I'd rather die than see myself without him. I'd rather kill myself than live without him. Was I going insane? Did I need serious help? After five beers, I went to sleep early. Good night, San Francisco, at exactly 6:30 p.m. I never wanted to wake up again. *Ever.*

CHAPTER 11

The Great Escape

I had a little headache from the beer last night. Oliver made breakfast while I showered. Then he took one too after he finished with his coffee and entire meal. We got all our bags at the door and made sure everything in the house was unplugged and clean. We said our prayers and threw all our bags in the truck and headed to the airport.

Last night was forgotten. We never looked back. We parked the truck and went to domestic. We had a five-hour flight to New York. We encountered a lady at the check-in who gave us a horrible time. We spent half an hour just talking to her about the rules and regulation. She told us that we couldn't fly to Portugal because we were entering Amsterdam. The pandemic in the Netherlands was horrible, and so Portugal did not allow people in, except for its citizens or at least if you had a place there or somehow worked in the country. I gave Oliver a signal not to ask any more questions, or else we wouldn't be able to leave San Francisco. I told her that we had an apartment in Lisbon. To my surprise, she zipped her mouth and only said, "Oh, okay."

I didn't understand why she was holding us when we were flying to New York now and not internationally. We also filled out an online form prior to our arrival in Lisbon.

Christ, this woman was getting into my nerves. Today, nobody messed with me. Oliver and I were going to Europe. We got our COVID vaccination and our negative COVID test results. I'd go off if anything happened just because people were uninformed about their real job description.

Next thing I know, Oliver and I were inside the plane, drinking soda and having almond garlic nuts that tasted wonderful. How I wish we got another bag of it. We watched two movies the entire flight to New York. I held my breath and was a bit concerned about what was going to happen on the next boarding flight. We had a two-hour layover in Amsterdam. I wished or hoped for the best. Oliver had been quite speechless when it came to questions and answers. Besides, with my fingers crossed, I really wanted Oliver to experience this travel.

This was it. Oliver and I were flying to Europe in two hours. We walked from the gate where we came in to the other gate flying to Amsterdam. It was B24. We used the bathroom before we settled in front of the gate. The entire day, we hadn't really eaten anything except the snacks we brought. We expected the international flight to service us dinner once we were high in the air. I just heard them call my name and Oliver's. We stood up and quickly walked toward the airline crew by the boarding gate.

We were asked if we were citizens in Portugal. Of course, that was a no. They asked us if we were flying for business. And again, that was a no. And our COVID testing? I mean, it was done. We were required to take another test because the test that we did had been more than two days ago. Once we reached Amsterdam, it would expire. So we had to do another test. They did not let us in the plane. My stomach was rumbling. I felt nauseated. I was so shocked. Speechless.

I felt like I was about to throw up from the five-hour flight. We came all the way here for nothing?

The guy said, "We can put you on a flight back to San Francisco for tomorrow and pay for your hotel for the night. You don't have to worry about the flight back."

I was not going back to San Francisco. Portugal's borders were closed to American citizens, so I asked the other guy for a solution, if there were any other European countries that were somehow open to Americans. I mean, come on. My bladder was desperate. My balls were screaming. And finally, he gave us two countries to choose from—the United Kingdom or Greece. Except in UK, we had to quarantine for fourteen days, or else we'd have to pay £200 each, according to one of the main guys speaking to us. In Athens, Greece, because we were vaccinated, we didn't have to stay inside our apartment. We could walk around the city freely. Okay. We were going to Greece then.

In a blink of an eye, the destination of our travel changed again. At this moment, they gave us a boarding pass from New York to Athens, Greece. Oliver just looked at me, all shocked. He didn't know what to say. I said five different countries for our destinations, and this one was not one of them. Him not knowing where the heck he was going made him speechless.

A shuttle bus from a hotel near the airport picked us up around 11:00 p.m. Lucky us, the restaurant in the hotel don't close until midnight. I didn't I ate anything good today, and I felt bad for Oliver being dragged around with my desperation to leave this country. A rigatoni pasta with a spoon of sauce. You must be kidding me. I did even have the energy left to complain. I didn't have any breath to say any words except point at the menu to the waiter. Oliver ordered a gigantic burger, and I was glad he was satisfied and full. I had no strength to brush my teeth or shower. I was frightened that Oliver might feel disgusted by me, but to my surprise, he actually ended up doing the same thing.

At this point, sleep was much more needed than whatever. Why did I feel so beaten up? I needed to get into the shower and immediately make two weeks' reservation in Athens. We needed an address to put on our documents. Oliver was ready to go and made two cups of coffee. It felt really good to have someone with you instead of being all alone. Oliver came toward me and gave me a hug and a kiss and handed me my cup of coffee. So I successfully booked us a two-week stay in an apartment in Athens. It had a kitchen and a balcony, which we were looking for. It also had an elevator. That was a plus. Knowing how Europe was, I was not walking four floors with my fifty-five-pound luggage, even if Oliver was with me. That would just not happen. We left the hotel at 11:00 a.m. and got a free ride back to the airport.

One thing I was thankful for was that the airlines paid for our one-night stay in New York. We only paid for our dinner last night, which was great. We did our coronavirus test right away when we got to the airport. Here was one thing I didn't understand with women who were inconsiderate toward other women. Oliver and I were waiting in line for our turn. This girl was so nice and friendly. I liked her personality, except that she was nice and friendly toward Oliver and not me. Oliver and I were together in line, and she told me, "I'm taking the man. You can go to my colleague behind me." I looked at her and didn't move. Then she took my paper and handed it to her colleague and told me again, "You have to go to her. She'll take your information." Then she turned around toward Oliver and gave him a huge smile and started questioning him about his travel to Greece and was giggling.

Was she flirting with him? I didn't want to overthink, but my instincts were telling me that she was. And because in my head she was flirting with my man, should I start exploding? I was born in the year of the dragon and was also a Taurus. Should I tell her this? Should I scare her? Should I start a catfight? My mental health right now was not normal. I was listening sharply to how she was acting the entire time, and after couple of minutes, she said, "Ah, my eyes. There is something in my eyes. I need a moment."

Right, she needed a freaking moment to scratch her eyes in one of the rooms. I thought Oliver was going to ask her if she was okay. But he never did. That's my man. Good job. And she came back acting all feminine, all cute. Was she kidding me? She did stop questioning Oliver and just told him to go to one of the rooms so one of the nurses could give him the test swab. Boom. The Greek gods backed me up. Zeus probably struck her eyes. Good thing she didn't go blind. I told the god not to overdo it. I was that nice. She was so lucky. After the nurse did the swab test, Oliver and I waited for half an hour behind the testing office. We both got a negative result. Thank God. We were both holding our breaths. We ate some donuts and drank coffee and waited for another five hours before our flight.

When we checked in our luggage, one of the girls from last night was there, and she took us off the line and took care of us. She gave us our boarding passes and took our luggage. We both sat in front of the gate, waiting for the boarding time. The only thing I was actually waiting for was one of the crew paging our names to go to the counter again. "Okay. Mr. Oliver and Ms. Amelie, you guys can't go to Europe at this moment." I'd seriously give up. That was it for me. I'd fly back to San Francisco. But they paged zone 2 to get in line, and that was us. The two girls working for the airline checking our boarding passes were so excited that we were finally flying out the country, and they did their best for us. I was so grateful for them.

After we got through them and started putting our backpacks on top of the cabin, I couldn't hold my tears of joy. I was so happy that Oliver's first international flight was with me, and I wanted to do everything for him to experience this trip at the most. I was so thrilled. It was a six-hour flight, and we arrived in Amsterdam for a two-hour layover. This was insane. Immigration brought us to one of the rooms, and no one wanted to speak to me. They only wanted to speak to Oliver. But why? I had all the information. He even told them to talk to me because he lacked information. Were they scared of me? Or was I just not good-looking and that's why they told him to tell me to just sit down? I could hear them very clearly. How dare them. It took us forty-five minutes to get out of the room. They asked Oliver for details and information about our return flight, the purpose of our trip, and where we would be staying. They wanted the address, and they called the lady who owned the apartment, Zasha. They asked Oliver about our job description, and they were quite suspicious of us. Okay. I believed we would be sent back to where we came from. Dutch people were very strict. I understand because of the pandemic. Who travels for fun when everything is going crazy around the world anyway? Me?

Oliver came back and said, "We are good to go." Wow. Was he joking? We got through Immigration. Amazing. Now we had to take the final flight to Athens. I had my fingers crossed the entire time, hoping that during boarding time, everything would go smoothly. We did have a recent COVID test. That actually cost $250 per person, which was seriously ridiculous. I thought that was corruption. I thought this pandemic is too much. They were demanding too much money from people, making the test as an excuse to get money from everyone. I was saying this because I did not have the money. Case closed.

I felt so beat up. It felt like my body went to war physically and mentally. Ugh. I couldn't wait to just get to bed either in our apartment in Athens or back in San Francisco in our bed. I didn't care anymore. Finally, we were inside the plane to Greece. We had three hours left. Oliver was astonished, just thinking about him stepping foot in Amsterdam. I was so sorry that Portugal and Amsterdam did not happen. I had no control over this pandemic. How I wish I could snap my fingers, and we could skip Immigration so we could see castles in Portugal and chill at the Chill Café in Amsterdam. I guess it was not meant for us to go that way. But the gods were waiting for us in Athens.

When the plane landed, we grabbed our luggage from the belt at number 9 and ran toward the bathroom. We were both dying to use the bathroom immediately. We almost forgot that we actually finally landed in Greece. We took a taxi to Nea Smyrni district where the apartment was. It was thirty minutes away from the airport. Both our phones were not working. I didn't understand why because every time I traveled out of the country, my phone always worked. I didn't know how I would call Zasha to let her know that we had arrived. Luckily, the taxi driver lent us his phone after we gave him an extra €10. Wow, finally, we were inside the building, and I couldn't wait to just hit the sack.

Zasha welcomed us to the apartment and to Greece. She actually did a warm welcome to Oliver because it was his first international flight. I experienced something fishy. This woman talked to Oliver the entire time when I was the one who made the reservation under my name, and I also used my debit card that had my name as well. I asked her questions, and she answered me but didn't even look at me. I started looking around, and she asked for our phone numbers in case we ended up needing something. She would come by and accommodate us with one phone call. She said this to Oliver and not to me, or perhaps she thought I was in the conversation? Why were these girls always intrigued with Oliver? I guess the main question was, why were they so inconsiderate when they knew he was with a girl? He was with someone. What if they were in my shoes? What if a girl flirted with their partner? How would they feel? I wanted to be blunt to her and just tell her to leave. We were fine. That's right, she better leave before I pull her underarm hair one by one with a tweezer.

Zasha asked me if I had any social media account so we could add each other. Oliver didn't have any in social media accounts. That's why she didn't have a choice but to add me. Sad for her. Zasha turned around and grabbed the doorknob and said goodbye to us. I was in the kitchen, and Oliver was standing by the sofa. Zasha turned to Oliver. Her right hand was still on the doorknob, and she said, "If you have questions on how to get to locations you want to go, I can help you and show you. I can help you how to catch the bus or the taxi." Was she serious right now? We were beaten up by our unplanned trip and wanted to crash and just rest, seriously.

"No, we are good. Thank you so much, Zasha," I said to her.

But she was looking at Oliver, and he said, "No, we're good. We'll definitely contact you if we need something or if we have any questions. Thank you, Zasha. Thank you so much."

Wow. What a day. And finally, she opened the door and left. Holy guacamole. I thought she'd never disappear. After settling down, Oliver and I went for a walk in the neighborhood and found this authentic Greek restaurant. We made sure we put our masks on. Everyone was wearing their masks, except those who were eating. What worried me was the language barrier. We'd end up playing the charade game, which I loved, so I thought I wouldn't have any problems with that. But most Greeks spoke English, which was great and made us feel at ease. Oliver ordered a couple of kebabs with Greek salad. After five minutes, five teenage boys ordered a gyro. Oliver and I looked at each other and went back to the guy who was cooking and ordered two of the gyros. Those looked better than the kebabs, and it was actually prepared faster. We took everything to go and ordered some Greek beer. We headed back to the apartment for only a ten-minute walk.

The neighborhood was really nice. Everyone around us were citizens, and we felt like we blended in. There were no other tourists besides us. Acropolis was thirteen minutes away by taxi from where we were, and the marina was ten minutes the opposite way from the apartment. What made my day was eating this souvlaki or gyros at the balcony, with a nice view of the clothes of the neighbors hanging because they just washed it. Oliver and I toasted the Greek lager and had a sip. Yum, the first bite of the gyros was delicious. It was insanely good. It had pork meat, lettuce, tomato, white sauce, and French fries wrapped in pita bread that was toasted. I didn't think I could drink more of this lager beer. It was just too heavy in the stomach. Oliver and I both took melatonin and went to bed. Good night on our first night even when it was extremely hot, because we thought that we only had a fan in the room, but we actually had an airconditioned room.

On our first day, everything was unexpected and unplanned, and it was a mess. A beautiful mess, I must say. Ugh. My body felt wasted. I was completely exhausted from the flight. I heard Oliver making a cup of coffee. It was his second cup, according to him. He only slept a little and was extremely excited for our very first day out in the city. I looked at my phone to check the time, and it was 12:30 p.m. Wait, what? I jumped off the bed and showered. Oliver made me a cup of coffee and put his pants on and his shoes. I came out of the bathroom ready to go. I finished the coffee he made me and put my shoes on, and we headed out.

We only had €1,000 cash, and the plan was to only use it for public transportation for the entire two weeks that we were there. We both used our debit cards and never our credit cards. I was glad that Oliver agreed to that idea, because we didn't want to go back to San Francisco in debt just to have fun. Because it was lunchtime, I was starving. Oliver had not eaten yet either. We found a restaurant that sold gyros near the taxi stand, and we ordered one each to fill our starving stomachs. We took a cab to the Acropolis, which was ten minutes away from where we were. The taxi dropped us off where the souvenir shops were at and where the rest of the taxi drivers were parked. Okay, I didn't see the great Acropolis. We had to walk for at least five minutes to the top. Wow, there it was.

There was no line to get in because of the travel ban that happened. I guess I really should thank this pandemic. Oliver and I purchased a ticket each for €10. We went inside. We walked on the marble tiles. I never thought I'd ever step foot in Greece. First of all, it was too far. Second, it was too expensive. This was all like a gift from heaven. We only stayed an hour and a half inside. I made sure I covered every angle of my pictures so that I wouldn't regret anything. We grabbed a frozen orange drink in front of the museum and went inside the museum souvenir store. All the busts of Hera, Alexander the Great, and so much more were all affordable and amazingly beautiful, but it was all worth more than €100. I didn't want to carry a heavy bust around on a walk, especially because it was out first day. I was glad Oliver agreed not to buy anything and focused on experiencing the city.

We walked outside the museum's vicinity and found more souvenir shops. We passed by this inviting restaurant facing the Acropolis with customers that are well-dressed. We walked a little bit farther down and went inside this souvenir store. A beautiful Greek lady welcome us and asked where we were from. When we said San Francisco, she said that no American tourists had come since the pandemic started because the border was closed, and Americans were not really allowed to travel for leisure. I thought that applied to every country. The first thing I asked her was if she had a Socrates head. She grabbed three different kinds and put it on the table for me to pick. I was so in awe. I remembered a girlfriend of mine five years ago, when her husband was working as a bartender in a ship. The boat he worked in went to Greece, and she asked me if I wanted anything from Athens. I said the head of Socrates, and he did get it for me as a gift from the both of them, except they broke up, and she never received any of the stuff back because she was in California and he lived in the Philippines. How difficult could a relationship be when both of you lived in two different continents? I always wish her well in this lifetime and am praying for her dearly.

Now I could get myself so many Socrates heads. How amazing was that? It was jaw-dropping. The owner of the shop just told us the total cost, and it seemed like she wanted us to buy her entire store. She just opened her store after more than a year, but us buying everything she had was just impossible to go back home for me and Oliver. Though all her stuff was beautiful and we wanted to help her, but €500?

We were done for today. I felt like going back to the apartment and just staying there for another two days, just so

I wouldn't have to spend. But after everything was put in the plastic bag, we decided to go back to the apartment because everything was heavy. Oliver bought three metal Spartan helmets in different sizes. I didn't say anything to him. Perhaps he was excited and happy, and I was very pleased with that. But my biggest concern was how in the world those helmets would reach San Francisco. Just the weight of it, that would cost us how much with the airline check-in luggage. I guess we could put it in the carry-on luggage. Okay. That just solved it.

When we stepped outside the souvenir shop, Oliver said to me in a whisper that we should go back to the museum in Acropolis to get that Alexander the Great bust, now that we were doing all the big-time purchases. I don't think I wanted to do that. Our pockets were hurting on our first day. I didn't think I could pin him down with what he wanted. He was willing to carry all the heavy stuff with us just to get back to the museum store, so you know what? We could do whatever he felt like doing. I was up for it.

The lady at the souvenir store gave me a gift, an amulet of the evil eye. I didn't think I received any gift from any stores I had been in, in my entire life. She was very sweet. Her husband was next door with his own business, selling coffee and pastries. He came over and told us that he could grab us a taxi because the taxi drivers by the Acropolis charged more. He told us to sit down on the chair and wait. We did confirm that we were heading back home. We only waited for seven minutes.

During those minutes of waiting, Oliver looked me in the eye and said firmly with confidence, "Amelie, we are going to the museum. I will tell him that we are going for a walk and he doesn't have to get us a cab. Okay?"

ARE YOU HAPPY?

Well, what could I say? When he talked to me like that, I mean, he was the boss at that moment. So I agreed. He stood up and took four steps toward the husband to tell him what he just said to me. When the husband saw him approaching, he told Oliver, "Sit down."

Oliver did not say one word to him. He turned around and sat beside me. I almost burst out laughing. I did hold it in, but I was crying and laughing inside. Oliver looked at me and started laughing. You said you're the boss? Okay. Go ahead.

The taxi came, and the husband said something to him three times in Greek. I wondered what it was. I assumed he was told not to scam us. We only paid €6, which was amazing because we paid €25 coming here. The taxi driver never said anything, but he looked shock. But now thinking how much the real fare is, I should be the one shocked that he didn't man up by giving us the change. But I admit that somehow, that was our fault by not being well-informed. He must have thought it was tip. Well, I was somewhat happy with our purchases but also not happy because we didn't get to explore more. Now we were back in the apartment. We were both battling jetlag, most especially Oliver.

At 10:30 p.m., we went outside for a walk, and it was the most pleasant walk I ever had with Oliver. It was quiet on the street, with a lot of people walking around and enjoying their stroll like us. There were a lot of restaurants and bars with people drinking and smoking. To my surprise, after thirty minutes of walking, Oliver said to me, "Let's buy a smoke."

I had never seen him smoke a cigarette once. He wanted to blend in with the Greeks. He wanted to smoke and drink like them. So we bought a cigarette and sat in one of the restaurants that had seats outside. We ordered one pint of

Heineken each and started smoking while watching Greek football. I have never encountered a community or bar or a restaurant with a lot of people and were very silent. But in each table, they were talking, but not loudly. They were very considerate toward other customers that were eating and also talking. It was a good kind of culture shock we experienced. It was completely different from California. We smoked half the box together just for this night and headed back to our nest. I could say that today was honestly fun. I did not explore alone. I ate with someone, walked and held hands, and rode the cab with someone. We had a laugh and talked. I made some plans not just for myself in regard to life but with someone with me. Yes, I was very happy.

It was two in the morning, and I was still up. I couldn't sleep, and neither could Oliver. I hated taking medicine or vitamins because I didn't want my body to get used to it. But at this instance, another melatonin was a must, and one last Greek lager before I closed my eyes should help.

Next thing I knew, it was 11:30 a.m. My god. I didn't want this to be my daily routine, waking up late every single day in this entire vacation. One thing Oliver loved doing was shopping and doing groceries. I saw bread and a coffee canister on the table and fresh kebab. I wanted say, "Stop with the buying because we still have another thirteen days, and right now, we are not working. There is no money coming in into our pockets." But if I did that, I'd turn into a controlling partner. Plus he was spending his money, not mine. Also, he was enjoying his vacation. "Wow, those look all good." Was I being too much? I walked toward Oliver and kissed him and gave him a hug. And the plan for today? "What do you want to do today?"

Oliver looked at me and threw me back my question. He didn't really have any idea what was there to see and do in Athens, except he wanted to go back to the museum and buy the bust that we weren't able to buy yesterday. We only had one luggage. We would end up buying another check-in luggage. And when I said this to him, he said excitingly, "It will be an honor to buy the other luggage just so we can get more heads and shop more souvenirs."

Okay. So I guess today we were going back to the Acropolis. But the question was, what were next week's activities? We couldn't shop every day. What was there for us to do in Greece. We couldn't backpack to another country because of this pandemic. How about Santorini? As far as I knew, it was really expensive there. It would be impossible. But why not do some searching?

Oliver typed the word *Santorini* in his search engine, and he was blown away and said, "I'll definitely pay for our flight. That's beautiful. How far is it from us?"

Okay, why not? It was very affordable. Three nights for $358, and it was in Oia. And how about the flight? Roundtrip per person cost $150. That sounded reasonable. And so we decided to go to Santorini next week for four days and three nights. I booked our flight first. I typed in our information, and Oliver gave me his debit card. It did not work. I used mine, and that went smoothly. His bank was being suspicious with his activities. I told him so many times to call his bank and let them know that he would be out of the country, which he never did.

"So we have a flight to Santorini next week Monday." And now I was booking the hotel. I couldn't believe this was possible. It cost less than $500 in Oia, in the area where you'd see the white and blue caves or buildings or whatever you called that. But I only saw those in magazines. I never thought I would be right here and could possibly go see it.

And I was not alone. I had a partner. No matter what this vacation would bring, I was happy and content.

I had to use my card because Oliver's card never worked, unless it was $300 worth of expenses. Then his card participated. I made him think that I used his card so he wouldn't feel bad. But the plan was for him to pay for our food and souvenirs. According to him, he wanted to be part of this trip, so he would definitely be part of it. I was so proud of the both of us. This was called partnership. And today was exactly the same as yesterday. We went to the Central Market on the north side of the Acropolis to look for more souvenirs, and we ended up at going back to the Acropolis Museum. We bought the bust of Hera and Zeus. No regrets at all.

While we walked toward the Acropolis, we passed by this Greek man in his late fifties playing a tiny guitar in the street. It was a beautiful music. Oliver put €2 in the man's hat while I took pictures and videos. The guy looked at me and gave me a signal, saying that I could take a picture of him and with him, that it was fine. So we did. Oliver and I took our turns getting pictures with him. And besides getting those two heads from the museum, I ended buying the two famous philosophers' busts at the souvenir shop in Central Market. I got Aristotle and Plato, together with Socrates that I got yesterday. Oliver purchased more souvenirs too. We ended up buying luggage to put all the things we bought. My expectations reached its point, which was the normal argument in my relationship. Except this time, Oliver yelled at me in the streets, even inside the taxicab. We were not in California, where it was normal to yell at each other, because arguments were considered normal. We were in Greece, and I had not seen one man raise his voice at a woman, and I felt so embarrassed that my man was yelling at me to get out of the taxi.

ARE YOU HAPPY?

We accidentally took a cab from the Central Market supposedly back to our apartment in Kallithea, and it happened that this guy never wore a mask, not once, and was smoking the entire time. Another guy approached us with a huge marble stone and was ready to throw it at the window or at our driver. He stepped outside and started screaming at the drunk guy, and everyone was holding him and keeping him away from the other guy so that there wouldn't be any fight. How I wish we could take the other cab behind him, except that there was a line, and he was the first one who was ready to leave. I didn't want to get in trouble skipping him or at least being prejudiced. He was a regular employee, so maybe I would just act normal and go with the flow? Shit. We were only eleven minutes away from our apartment, so maybe I didn't have to complain to him about him smoking and him needing to actually wear a mask for consideration. He stopped at this guy hanging out on the street with a minivan full of pistachio nuts. One of the guys put some on the taxi driver's hand, and then he asked where Kallithea was. Then he sped up and gave Oliver the chunk of pistachio nuts. Oliver almost ate it, except I gave him the signal to not eat it. It was on the streets. How many hands had touched it? And we didn't know how dirty it was. Twice I had to tell Oliver. It was kind of tempting, but we didn't want to get sick. So he poured it out into his back pocket.

The driver took a different route, so I reacted, and he said that he was taking the short route. Oliver and I just let him do what he wanted to do, of course. He was the driver? It had been thirty minutes. I raised my voice at the driver and said, "You are taking us farther and farther from where we actually live."

Oliver said that we would get off on this block, which we did. This was unbelievable. What happened to the evil eye? I thought that it was supposed to be a lucky charm or an amulet? I had it in my pocket since day 1 of this trip. Or maybe this didn't work on drunk people? When we got off the cab, Oliver took the luggage, and the driver asked for €10. Seriously?

I said, "No, €5. It's actually €7 total. Why are you asking for €10 when you didn't even drop us at our apartment?" I started raising my voice at this cab driver. He was seriously messing with us, and I took a picture of his plate number and his face. He got mad at me, but Oliver got really irritated and scared because he was in the middle of us. He didn't want to go to jail if anything happened. If that taxi driver hit me, of course Oliver would have to defend me, and he was so frightened that he might go to jail. So long story short, he took his anger out on me by yelling at me the entire time. He asked me for directions to head back to the apartment, so I typed it in to the GPS, but it was taking forever to load. In a second, I could not answer Oliver's question.

He yelled, "I only ask you one question, and you can't even answer me."

Right at the corner, where people were standing in the coffee shop and vehicles with their window down because of the heat, everyone heard him and stared at me like I did something wrong to him. Okay, people of Greece, I did not cheat on him. Oliver's reaction was extreme, which was weird for me. It might be right or normal to everyone else. I asked him to stay on one side and wait for the phone to load instead of walking without any directions. But he didn't want to listen to me. Perhaps I had been controlling every situation in this relationship, and maybe he wanted to feel superior? Okay, go ahead and keep walking.

He said, "I am done with this fucking trip." And with that, he walked out on me. He was dragging the suitcase we got from the Central Market, and if he could throw it back and forth, left to right, he would have, except that it was extremely heavy because of Hera's head that we bought from the Acropolis Museum. It would be very sad if the head broke. That was €120.

I doubt I'd be coming back to Greece anytime soon after this vacation. I followed him around everywhere he turned, and I must say we had been walking for forty-five minutes now with no directions. He was very irritated and repeatedly said that he was done with this stupid trip. I felt horrible. He has been complaining since last night—actually, the entire evening—that he couldn't sleep. It was called jetlag, and he had not experienced it in his entire life.

I guess this trip would never happen again. He was irritated that he couldn't sleep since we got here, and we were having difficulty finding our apartment. I wanted to tell him, "Please leave tonight or tomorrow. You have an extra $620 voucher from an airline. You can leave anytime. I want to be alone. This vacation is for me to rest, to relax, not for anyone to raise their voice at me."

He was tremendously upset with me for telling him not to buy the luggage and to wait. Maybe we'd find something nicer or better. He bought luggage from the street. Okay, go ahead. I didn't understand what was wrong with what I said, but he could buy whatever he wanted. I did not control you. I just said that we might find something else that was actually better quality. And after a while, he actually said to me that he was done being out, and he wanted to head back to the apartment. But we just got out of the apartment, and now he wanted to head back?

It was our third day, and I had not seen anything in Athens besides the Acropolis. This was not a vacation for me, not a totally relaxing trip. It was all tension, pressure, and irritation since day 1. Maybe I shouldn't have forced this trip, not knowing that it would end up like this. I could have cancelled it and disappeared on him. I wish I took him back to San Francisco to his house and flew all by myself and stayed in Greece for a month or two. Did I have any regrets? Yes. I had a very heavy burden in my chest. How I wish I could have traveled alone as usual.

I threw my phone on the ground because of my irritation, and Oliver got madder. If my phone broke, then we wouldn't have any form of communication. But didn't he get it? That's what I wanted to happen. I didn't want the phone because he asked too many questions and demanded answers in seconds. When I couldn't answer, he got upset. Hold on, he had a phone. Why was he putting the pressure on me? After being in three cabs, we finally reached the apartment. After the taxi driver helped us with luggage, Oliver thanked the guy. When he turned around and saw me, he yelled at me again while he opened the apartment door. The entire time he was yelling at me, the only thing that ran in my head was *I want to run away from you, Oliver. I want to disappear.*

I wanted to go to the bathroom and cry. I wanted to cry really bad. I thought this trip was a way to heal this relationship. I doubt that. Not once did I raise my voice at him since this vacation started, but he took advantage of it and raised his voice at me. Should I be back to myself and raise my voice at him too? I tried. I think that I did my best. I didn't think I wanted to be in this relationship. And the host of the apartment we were staying at was obviously flirting with Oliver. I ignored it, and after three days, I asked my girlfriend Tiffany back in California, "What do you think about booking a stay in this Airbnb with your name on it and you pay for it, but the host doesn't even speak to you, only to your boyfriend or, hey, your fiancé? And she was about to leave, right hand already on the doorknob, and she turned around and looked back at your partner and said if he needed any help finding attraction sites or bus routes in the area, she could definitely help. And not did she once look at you."

Tiffany, without a doubt, said straight up to my ears, "She is obviously flirting with Oliver."

I mean, where was her respect? Did she rent this place to pick up guys? How I wish I could have traveled all alone. I never had this problem with any of my escapades. I felt like shit right now. I was at the balcony listening to the symphony while drinking this Greek white wine. I didn't understand what it was because it was written in Greek. The goat cheese tasted wonderful. Olives were extremely tasty, and the salami was yum. I wanted to sleep in the balcony than go inside where Oliver was. My phone beeped. He texted me. "I love you, Amelie."

I felt seriously numb. How was I supposed to feel a thing after he yelled at me? I had no face in the neighborhood. My tears wanted to drop in the last two hours. We had four more days in this apartment before we flew to Santorini on Monday. I was scared and bothered by what happened today. I guess I was staying in for another couple of days. Besides, we didn't do any sightseeing. We woke up at twelve noon and went to the souvenir shop. What a vacation. The best I ever had, to be honest. We didn't go to any museums. Screw me, right? Was the counselor or psychologist right? It had been a month now since I talked to him. He told me that this relationship wouldn't go anywhere and might actually get worse. Oliver never raised his voice at me. Encountering him today and the way he was to me with his voice and with regret with this travel, my only question was, "How do I get out of this relationship, and where do I go?"

I was so scared to be alone. I was so frightened to move to a different place again. I didn't know what to do anymore. I wanted to leave Oliver in this apartment and get another one for myself, but how? If I did that, that simply meant we were really done. But wasn't that what I wanted? Why couldn't I do it? Two hours later, Tiffany sent me an email, asking me to call her. I went to the hallway and sat on the stairs. I couldn't hold my tears, so I started crying while talking to Tiffany. After two minutes, Oliver went outside and told me to get back inside the room.

"Who are you talking to secretly? You're talking to a guy?"

Wait, what? Why jump to conclusions without any evidence? He just accused me. I threw my cell phone at the closet mirror because of my irritation. And for a moment there, it scared the crap out of me. I thought that the mirror would break and I'd have to pay for a huge mirror before flying back to San Francisco.

Oliver walked toward me and said to me, "You're a liar bitch. You're a bitch." What he just said to me went straight to my heart. He looked me in the eyes and said it very clearly. It felt like he stabbed me in the chest. What did I ever do to him today? Did I say anything wrong? All I knew was that I got upset and wanted to beat that taxi driver, and the only reason Oliver was giving me right now for his complete madness was that when he asked me to get off the cab, according to him, I didn't get off. That was the only reason? This was why he told me I was a liar bitch?

"I'm done with this relationship. Book me a flight for tomorrow. I'm flying back to San Francisco. I'm done."

Okay. "I'll book you a one-way flight back to San Francisco right now. If that is your wish, then I'll give you what you want."

After five minutes, he said, "No, you are not getting me a flight back. I'll suck it up until we fly back together."

I was confused. Did he want to leave or not? I finished my wine, watching Oliver's favorite sci-fi movies. I was sitting in a chair by the counter sink. I couldn't breathe. I just wanted to cry, and my chest wanted to explode. This apartment was seriously horrible. The stove did not work, the light bulbs were shutting on us one by one, and there was no real knife, only a butter knife. Wow. Thanks a lot. I was in a suicidal mood, and the wine was all finished. I went to bed, and Oliver went to the sofa.

Next morning? Right. There were fresh white flowers on the table in front of me. He said his apologies like the usual, for at least two years now. I didn't talk to him, and I did not want to hear him. It was 2:00 p.m., and he forced his sorry words at me and demanded me to brush off whatever he said to me last night. It would be insane to just brush it off like nothing happened. That was yesterday. Today was a new day. Yes, he was right, except when I didn't accept his apologies the tenth time today, he called me an asshole.

"You're an asshole. Book me a flight back to San Francisco right now. Here's my credit card. Which suitcase am I bringing back? I don't want any of the souvenirs. I don't want any memory of you."

A new day? Could you really call this day a new day? And I thought that I was in the land of the gods. Where the heck was Zeus, Athena? Or how about Hades? Where were my protectors? My spiritual security guards? I was going crazy. What's with the evil eye? The amulet didn't seem like it was working at all. All my dreams before this vacation were telling me something. I never had dreams like that. It was back-to-back. And it was also clear, like I was awake and everything was happening. It was weird. I needed to call the storage back in San Francisco and book one for when I got back. What was I going to do with a place to live? I made my life look wonderful whenever I talked to my friends, but the truth was that I was no one. I had nothing too, besides the junk I had, which were my furniture and books. And now these giant Aristotle and Socrates heads. What was I going to do with this stuff? Put it all in the storage?

The word *depression* was knocking on my door again. I didn't know what to do. I cried about everything last night while trying my best to not cut myself with the stupid butter knife. There were no tears in my eyes. I felt numb. I tried to find Oliver a flight back again, but he kept talking down to me and said, "Everything is about you. It's always about you. Even the way I talk to you, I have to watch my mouth so you won't be upset."

The thing was, if he talked to me to how he wanted, this was how he wanted to speak to me. By calling me names. I didn't think I was controlling him on how he should speak to me, but he should at least show me respect. Who calls their partner a bitch anyway? His wife called me a bitch. Now he calls me a bitch. And they were both educated. I was really speechless.

I tried to stay away from Oliver, but he didn't accept what I wanted and told me, "You're stuck with me forever." How about if I kill myself? I wouldn't be stuck with you forever. He said no again on booking a flight back to San Francisco. "Amelie, I want you and I love you. I love you so much. Please, just hold my hand. Come back inside the room."

Why? I was honestly confused. I was seriously astonished at what was happening. Why was I in this situation? What was really going on? I thought this trip was to fix this relationship. I didn't want to be in this relationship anymore.

I honestly didn't. How do I get out? What do you want from me, Oliver?

"If you want to go back to San Francisco, please do. I'll buy you a flight right now. If you want to stay, then stay. There is no need for foul words on a vacation. I don't understand why you have to force me to accept your apologies when my wounds are all fresh. It's two days in a row. I'm speechless and have this big question in my head of what I ever did to you for you to call me names."

The entire day, we stayed inside the apartment. I ignored him and didn't feeling like saying a word. Do you think what he is going through is called jetlag? Because I didn't want to believe my guts, thinking that it was called control. But why? At this moment? I kept myself busy by packing one of the luggage. I put the busts inside and wrapped it with my shirts and locked it. Now it was ready to fly back home.

I took a melatonin around 7:00 p.m. I had no reason for me to be aware and awake this day. But my concern was tomorrow. What could I do tomorrow alone without Oliver? I didn't want to think about that. I didn't want to worry myself thinking about what I was going to do when I got back to San Francisco. I was on a trip, and I would cherish this unforgettable vacation. It was very much memorable because of how things were turning out. I would let his hurtful words and sensitivity enter my right ears and go out the left ears. But I must say, I was looking forward to the next day, and I hoped I would feel much better than today. I needed to stop taking the sleeping pill. It was making me sleep and sleep and sleep twenty-four seven. I was missing Athens.

I woke up around 1:00 p.m., and Oliver said that he would make me a cup of coffee. I said, "No, thank you." I put my swimsuit on and got ready to go to the beach. It was only ten minutes away from the apartment. Oliver asked me where I was going. Why would I tell him? Had I gone mad? Why was I still in the same place with him? I answered him because I was an idiot. "I'm going to the beach that's ten minutes away. If you want to come, then come. If not, then stay here and do what you want."

He jumped from the bed and changed quickly and put his sandals on. I guess my expectations of being alone today in the beach was impossible. He paid for our entrance fee of €5 each. I felt so cold toward Oliver. I just hope I could be chill like the Greeks in hard times. We tried to find a seat with an umbrella. It was just too hot today, and the plan was to not burn.

We found us a spot, but Oliver said, "Let's go get our drinks before we sit."

I didn't really feel like drinking at this hour. I just woke up and just had my coffee. I told Oliver about this and he said no.

"Amelie, no. I am not walking by myself to the bar to get my drink. You are coming with me. Don't start arguing with me."

But why did I have to go with him when the bar was actually a two-minute walk from where the chair was? I didn't even say anything wrong except that I wanted to sit here, and I didn't want any drinks. I just wanted to sit down and get some fresh air, but why couldn't I? He wasn't going to accept my no. He raised his voice at me in the beach. So I ended up walking to the bar with him because I didn't like people looking at us making a scene. It was embarrassing. He tried to grab my hand as we walked, but I pulled my arms close together. I sat at the stool and did not say a word to him. When he asked me if I wanted a beer, that just really upset me because I said to him I just had coffee an hour ago, and it was still early for me. And what did he say?

"Amelie, just grab something to drink so you don't have to walk back here later. Besides, we're already here. How about a wine bottle?"

I didn't know what to say to him anymore. I felt like I was wrong in every angle of this situation and that I did need to respond to his questions and do exactly what he wanted. But why? He bought a bottle of white wine, which came with a plate of different varieties of fruits. I could feel my nerves sparking right now. I was so upset, and I felt like I was forced. Wait, I was definitely forced. Could I sit on the chair now? I felt that my day was ruined. I was so not in the mood. It had been a week, and so far everything was just going sour.

Oliver opened the bottle of wine and poured some in the glass and ask me if I wanted some. The heck. Why not? Why not get wasted? There was no point on being excited at this circumstance. Okay. Oliver was starting with this negative conversation. "You're a phony liar."

I was honestly speechless. I didn't know what to say to him. I looked at him with no words. I got up and walked toward the bathroom, and when I came back, he was browsing on my phone, looking for messages from guys because he thought that I was cheating on him. He didn't find anything and saw me coming behind him and threw my phone on my seat. I grabbed my seat and carried it to move to the other side of the umbrella, where I didn't have to see him and hear him. He followed me. He sat on the sand. He started ranting and wouldn't stop.

"Oliver, if you want to leave, please do. Don't ruin my day as it is already somewhat ruined. Please go do whatever you want to do. Go back to the apartment or go back to San Francisco. Please go." This was getting ridiculous.

"That's what you've been wanting. To be alone and not have me in the picture so you can flirt with guys here. I get it,

Amelie. I am giving you what you want. A luxurious vacation all by yourself."

What did I ever do to him? Was he not being selfish to me? This was the third day that he called me different names. He got up and left. I wish it was all real. I just hope that he wouldn't come back. I stood up and carried my seat back under the umbrella to my original spot. I went to the bar and ordered another bottle of wine. My phone rang. I hope I didn't have to answer him, but I brought him here. So I would not ignore him even though was an asshole to me for days now.

"I ordered another bottle of wine," I said to him.

He replied, "Okay. I'm coming back." He was in the cab already, halfway back to the apartment. Seriously? Was he out of his mind? He was acting like a child. Did he just want attention? We came to Greece to relax, but I could see this entire thing was not helping him at all. Was this part of control and manipulation? Because if it was, I would not follow him and beg him for an apology when I didn't do anything wrong. Lord, I just wanted a peaceful vacation. Why did this happen? He sat on my left side, where sat earlier. The waiter came with my wine bottle and a fruit bowl. Oliver gave him a tip of €5.

I was feeling the wine in my system and was a little buzzed. Good thing I was in this state right now because everything I said to him was now a comedy, and it was all laughter. The only horrible thing was that I didn't remember what happened that night. I woke up at 2:00 a.m. How did I get back to the apartment? My forehead had a small bruise, my knees and elbows had small scratches, and I was naked. I didn't remember anything. I made love with Oliver that night. But did I pass out in the beach? That must be embarrassing. How did Oliver get me in the cab and bring me back home? I was so irritated. I turned on all the lights and started banging everything in the kitchen. Perhaps I was starving. I didn't really eat anything the entire day yesterday because after I had that coffee, Oliver got us a bottle of wine. Then I passed out.

I was with a wrong person. Obviously. He didn't say anything to me while I banged everything. Okay, what did happen last night? Why was it that all of a sudden, he was afraid of me? He was calm with soft voice. He offered me some food that he could cook for me. Was he kidding me? My entire body was in pain, most especially after making love with him and not being aware 100 percent that night. It took me a while to settle down. After all those horrifying words that he said to me for days, I made love to him. Where did my pride go when I was drunk? This was insanity. I was disgusted with myself. I tried to go back to sleep after I had some scrambled eggs and toast with the Greek strawberry jam and an orange juice.

Oliver was just completely different. I was not even going to ask him because I know that he would not tell me the truth. Even if he did tell me, it would be half the truth. We only had one day left before we flew to Santorini.

I packed everything, getting the luggage ready to fly back to San Francisco. I put it in the closet, just in case the owner of the apartment came to check the unit while we were gone. We went for a walk to our favorite spot for gyros. We ordered a couple and them took back with us to the unit. I was glad that our flight was in the afternoon tomorrow. I had the entire time to rest from being drunk. How I wish I could contain my tongue from asking Oliver what exactly happened that night.

I took out my journal and started to scribble. I made a cup of coffee and sat in the balcony because I didn't think I honestly wanted to see Oliver's face. He thought that everything was back to normal, that we were both fine because we made love. I was not even aware, so how could things be fine? But just with like the wine I drank, I got sober the next day. There was something wrong with my mental health. No matter how much people did me wrong, I forgot about it.

Oliver and I walked fifteen minutes to the cab terminal and headed to the airport. My main concern was them having us take another COVID test, and that would ruin this day. But luckily, we were vaccinated just last week. We did the second booster shot, and they accepted that and gave us our boarding passes. I was holding my breath until I stepped foot in Santorini. So far, everything was going well. We had to take a bus to the plane, and we got through the boarding door, yes. I was going to Santorini. Oh my god. A propeller? They must be kidding me. I tried my best not to pee inside the plane. I only saw this in movies. And then after a while, there would be a bird flying on the opposite side and would come across the propeller. Then the propeller would start acting up and break. The plane would then crash, and things exploded. *Boom*. Then that was it. My last memory would be when I was in Athens, flying to Santorini, and I was with Oliver. And my parents would find out that there was a plane that crashed in Greece, and I was in it. And my two-by-two picture would be on the news. That was an extreme imagination, but dying in another country where all the gods were would be spectacular.

I looked at Oliver, and he didn't look happy. He looked intense and quite worried. I held his hands and looked at him. I nodded and said, "We'll be fine. Don't worry. If you die, I die, with the rest of the people that are with us."

He laughed and said, "Amelie, I don't want to die yet. I have my house that is waiting for us to come back. I need to finalize this divorce that's been going on for years now." He had a point. And a damn good one. We landed on the island of Santorini safely. I was still holding my breath. I didn't know how things would go here and what to expect. And I didn't want to jinx anything. I really prayed that everything would be fine and Oliver would be calm and relaxed. If only I could give him a marijuana every time he was cranky. That would be a blast.

A lady from the hotel we booked pick us up. She was a blond girl. She talked to Oliver the entire time. I found it very odd that everyone would rather speak to Oliver, and they didn't even look me in the eye. It was really weird. We rode in her smart car for thirty minutes from the airport to Oia, and we heard her speak about the island and the things that we could do, which was very interesting. Her English was good for a second language. She had a thick accent. We ended up renting a smart car for two days. The blond girl would bring it first thing in the morning around 9:00 a.m. She told us to follow her, and we did. Wow. Both Oliver and I were speechless. It felt like we were back in San Francisco and browsing pictures of Greece. It didn't feel real. We were not supposed to be here because the flight was very expensive. There were just no words. Whatever the pictures showed us about Santorini, it was exactly the same in real life. It was wonderful. The white and blue walls were beautiful.

I tried not to be desperate and take pictures quickly. Maybe one or two hidden shots perhaps? I couldn't help it. My hands were just itchy. Good thing I was walking behind the two of them. We entered a tiny gate and walked down the stairs of the white and gray steps. The blond girl pushed a wooden double door open and said, "This is your room. If you need anything, here is my number. I will bring the smart car tomorrow at 9:00 a.m. This wine bottle is for you guys as your welcome gift. Welcome to Santorini."

The blond girl was a pro. She was detailed and very much comforting, except that everything she did had its payment. I guess that was how she earned a living. But I would definitely vote for her as the best tour guide in the island. Oliver and I went inside the room, and it was a cave bedroom with a living room and a fridge with a kitchen table that had four chairs. Now this was what I called a vacation. It had a front balcony overseeing the entire Aegean Sea and the volcano. How insane could that be? I didn't think I could just sit down and relax. I was glad that Oliver felt the same way. We went out for a walk straight to the souvenir shops and hunted for dinner to take back to the room. The sunset was spectacular. We ate our dinner at the balcony where we got to watch the sunset. We opened the red wine to celebrate. So far, everything was wonderful. Since we came to Greece, I didn't really slept straight. The bed in Athens was not that comfortable. And tonight, I was so relaxed. We upgraded our room with a jacuzzi.

The blond girl came that morning with the smart car. We found a restaurant for breakfast that just opened. Lucky us. We woke up around 7:30 a.m., and all the restaurants and shops didn't open until 11:00 a.m. But this restaurant was fantastic. It overlooked to the entire island, and the volcano was in front of it. We ordered two cups of coffee and scrambled eggs with vegetables in it. I forgot what it was called. Everything in life had its own label, even an egg. What did you think about that? Wasn't that insane?

It was 9:00 a.m. Oliver paid for our breakfast while I finished my second cup of coffee. Oliver asked the waiter to take our picture, and the guy was so kind to raise the cover so that we had the view as our background. I never smiled in pictures. And on the third shot, the guy told me that I had to smile and show how happy I was. I did. How could you say no to him after he said yes on taking our photo? Right? It was give and take, I guess. He didn't seem like he was just a waiter but an owner. People in this country were very humble and relaxed. How I wish I could adapt. The best souvenir I could ever have for the rest of my life would be the word *humbleness*.

We walked back to the room, and the blond girl was there, waiting for us with a smile. We grabbed all our belongings and followed her to the upgraded room, which was a six-minute walk because of the tiny streets and stairs. And the room was not downstairs but upstairs. The room was very beautiful with a beautiful view. It had a wooden double door with a mirror where you could see the outside and the Aegean Sea while you were in bed. And the balcony had the jacuzzi, good for four people. It had two chairs and a table with a long beach chair where you could sunbathe. How cool was this? It felt like I was on my honeymoon. How I wish.

The blond girl only allowed us to drop our stuff, and we had to follow her quickly to know where the smart car was parked because she had another appointment. It was a top-down orange smart car. This was amazing. Oliver was the driver. My driver's license expired two weeks ago. He signed his life away, and we paid the blond girl in exchange for the key. We would keep the car for two days. That sounded good enough for us to tour the island. We parked the car somewhere else where we would remember. We headed back to the room. I put my two-piece on and got inside the jacuzzi. Oliver popped the white wine open and put on his swim shorts. I never wanted to wake up from this dream. I wish I was in a movie where I could pause this moment.

Oliver admitted that this was more of a honeymoon than the honeymoon he had with his ex-wife. How intriguing. Now I was curious. I asked him, "How was that? Where did you go with her? What did you guys do?"

He didn't seem very happy. He and that witch went to Honolulu for four days and three nights. They went swimming, and he tried surfing. He did not succeed and ended up cancelling it. And that was it? Maybe that was her dream honeymoon. Hawaii? I couldn't poop on her happiness, could I? I mean, that was none of my business. But for a person who earned a good chunk of money, I didn't really get it. This is what I mean, Oliver. I give you the very best of me, yet you are rude toward me. Where is justice when you need it?

But I didn't tell him this. I had all these thoughts in the back of my head. I didn't want to argue and fight again. But it did amaze me that I was being treated this way. Was I being punished for everything I had done in life? Good thing our conversation was calm, and there was no tension so far. Oliver was thankful the entire time and could not believe that he was here. He only saw this place in travel magazines at his doctor's office.

My plan for this entire day was to be in the jacuzzi with a bottle of white wine and walk around the island for souvenirs. I made a surprise reservation for a speedboat. We would get to drive it without a skipper. And this would be the entire day's activity for tomorrow. It was a thirty-minute drive away from Oia, but the good thing was that we had a car to drive on our own time without being pressured by anyone. I never liked group tours. You had to be nice to other people, and you had to conduct yourself with proper manners so that nobody would look down on you. And you had to wait for them when they were late. I just couldn't do that and be in the same huge boat with other people.

I waited for a little while before I told Oliver about what I did. I mean, he was tagging along with me, wasn't he? If he didn't want to go, then I would get to drive the boat all by myself in the Aegean Sea. We went and walked on the tight street of Oia and went inside each souvenir shop. I saw a big blanket that was white and blue with a fish design and the famous Greek culture design they had in everything. I wanted to buy it, but Oliver gave it to me as a gift. I understood that he was sincerely apologetic, but I only wanted him to be nice to me and not say hurtful words and show his love through actions, not through material stuff.

"Thank you, Oliver."

I was never used to someone buying me things. It made me feel weird. But was I happy? Super. We purchased some shirts and small knickknacks. There was more stuff to carry back home. We saw a painting worth €300 and agreed to buy it. Oliver wanted to buy it for me as a gift and insisted it. He swiped his bank card, and it didn't work. After three swipes, he checked his online banking, and his house property tax was deducted just last night. Now he was more unsettled than ever because he had no money. But the good thing about it was that he was nicer to me. I paid for the painting, but he told me we didn't have to buy it continuously. But I wanted it.

"I am not asking you to buy it. I want to buy it. I will buy it."

He was so concerned because we still had another one week in Greece, and he wanted to put whatever money I had on the side in case of an emergency. He wanted to pay for everything while we were in the island, but he should be at peace that every bill was paid back home. I didn't tell him that I had money and to not worry. I just told him, "I got you." I smiled at him.

He was so scared. I told him finally that I got us a boat and he could be a skipper for the entire day while I sunbathed and pigged out. I actually hired him. Wasn't he just one lucky cricket? I thought that somehow helped distract him. I repeated, "Oliver, don't worry. I got you."

He didn't even want to eat anything except a can of sardines. He was fine, he said. We ordered some pasta and a paella from a nice Greek restaurant at the corner near the main entrance of Oia. I invited him here, so I would not let him starve. Even if he was rude tow me, he did love me. Do you think he does? I was so confused. He should sleep outside tonight. How I wish there was a doghouse outside the hotel room.

I didn't know why I loved him when he was broke and rude to me. But because my main concern with a partner was companionship and someone to hug me and tell me that I was not alone, then I didn't really care about the rest anymore. And he did give me that love. He hugged me and made me feel that I was loved and that I was not in a dark room alone.

He asked me if I was all right. The only thing was that he asked me too much if I was okay. Was he making sure that I was fine because he was worried I would leave him? Well, I should leave him because of how he treated me. Everyone told me to walk out on him, even the psychologist. I didn't really know why. Once I leave Oliver, would I regret it later on in life? Didn't I ask God for a partner? And now that I was given a man, a partner, I would just walk away. Was this why I was cursed? Because of how I acted on my decisions and in general with life? I guess I believed in karma. As long as I did good toward him and took care of him, I'd let Hades take care of my hurt and pain. For sure he would drag all those people who acted like Ursula from *The Little Mermaid* toward me down to the underworld. I couldn't wait for that day the witch would reunite with the god Hades and for her to finally stop stalking me on social media.

On the third day, I put on a Tiffany-colored two-piece, my short shorts, and tank top. It was honestly warm in Santorini, which was the opposite of the water. It was perfect. Oliver was the driver. We stopped by the grocery store to buy a bottle of wine and six cans of beer with breakfast and other snacks. It was early morning, and we were buying booze already. That's because we would be stuck in the boat for the entire day. We wanted to make sure we had the goods. We stopped at the gasoline store to fill the gas tank, and we just paid $50. Were they insane? Did they fool us? But the gasoline tank did say $50. This was absurd. Now my driver was flipping out.

"Don't blame me for the gas price because I did not price that. If you think about it, we are in an island, and everything here is imported. That's why things are very expensive." Geez. Was I a punching bag?

"Amelie, I'm just sharing my point of view." But the tension, dude. The way he was telling me, it was like he was blaming me.

I took a deep breath and looked for a radio station, and I had no luck. I couldn't even hook my phone to the car. I started humming and making up words. "Oh, you piece of shit. Baby, you need your nuts punched to the right and to the left. You wonderful creature."

Oliver started cracking up and laughing. There you go. At least something made him happy. The owner of the speedboat we rented was standing by the boats, waiting for us. What amazed me was the attitude of the people in this country. They were very friendly and welcoming. The guy showed us the map. For thirty minutes, he told us how to maneuver the boat. Good thing Oliver listened really carefully, because the only thing that was inside my head was taking the best pictures of myself with my swimsuit on, of course. It would be a solo photo without Oliver in it. He was the skipper and the photographer. And what picture should I pick out to post on social media? I needed a sexy picture. This was once in a lifetime.

I couldn't believe I trusted Oliver to drive the speedboat, and he never had any experience. Basing his driving skills in San Francisco, he was a scary driver who honked at everyone and threw his hand at people when making a mistake, as an apology, or whenever he was upset with ridiculous drivers around him. But at this moment, it was either I drive the boat or I shut up and be thankful that Oliver was actually here with me, having fun driving the boat. He was excited to be here. At this moment, the only thing I waited for was to vomit. I hated being seasick. This was so unexpected. I thought I was going to have fun and drink a glass of wine and do a little pictorial, but I guess not.

I tried my best not to spit but snap here and there with my phone, taking couple pictures. It took us an hour and a half from the dock toward the volcano that was so far but did not seem like it. I couldn't do this anymore. I didn't want to ruin this day.

"Oliver, we will need to park somewhere. We need to take a break. I am getting nauseated."

The water was so deep and dark blue. I was quite frightened that a shark might pop out of nowhere. Our boat was not that big. Oliver started driving again and passed the volcano for another half an hour to the other island and parked. He tried to grab the orange ball that was floating on the water, and because he missed it, I tried to grab it. I ended up scratching my hands, and he started getting irritated at me because I couldn't get it.

"We need to tie the boat in that thing with the rope. Why can't you just tie the rope in it?"

Well, how do I know? I never drove a boat. I never parked a boat in my entire life. I could parallel park a car, but goddamn, Oliver. There were a couple of Greek men standing at the dock, looking at us. It was quite embarrassing to ask them for help, but it did seem like they were waiting for us to holler at them. They were ready to jump to their boats and start rowing, but finally, Oliver got the tie into the floating ball. Thank heavens. I went to the front of the boat because I didn't want to hear from him. I was just so upset that he demanded me to grab the floating round ball when it was actually tied under the water, and there was no way you could remove that.

I looked so stupid in front of those Greek people. Besides being a woman and not knowing anything about boats, what else could I be stupid with? I removed my shorts and tank top and made sure my butt was eating my underwear so it would look like a thong. How sexy was that? With my bulging stomach because of my love for Guinness beer? Sure, why not.

Oliver approached me and offered me a beer. He had three cans of Heineken already, and this was his fourth one. I just hope he won't knock out or something because I was not willing to drive this boat back to the dock. He knew that I was so sensitive, yet he continued to be the way he was toward me. Should I ignore how he was to me just now? Was I overreacting? Should I ask him if he wanted to box right now? Should I MMA fight him? Maybe not. I would rather get a tan on my butt and underarms than entertain my irritation with him. I couldn't drink with him anyway because

I felt like throwing up because of the movement of the boat on the water. I couldn't even eat. I just drank from the water bottle that was in his backpack.

Oliver looked very much concerned. I think it was because of his financial state. I would try my best not to poke him. I couldn't even make a joke to him right now. I mean, I couldn't even speak properly because of my current state. Instead, I gave my phone to Oliver and asked him to take a lot of pictures while I did a sexy pose. It's not that I didn't care about his bills and that I was not willing to help him, but he had a lawyer who needed to be paid and his house mortgage. Wasn't that his baggage? I had no baggage, so I'd enjoy myself in this vacation. And if he wanted to think about his problem back in San Francisco, then I couldn't do anything about that.

We stayed at the same spot for two hours and thirty minutes. We just lay down with our towel. The owner of the boat said that there were pillows inside the boat. I didn't know if he was joking or not, but there was no pillow inside. I used Oliver's chest as my pillow and my towel as a blanket. There was another boat that came, a big one with bunch of tourists. If we didn't rent a boat; we would have ended in that huge boat with the rest of the people. I was so happy with the privacy we had, even though Oliver and I were always like cats and dogs. I was starting to get a tan, and my skin was getting dark, obviously. Oliver and I decided to go back to the red beach sand toward the dock. I didn't think we'd end up staying in the boat until 7:00 p.m. It was only 2:00 p.m., and we wanted to be in bed for a nap. Was this how it felt to get old? I mean, I was only thirty-three, but I was feeling aches and pains all over my body.

I told my mom about my symptoms, and she said, "You need to check your uric acid levels." And after I explained more information about what I was feeling for quite some time now, she finally said, "Well, say hello to the arthritis world." When she said that to me, I thought, *I knew it all along.* I did have it at a young age. I remember going to my primary doctor two years ago and talked to her about my concern, but she guaranteed that I was too young, and it was impossible for me to develop arthritis. I asked her about me doing a test for rheumatoid arthritis, and the funny part was that she did not have me do any of the tests for it. Instead, she had me do other tests, and her conclusion, after we received the test results, was "Amelie, the biggest concern is for you to do some exercises every single week. If you can do it every day, then that's better. And you need to quit eating food that contains a lot of fats. But other than that, you are very healthy."

I didn't think I was catching up with her. I did not get the result that I asked for. I didn't get the answers I was looking for. Should I sue her? No. She was too nice to be sued. And other than that, she was way too young. She looked like she just graduated med school and was trying her best to give me the right answers. The problem was that I didn't need her to be nice to me. I needed her to look me in the eyes and say, "Look, woman, whoever and whatever you are, you are healthy. You need to keep your mind active. Go back to school and get something out of your life instead of thinking that you have rheumatoid arthritis. If not, then go screw yourself and stop wasting my time."

I guess I needed to look for another primary physician who older and was about to retire and didn't give a damn about people's complaints and instead tell them the truth. Or maybe it was an underlying disease that required more testing. I just hope I wouldn't die any time soon.

Oliver and I started heading back to the red sand beach and stayed there for almost three hours. One thing that irritated me was that every time I said something, he got defensive. After a while, he would say, "I'm sorry. You're right."

Of course, I was right. When did I made a mistake in this relationship? "Oliver, don't you think we are too close to the shore? There are lots of rocks at the bottom, and I can see them," I told him.

He said, "Amelie, relax. I got it. You can see the rocks at the bottom, but that doesn't mean we are in the shallow part."

Not even a minute after, *boom*. I heard a scratch. The propeller scraped one of the rocks at the bottom. I looked at him and didn't say a word because he would raise his voice at me and say my name over and over again. After he got us in a little deeper spot, he threw the anchor down.

"Amelie, don't worry. It's nothing."

I didn't argue with him. I kept my cool. My guts told me that there would be a problem. And my chest was palpitating, like I just had two energy drinks. I didn't even bother thinking about what was going to happen later when we returned the boat.

"I am going for a swim, if you want to go too." I knew the water was cold, but I would not just sit in the boat the entire day. This was the Aegean Sea. I needed to be baptized by it. Oliver went down first. We pulled the ladder down beside the propeller and climbed down up to his chest and quickly dipped his entire body, including his head. He grabbed the ladder and promptly got back inside the boat.

"It's freezing cold. I am not going back into that water. That's it. I am done. I am baptized by this country." Wow. Okay.

"Go to the front of the boat. Sit under the sun so you won't get cold." I gave him his towel and the extra towel the boat provided. Now I was concerned if I would be able to tolerate the chilly water, but because I bragged too much about being blessed by this country's water, I had to go in. And so I did. The water was cold, but it was so fresh. It was amazing. It was like drinking water, but you couldn't drink it because it was salty. The water was so clear. It was remarkable. For less than $400 roundtrip ticket from San Francisco to Greece? This was one of the most wonderful gifts I ever received from God. It was extraordinary. But because it was freezing, I had to sit with Oliver at the front of the boat.

Three Catamaran boats came in with lots of people in it. Good thing they parked on the other side, far from us. If ever they parked close, because their boat was bigger, everyone there would see everything that we were doing. It was not that we were doing something special or horrifying, but that would suck though.

"Do you want to stay in the boat until 7:00 p.m.?" Oliver was getting bored and wanted to head back. I could just sit here until tonight, but he was right. There was no point in staying here. My entire face and shoulders were red already and hurting from the heat. So I sent the owner of the boat a text message saying that we would be heading back in an hour. And in five minutes, we received a confirmation from him saying, "I will see you guys soon."

I went to the water three more times. How I wish Oliver swam with me, but he couldn't tolerate the chilly water. But at least he tried for me. Oliver pulled the anchor up, and I started tidying up the boat before we returned it. It took us between thirty to forty-five minutes to go back to the dock. Oliver tried to enjoy being a skipper for less than an hour. I tried to get more tan on me. While approaching the dock, here we go again.

"Oliver, you are getting near the dock. You're going to end up breaking the propeller."

As usual, he got defensive. "Amelie, please, I got this. It's not going to scrape."

Boom. I heard the propeller scratch the bottom cement. Why couldn't he listen to me? Why was it that he never heard me out? Every time I said something, I'd get shut down quickly by his defensive self. The owner saw what happened, and he jumped off his truck and ran toward us. This was so not good. He jumped inside the boat and took over the steering wheel. I didn't know what to tell him, but obviously, we would have to pay for the propeller if ever it was ruined. He let us out with all of our stuff and put the speedboat in a rack. He connected it to his truck and pulled it off the water. He looked at the propeller and asked us to come and see, and it was damaged. One of the faces was destroyed. He asked us where we were and how it cracked like that. I looked at Oliver and didn't even say a word.

The owner of the boat said, "The deposit money will be used to buy a new propeller. It costs around €160 to €200. I will return your €25." He was going to give us cash then said, "Hold on."

He never returned us the €25. Did I even care at this moment? Not really. I had no energy to argue with the owner of the boat. Plus I was exhausted right now. When Oliver and I got inside the car, he kept saying that he would pay me back for breaking the propeller.

"It's fine. Don't worry about it. Stop telling me you will pay me back. We are on a vacation. Let's just get in the jacuzzi when we get back to the room."

ARE YOU HAPPY?

First of all, I invited him to a vacation. And second of all, he never drove a boat ever in his entire life, and I demanded Oliver to drive it. So what right did I have to get mad or upset with him? I didn't have any authority whatsoever. At least it helped calm him down. We stopped by the same restaurant we went to yesterday and ordered the shrimp rice and Italian spaghetti. We jumped in the jacuzzi, and Oliver looked down because of his financial crisis. He wanted money to pay for everything and to do extra activities. But the main goal of this vacation was to relax. We already paid for all the hotels and flights. We just needed money for the cab and food for the rest of the time we were here. And how about when we got back? I had no idea. I would have to go back to work right away. Perhaps I was also broke. We spent the rest of the evening in the jacuzzi, talking about our experience in the boat. We shared pictures and shared our dinner with each other.

He started touching my hands slowly back and forth. I put my legs on top of his legs while he drank his white wine. He kissed my hands, shoulders, forehead, cheeks, lips, then my neck. It led us to the bed. Then things got all censored.

"Are you happy?" Oliver asked.

"Yes. I'm very happy," I replied. I asked him the same question. "Are you happy, Oliver?"

He said he was extremely happy. No one had ever done these kinds of things for him. He was speechless and overwhelmed. I had not traveled with any man in my entire life besides my parents and my brother, Chris. If Oliver was very grateful, I was too. Knowing that I was not alone was a big factor for me. I was scared to be alone. I didn't want to be alone again. As I could see, this irritation we had toward each other and raising voices was all part of the relationship. As long as we were not hurting each other physically. I did love Oliver sincerely.

A dear friend of mine asked me, "Well, how about a relationship that is emotionally draining? And yours definitely is one." She was right. But thinking about it, I was still alive. Was I right or not? I guess we all had different minds, and the way we all felt about certain stuff was just completely peculiar. This was why most people thought of me as a bizarre gal. I had to admit, though, that every time Oliver and I hugged each other, it honestly felt like home.

Today was our last day in Santorini, but our flight was not until midnight. We had to make sure we arrived at the airport to meet the blond girl around 9:00 p.m. for her to pick the vehicle up.

"Good morning, love," Oliver said to me.

I went to him, hugged him, and replied, "Good morning, baby."

I thought that the god of love, Eros, came with us here in Santorini. I was happy. We did our last walk in Oia after we put all our belongings in the trunk. Because it was our last day, I wanted to splurge.

"I demand for us to eat in a nice expensive restaurant, and I will pay for it. I don't want you to worry about it. We will put €100 for good food." He didn't say no to me.

"I don't think I still want to be in Oia. How about Thira? There might be good restaurants there." I guess he was right. We stayed in Oia the entire, and I forgot that there were other good spots in the island. We started heading to Thira. We ended up taking the dangerous road that only one vehicle at a time could go through, and that took us longer. It was actually good, I think, because we were killing time. For the first restaurant we went to, the map on my phone brought us in a lot of shortcuts, and we got a little bit lost. Oliver asked some construction men at the road, and it happened that they were closed. So we had to look for another restaurant that was open, and we were getting seriously hungry.

We typed in *Thira* this time instead of the restaurant, and it finally brought us to a different scenery. There were a lot of restaurants and more souvenir shops. We parked the car beside this small clinic. I didn't know if it was an emergency hospital or a regular hospital, but it was definitely a small clinic. There was a Mexican restaurant in Santorini. How cool was that? We found a restaurant that was inside and couldn't really see. It was hiding behind the trees and plants with lots of beautiful flowers. It was packed with people. Sophisticated tourists were dressed up in cute outfits and jewelry. I wanted to eat here.

"Anywhere you want. I'm just following you. You're paying anyway."

Okay. We found the spot then. We sat down and ordered. We spent at least €80. I ordered lamb meat with potato and carrots, and Oliver got salad and salmon with a beer, and my latte was delish. We asked for too much food. I couldn't even enjoy the lamb meat I got. We ordered a huge plate of the Greek salad, and I mainly ate the salad. So I had to pack the lamb to go, and maybe when we got back to Athens, I could eat this in the apartment. Oliver insisted to carry the lamb for me. I doubted him at first, but I didn't want to be rude. I gave him the bag. The entire time we were walking around, I wasn't paying attention to the bag because when I looked at it, I could see the sauce in the plastic bag and not inside the Styrofoam.

I raised my voice at him. "Give me the plastic bag!" I demanded that he give me that bag, or else I would go crazy in the street. For the love of the lamb? That was an expensive food, and I was saving the sauce. I didn't want to waste anything. I traded a plastic bag with him, and we stopped by the ice cream shop for a gelato. We had so much time to kill still. Oliver didn't want to be in the small car for six to eight hours.

We got a hotel room in Thira for €40. It was not bad. We didn't even have to move the car elsewhere. The hotel seemed like a family-owned business. I guess everything here in the island was a family-owned business. They offered us coffee and other drinks for free. They were a bunch of kind people. Oliver showered when we got inside the room, and I could not take it anymore. I fell asleep for a couple hours, and so did Oliver. My alarm went off, and I jumped on my feet and took a shower. I gathered all our stuff again as usual. I did what I was good at—rush and nag Oliver to hurry up.

"Do you have your lamb meat? Make sure you don't leave that behind," he said.

"Thank you for reminding me. That would be a huge waste of money if ever I left it behind."

It was dark outside, and the blond lady sent us a message that she was on her way to the airport. And we were too. We were only ten minutes away from Santorini International Airport. It was weird. The airport seemed to empty. Maybe the passengers would come late and we were just early. After fifteen minutes of waiting, the blond girl came, and we handed her the car keys. She was the best, but so long for now until next time.

We walked inside, and a security guard approached us and asked where we were heading. Oliver told him that we had a flight at midnight to Athens, and the security guard told us that the last flight was around 8:00 p.m. There were no other flights for tonight. Wait, what? We showed him our ticket, and he explained to us that the flight was actually last night, not tonight. So we missed our flight for one day, and not just that. We missed our nonrefundable flight, and we had to wait until tomorrow to book another one. And the sad part was that there was no taxi outside the airport. We were so screwed. I didn't know what to tell Oliver. He was outraged at the moment. I couldn't blame him.

"I got us. Don't worry." When I said this to him, he got more irritated.

"How can you be calm when we are a mess right now? There is nothing we can do. I don't have money right now to buy another plane ticket. There is no taxi. Where are we going right now? Stay in the airport?"

No, definitely not staying in the airport. "We are going back to the hotel. We paid for the room until tomorrow, so we can go back there. The last rental car right in front of us is about to close, so I suggest you run there with your long legs instead of arguing with me and going off, because none of this was my plan. And in regard to the flight, don't even worry about it. We will leave tomorrow. I got us."

We got a small vehicle and paid for it for one day. The owner of the hotel gave us back the room key and said, "Welcome back. Your room is waiting for you." It was kind of him to say that, and he even made me a cup of coffee.

When we got inside the room, I booked us a flight with a different airline at 11:00 a.m. for the next day. We went to sleep. I must say, it was comfortable. Not that I wanted any of this to happen, but being left behind in Santorini for the next two days was wonderful.

Finally, it was the next day. Oliver was getting homesick and just wanted to go home. I think the two-week vacation in Greece was a bad idea for him. We got our boarding passes and got through Immigration. I was still praying that something should come up for our flight not to happen. But that might blow Oliver's fuse. And it would not be good. I couldn't believe this trip was about to end. We were on the verge of it.

We rented a car in Athens because our flight tomorrow back to San Francisco was at 6:00 a.m., and we had to leave the apartment around 3:30 a.m. because it would take us half an hour to get to the airport. And I doubt that there would be any taxis that early. Plus we had two fifty-pound check-in luggage, two carry-ons, and another two handbags full of souvenirs which I would claim as our carry-on luggage.

I couldn't believe we got here with one check-in luggage and one carry-on luggage, and now we had so much stuff. It was making things difficult for us to leave. When we got inside the vehicle, I typed our apartment address on the phone map. Oliver started having pain on his sciatic lower back, and he ran out of hydrocodone. Tylenol did not work on him. What to do? He only brought enough medicine for two weeks. How I wish I brought some with me for him. I never thought about it. Ugh. He couldn't move, and we had to wait. This was why he was having difficulty walking today. He was not even supposed to lift heavy stuff, but he ignored it. I understood that he wanted to do most of the things for me, especially carrying heavy stuff because he was the man, he said. Still, balance it out. I couldn't tell him anything, especially right now. I had to show him that I was just here and would do whatever he needed. As long as I could accommodate it, I would do it.

He declined for me to drive from the airport to the apartment. He wanted to drive but needed a few more minutes to stretch his back and take a moment of silence. I felt bad for him. How I wish I could touch his pain and that it might go away. But this time, the employees of the car rental were staring at us for just being inside the vehicle for quite some time now. I found the acetaminophen and gave Oliver two tablets, and he started driving. We went straight to the gyro restaurant at the other street of our apartment.

We parked the car in front of them, and after we had our dinner, we walked back to the unit with our stuff.

I wondered how difficult it was to be a man. You had to do everything for the girl you love. You wouldn't want the girl to have difficulty carrying bags. You drop them off right in front of the house instead of having them walk a couple of blocks. I personally preferred walking so I could get exercise. It would suck to always sit and stand. I rearranged our luggage and got everything ready for tomorrow. I put the clothes Oliver would wear tomorrow on a chair on his side of bed. I sat on the bed and contemplated everything that happened within the last two weeks of this vacation. Did I enjoy the entire trip? Let me see. I needed a moment to ask how my heart felt. My biggest concern was when I got back, I would have to pack all my stuff and put it in the storage. According to Oliver, we were done. So clearly, I needed a plan because I didn't want to be kicked out. That would be embarrassing. I just hope he wouldn't throw my stuff on the street because I would end up going back and forth catching it, like playing tennis like an idiot.

Living in the neighborhood with Oliver, I was quite sure the neighbors knew me already. This was one of those neighborhoods that had three-story buildings with triplexes, where people rented and put their computer desks by the window and watch people walk by the street. I did the same thing. In Oliver's Victorian house, in the living room, I took everything out that was blocking the window and put a round table and two stools. That was where I sat every morning to drink my coffee and read the daily newspaper and my novel. It was fun watching people pass by. But now I had to look for a new place to live. And the only thing I could think of was visiting my parents in Las Vegas for a month. After, I'd apply for this caregiving job in London. So while I waited for the result of my application, I would take a leave to see my folks. It would be a bloody move, but if I thought about it, it would be stress-free. I would be single again. I could do whatever I wanted and go anywhere I wanted. But there was one thing too—I would be alone again. It would be a new search. "Hi, it's me, Amelie. How are you?" I get it. I didn't have to meet anyone or be with anyone. But the problem was, with the loneliness you get after a while of being alone, depression comes knocking at your door. Sadness was unexplainable. Good night to the fun times and all the efforts I put into this relationship.

As my alarm went off, I heard banging in the kitchen. Oliver was having his second cup of coffee, as usual. I couldn't believe he was up earlier than me. Before I went to bed last night, I planned to shower early in the morning before we left. But that did not happen. I was not trying to be disgusting and not care about my hygiene. I just felt exhausted. I didn't know why. I was probably tired thinking about being broke. We brought all our luggage outside the apartment door and made sure everything was tidy. I put all towels on the bathroom floor, and Oliver left the unit keys on the table and locked the room.

I thought that the luggage wouldn't fit in the car because it was a tiny vehicle, but I had my fingers crossed the entire time we were in the process of renting it yesterday. Oliver's lower back was aching again. Oh my god. What could I do? Tylenol or any kind of painkiller did not work. The only thing that worked on him was a prescription from his doctor. How I wish I booked us a one-week vacation, not two. I'm so sorry, Oliver. He dropped me off the departure door with all the luggage, and he returned the car downstairs. It took him a while to come back to me because of the pain he was feeling, and the parking was quite far to walk. The airline was open for check-in. I thought that we would be late. We made it in time. When we got to the ticketing lady, she asked us for a negative COVID test form. We didn't have it. I knew it. I did say this to Oliver, but he insisted that we shouldn't go to any of the clinics here in Greece because they wouldn't even understand us, and he was concerned that we might get sick from random people going in and out of the hospital. Okay. But now what? The next flight wouldn't be until tomorrow morning, and this time it had two layovers in Amsterdam and Los Angeles. We needed to do the test first before we could fly.

I didn't' want to look at Oliver. This was bad. Seriously bad. The lady booked us a flight the next day. I assured Oliver that everything would be fine. I sincerely apologized for this horrific trip. He was going off. He didn't have money to book us a hotel for tonight, and we didn't have a vehicle any longer. He didn't have money to buy us food.

"I got us covered. It's okay. I just got us a hotel. It's all the way to the east side of the city. We will just take the taxi after we are done with the test." It was 6:15 a.m., and we are left by the plane again. This was the third time. Apparently, we were not alone. There were a couple of Americans who were left behind because they assumed that because they were heading back home, they didn't need to do the testing. The hotel was supposedly fifteen minutes away from the airport, and this freaking genius took me as a stupid person. He took a different route that took us forty minutes to get to the hotel, and Oliver was going crazy on me because of the pain he was having on his back. When we reached the hotel, it was actually a resort. Look at that. It was a beautiful resort beside the beach, the Aegean Sea. They offered us free breakfast buffet. The taxi driver just told me that I had to give him €40. Was he crazy? The total cost was supposedly €25, but Oliver was on my face, and this freaking guy was a hassler and wants to leave. Oliver told me with an attitude to pay already and just forget about everything. Right, because he was not the one paying. It was me. I gave the taxi driver €40 as he wished, but I cursed him tremendously. I cursed his eyes. I cursed his nose that it would get swollen badly. I cursed his mouth, his teeth, and his hairy legs. I cursed his moustache. How I wish I had a voodoo doll where I could fart on it every single day. He would smell like a rotten egg, and no one would go near him. Huh. Then he'd lose his job as a taxi driver. And off he went. Great. What a great man he was.

The receptionist gave us the key and showed us the breakfast room. He helped us with our luggage to the seventh floor. With the super tiny elevator? We ended up putting everything in one elevator, while Oliver and I went and rode the other elevator. Wait a minute. I couldn't move my left leg. I thought my lower back was messed up too. I didn't want to put pressure on Oliver, so I couldn't tell him about it.

"What are you doing, Amelie? Let's go. Hurry up," he told me.

"I'm having cramps. Go ahead. I'll be there," I said to him. I stressed my muscles too much by lifting a heavy backpack with a bunch of busts. I was in so much pain. What should I do? I needed to take things slow. Good thing I had my Motrin. That should help me. But the main concern was getting to the room. I thought this was the finale of our vacation, and obviously, next time, I really couldn't do a two-week trip because I was clearly getting old, and backpacking was just impossible. I knew that I was in my early thirties, but I fell off long stairs before, and as a health care worker, I was required to transfer my clients from the bed to the wheelchair. We were lucky if there was a Hoyer lift. And what was fun about my job was when I encountered a person with

Alzheimer's disease. I had this lovely lady who told me I was too nice to her, that she appreciated everything that I did for her and she loved me. After an hour, just an hour, she grabbed my arms really tightly and hit me with a pillow continuously. The only thing that was in my head while she was doing that to me was *I must deserve this kind of life for her to call me a bitch and an asshole and for her to punch and scratch me.* But hey, she was not the only one. Even Agatha the witch called me a bitch. I just wish I would die in this lifetime and be reborn. And what if I ended up being reborn? What kind of life would I want to have? A simple life, perhaps? Away from the city and the ridiculous dramas? My own drama was already consuming me. I couldn't take another person's personal issue.

Finally, I stretched on the bed. I took two Motrin pills and fell asleep. I opened my eyes and reached for my phone to check the time. It was 1:15 p.m. Was my phone broken? I just missed the entire morning sleeping at the resort. I turned to my left side, and Oliver was lying down too and was in pain. He took two Motrin at the same time I took mine, according to him. I wouldn't know. I passed out. I should drill him by saying, "No, you are lying. You did not take any Motrin." I should give him a hard time when things were already a mess. What a great idea, Amelie.

"Let's go for a walk. I need to see if it will help my lower back. So we can see the resort too." Okay. That sounded good to me.

I brushed my teeth and put my shoes on. I was ready to go. I never combed my hair. My skin was much more important than my hair. It was a bad mentality because women's hair was very crucial to their appearance. I must admit, I was very lazy when it came to brushing my hair, and it was very obvious when you'd see me. The resort was pretty much empty. They probably got affected by the pandemic. It felt like we were VIP guests. We had the entire place to ourselves. One thing that I found really cool about this country was the marble tiles they used on the ground for people to walk on. And the houses were built in marble and tiles. The handicraft and dedication they had for a strong structure and beautiful foundation was remarkable.

Oliver and I went outside toward the beach. There were two guys doing a race from the resort to the other side. I looked at Oliver with a big smile, and he said to me, "No. I am not going in the water. I am not swimming with my lower back being this way. Besides, the water is freezing cold. If you want to go for a swim, you can go for it. I'm going back to the room and lay down. I'll rest my back for tomorrow's long and never-ending flight." Bummer.

How fun could this day be? This was our last day, and we were stuck inside the room the whole day and night. I didn't want to go in to the water without him. What if there was a jellyfish? A shark? I'd be in the water, and I couldn't even see what was going on around me. We started heading back, and there was a cat that kept following us. He kept petting it. That's why it wouldn't leave. I was allergic to cats. He held the cat like it was his very own, then he would hold my face later and cuddle with me. Where do you think the cat's would hair go? On my wonderful and beautiful face. Fantastic. Should I say a thing? Or should I just beat him up? He loved cats. He saved a cat named Roxy from a shelter, and he slept with it every single night before I came into his life. The cat must have hated me for ruining her life.

For the rest of the evening, we stayed inside our room. Good thing I still had the lamb meat. It was still delicious. Oliver and I shared it and had a soda with bread that we brought with us from a week ago. When you had money, you had wine and expensive food. But on your last day, it was always a cheeseburger with water, no fries. We watched horror movies the entire night until we both fell asleep. Odd that I didn't turn into a psychopath like the ladies I saw in movies. Most especially with what I was going through with Oliver. What if he woke up and I started acting like a white lady with all my hair brushed in front of my face? Didn't seem like he had a heart problem, so it was okay to do this to him.

Good morning, Athens. This was it. We were going back home to San Francisco. And we were going to Amsterdam. I just hoped they wouldn't give us any difficulty. I just wanted to go home now. The hotel prepared us a driver to drive us to the airport at 3:00 a.m. And you know what was hilarious? It only took us fifteen minutes. Unlike the other driver yesterday morning. It took us forty minutes. He was a horrible person. The lady at the check-in counter wouldn't take our luggage because it was over the weight limit. I thought that I was overweight. I guess my life was not that horrible. Both our luggage was seventy kilograms, and she wanted us to pay more than €200.

"We don't have any money anymore. We were supposed to leave yesterday, but we needed to do a €60 coronavirus test each, and we needed to get a hotel room. Plus the taxi and food. We just want to get back home." My puppy eyes did work. The main manager only had us pay €50 for each luggage. Wasn't that amazing? I guess I was the only one excited with all this back-to-back mess that went on with this trip, because Oliver's mind was on the long flight back home.

"I can't wait to get back home," he spoke. "I can't wait to be back on our bed. I miss our soft $1,500 mattress. I want to be in my nightgown watching horror movies with my wine."

Hey, you are not the only who wants to go home. I want to be back too. And you are not the only one with a ruined back.

Although Oliver's back was much worse. I felt sorry for him. I did dedicate my life to him, and even when the day would come that he had to wear a diaper, I promised the gods that I would change his poop diaper for him. That's how much I loved him. I guess that was not happening? I didn't even want to think about it anymore. Praise all the gods, we were finally in the plane. Oliver tried to lay in one of the seats but only rested for half an hour. His back was really bothering him badly. I thanked him for going with me on this trip. It was a big deal, and this was the very first time I traveled with a guy. Even though it was somehow rough, it was still a successful vacation. And when we reached the second layover, which was in Los Angeles, California, we had to go through the inspection. They checked our baggage, and we were required to open it because they saw something sharp and long inside our bags. It was actually the bust of the gods. It had a stick for it to stand. The problem now was that Oliver could not find his keys. He could not open the luggage he had. And now he was behind me, all upset. "I did not hide your keys, Oliver," I said to myself.

"Amelie, where did you put my keys? You were the one packing everything. My truck keys are missing, and I can't find it." He was going back and forth on the luggage and me. Everyone was looking at us, even other people who were going through the baggage check.

"Have them break the lock so they can see what is inside the suitcase," I told him.

He replied, "Amelie, they don't do that here at the airport. Where are my truck keys? The luggage key is with it. Oh my god, Amelie."

Amelie this, Amelie that. I went to where his luggage was, and I asked the guy to give it to me because he was keeping it inside with them until it got checked. When he put it in front of me, I opened the pocket, and it was there. The keys, including his house and truck keys. Why did I put it there? Because the key chain was too heavy. It was full of different keys, and he did not have to carry it in his backpack because of his lower back. Yup, that's right, so he could roll the luggage around the ground easily. I gave the key to the guy, and he was able to open it and see what was inside. I grabbed all my stuff and started walking toward the boarding door for our final flight to San Francisco. After that, Oliver calmed down and tried to hold my hands, but I snapped my arms and walked faster, and I walked a different route.

This time, I did not care if I walked out on him. We were back in California. He had his boarding pass, so he could find his own way back home. All the stress and pressure after that beautiful trip? It was insane. During the entire flight, he kept touching me, even my finger. I was so irritated with him. He should have left me alone because I would turn into Anderson Silva and use all different karate chops I could to make sure he had both eyes darker than the elephant's butthole. And I didn't think he'd want that.

Yes. We were back home. I felt so relieved. We grabbed our suitcases and looked for Oliver's truck. I had to pay for the parking at the airport, yet the entire time, he was rude to me. What if I didn't pay for it? I couldn't do that because I'd end walking back home. Plus it was his house I was going straight to. Not just that. He would be stuck at parking until he paid it off. And the conclusion? I paid for it because at some point, I was aware that there were times I was a douchebag toward him. I thought that he took advantage of this trip to be a jerk to me because he knew that I wouldn't fight him. The funny part was now he was calm and super nice and sweet to me. He ordered me my favorite food. We stopped by the Chinese restaurant that was a five-minute drive away from the house. I thought he didn't have any money. The next day, he got me a bouquet of flowers, and he even put the vase beside it on the kitchen table with a card.

"Okay, Oliver. I understand what you said to me back in Athens. You want to split and you are done with this relationship. Please, do give me time because right now, I don't have money to move out and look for a new place. At least a month. You won't even see me because I will be working twenty-four seven. I just need to leave all my stuff here temporarily," I told him.

He did need to spare me some time. He couldn't just kick me out of his house. I had so many stuff, and I needed $3,000 just to hire a moving company, plus the storage and the first month's rent and the deposit. It felt like the end of the world. Where were the zombies when I needed them to attack me and bite my arms and take my eyeballs out? I had nowhere to go. I needed to submit that application form for employment to the agency in London. But first, I needed to rest extremely bad. My lower back was not yet healed.

"Amelie, you are not leaving me. Please, it was my first international flight. I was stressed out and felt pressured. Please don't leave me."

Wait. Was he insane? He told me he was done. Now he did not want me to leave him. I didn't understand. Saying things that you don't mean in a relationship, was that even legal? Where was the love there? He did that during the vacation because he knew I made a promise that I would not leave him no matter what. And how about now? Because we were back, now he was worried that I would really leave him. Were his screws loose? I mean, Oliver, come on. You can just say it because there are a lot of screwdrivers in the garage, and I can help you with tightening your screws.

I was so confused. Was he making fun of me, of my life? I hated it. I grabbed some boxes from the garage and taped the bottom. I boxed all my books in the bookshelf while I listened to him ask me not to leave. He was very sorry. I turned around and looked him in the eye, irritated. His eyes were sincere, but I didn't get it. Should he not be mad with Agatha because she was making his life horrible and I was only trying to give love to him the entire time? I got it. Nobody cared. That's how life was. You needed to only care about yourself.

"I care too much about you. I'm done thinking about you every single time. I'm still a mistress by law. I'm so sick of it. I'm so tired of this situation that I am in. And the entire time we were on a vacation, you were very rude toward me. I seriously don't understand what I did to you," I told him, my voice up high and my eyebrows furrowed. I had been engaged to Oliver for exactly a year now, yet I couldn't even announce it to friends and family because he was still married by law, by paper. So was I not embarrassing myself when I did that? I knew he chose me. I had him by my side, but the main question was, would he not walk away from me later on and go back to Agatha? Where were the securities? I would end up giving my whole heart, yet it would just be broken in the end. Nope. He couldn't even tell me what I did wrong. Instead, he apologized that he has been an ass since the day we met. What are you doing here, Amelie?

CHAPTER 12

Almost Done

I was preparing my client's breakfast on a Tuesday morning. I brewed some coffee for her and me for us to drink at 7:00 a.m. and read the daily newspaper. It was my routine with her for three months now. It was very sweet. She had a big heart, and she was in her nineties. My phone rang. It was Oliver. I stepped outside to answer it, and he said that he had good news for me.

"What do you want?" I said to him.

"Amelie, Agatha finally signed the papers. I'm free. You are not a mistress. Never ever say that again. I love you so much, Amelie."

Really? This was crazy, but it did feel like a thorn in my chest was pulled out. I could breathe well with fresh air. "Really? What happened?" I ask him.

He replied, "Well, I called her attorney and said that I agreed to what she wants, which is to sell my house and give her half. You're right. I can't do this any longer either. It's too tiring and suffocating. I don't care wherever I end up in, as long as I am with you." Wait, what? But why? His house was worth more than a million, and he was willing to give it up just to be with me? What could I say?

But the problem was this. "You will just give me a headache, Oliver. And you have been pissing me off since the day we met. I guess we can look for an apartment?" Oh my god. Why couldn't I say no to him? I was such an idiot. I get it. Everyone who knew me just wanted to bitch slap me for not thinking straight. But as far as I knew, I never did think straight in my entire life. I did love Oliver, and I thought about the first months I had known him. I never knew he owned a home and a vehicle. I thought that he was bunking at his parents' house. And that knowledge I had about him lasted six months. I never really cared about whatever he had. What I cared about were the caresses he gave, the way he hugged me and kissed me, the way he did me and when he breathed in me. Okay, I will stop now. But every time I got upset or pretended that I was irritated, he always brought me flowers to calm me down. Was I being shallow? I guess I was being a girl, was I not? Well, guess what, not all men know the word *flowers*, so receiving it made my heart fat. But I just went back to his arms again. Nothing new.

Oliver said, "Let me call you back. Amelie, we will sell this house. We will sell our house. I need to speak to the attorney and to the broker. Then I will call you back. I love you so much, Amelie. Are you happy?"

Was I happy? Well, yes, I was. That was great news. I was happy for him. I mean, if that was what he really wanted to happen. To think that was just a house. It was a material thing that cost him his happiness and caused the ex-wife to go insane. Well, if he got rid of her completely and came to me all fresh and single, he could start courting me properly. Why not? I would love to start fresh with Oliver. Was I demanding too much from him? I didn't think I was because I was in this situation because I loved him, and I didn't mind going through a thunderstorm just to be with him. I did think he was capable of providing peace in this relationship, which was the only thing I was asking for. I wanted to have a normal partnership that I could announce to the world who I was really and who he was to me.

Oliver called me the next day with another good news. "Hey, my love." My morning with him was sweet as always with his greetings, but the day ended with us battling and arguing on who was right.

"What is it?" I replied to him. Yes, I was blunt and straightforward, but according to him, it was one of those characteristics of mine that he really loved.

"I spoke to my dad last night. And he is selling us his house here in the city. We don't have to look for a realtor and houses elsewhere. We have a house now. It has three bedrooms and one bathroom. I am giving it to you, Amelie."

Just like that, the blessings he was receiving was a never-ending goodness from God. As he went through his divorce, I was there the entire time. And as he lost his home with thirty years of investment, his father caught him and saved him. He had a more expensive home and much bigger house that was at the corner of the street. I remembered stopping by that home once when we were passing by so he could point it at me just to show the outside, and it just so happened that his older brother was outside fixing his car. Oliver pulled over to say hi to him and introduced me to him.

He was a very nice and friendly man. I heard him tell Oliver, "Take care of this one."

"Yes, that's right, Oliver. You better take care of me," I said to myself. Glenn was actually the first family of his that I met. But he was getting that house, and I was very happy for him. Could you imagine? Agatha tried to bring him down to the ground but didn't know that he would actually be in a better situation. It was honestly frightening to meet someone like her. They ruined your life because they were unhappy with theirs.

"Oliver, I am worried about my best friend Agatha. You are actually making her madder at me because of what you are doing." Wait, what wrong did he do now, Amelie? Well, as you can see, he would live with me in a nicer home and more expensive house. That was the biggest mistake he was making. What if she attacked me again or harassed me? She was mad.

After a couple of days of working, I went home, and Oliver open the door and said, "Do you have a couple of minutes?"

What was going on? "Yes, why? What is wrong?" I said to him.

"My parents want to meet you. We are going upstairs next door."

Was joking. Right now? After two years in this relationship, I was finally meeting Oliver's parents. Do I want too? Should I? What if I ended up telling his parents that their son actually needed a beating? They wouldn't like me. I didn't work in the management department in a hospital like Oliver's ex-wife. I was just a health care worker. They might look down on me because I was not earning a good amount of money annually. Plus I was a half-breed, English and Filipino.

"Hey, Amelie, let's go. Put your shoes on."

What the heck. So demanding. Why was he rushing to bring me in front of his parents when I looked like this? I wore a huge red shirt and yoga pants, my toenails not polished neatly. My hair was not brushed, and I had not prepared a speech. For sure they would ask me what I did in life.

"Okay. I'm ready." No, I was not. Oh god. He was holding my hands firmly. Was he making sure I wouldn't run away? Way to go. I'm so proud of you.

He hit the buzz button, and he spoke in the speaker, saying, "It's us." Apparently, his parents lived in a multifamily home and were on the third floor. And on the second floor was his brother and his family. The first floor was empty. We were buzzed in. I looked up, and there were twenty-five steps to see his parents.

"Please don't push me. I don't want to die. At least not yet."

Oliver started laughing. Oh no, I could see his dads' two legs. He was wearing cozy red pajama pants. I looked up and saw him smiling at him with his arms wide open for a hug.

I said, "Hello, sir." I went straight to his dad and gave him a hug. I wrapped my arms around him. I almost lifted him up. Good thing I did not. If I was his caregiver, he would probably end up firing me.

"Welcome to our family, Amelie. Please be yourself. Come. My wife is inside the bedroom," he spoke.

"Thank you, sir," I replied to him. Wow. He was super sweet, like a papa bear. He was super soft to hug. He was so sincere when he hugged me, and the way he looked me in the eye was crazy. He was not faking it, I guaranteed. Was I paranoid or what?

Oliver pulled my arms toward the bedroom, and his mother was on the bed, laying down and watching television. She was bedridden and couldn't walk anymore because of some medical issues. I waved my hands at her and said, "Hello." While saying that, I tilted my head down a little bit to show her my respect. I was so nervous. I would hold my breath until I left their house. Then after that would be the only time I would inhale.

His mom asked me to sit down on a chair, and so I did. His dad sat across from me. They were staring at me but happily, with smiles on their faces. I felt sad. I just wanted to hug them and say, "I will be your caregiver for life. Don't even worry about anything." But I didn't say it. I tried my best to keep my mouth shut. I spoke highly about politics, and that would definitely get me in trouble. I should have told Oliver to bring duct tape to put on my mouth just in case I said something unpleasant.

His mom asked what I was, and Oliver said, "Oh, she is half Filipino and half English."

She replied, "That is why she is very pretty. The combination she has."

I didn't know what to say, really. She was very kind to say that. She explained to me the kind of disease she had that made it difficult for her to move around, even sitting at the edge of the bed for her to eat her meals. Her muscles and joints were beyond bearing. While I listened to her, I could feel that she wanted me to be there for her, that she needed help not just physically but emotionally.

Oliver just started bragging about me being a health care worker and that I knew so much. He told them all my stories about my clients, the good stuff, and the rants that he heard, especially about my Alzheimer clients.

"Oh, Amelie has so many stories and has so many experiences with different clients, with different kinds people, and different kinds of diseases."

Okay, Oliver, wait a minute. Was he introducing me to them as a health care worker or his new partner? It felt like I was being interrogated or interviewed for a new client.

His dad said, "My wife and I, we have been together for sixty years now through thick and thin. I hope that you guys stick together the same way we did." He said it a beautiful smile in his face. Wait, I wish Oliver was listening to him properly because I was the innocent one in here.

I wish I could tell his parents, "Oh, Oliver does need a beating sometimes." But I couldn't. They might think that I was idiotic or senseless. I loved Oliver's parents. Both of them were loving and sweet toward him.

They said, "Come up here whenever you want or like. The door is open for you."

I replied to Oliver's dad, "Thank you, Sir. Thank you so much." I gave him a big hug and gave his mom a peck on her forehead. I was so worried that I would end up hurting her if I touched her.

She said to me, "You can give me a peck on my cheek. My entire body just gets really painful."

We started heading out. Good thing Oliver grabbed my hands, or else I would have grabbed the vacuum and mopped and started cleaning his parents' house. The entire time we were walking back to Oliver's house, he kept saying, "I love you, Amelie. Forever. Please never say that you are a mistress ever again. I am a free man now, and I have brought you in front of my parents as my partner."

Yes, you are right, Oliver. You definitely are a single man now. I mean, not really because he was engaged with me. He had beautiful parents and a beautiful welcoming family. And what I noticed the most was that they were very humble people. They never talked about politics, about their achievements, about their homes, about their money. They had wonderful hearts. When we got back inside the house, Oliver said that his parents were not that way toward his ex-wife. He could tell his mother liked me. If that was the case, then

I praised my God and all other gods, especially the Greek gods. I even praised the spirits that were always guiding me and Oliver and even the bad spirits that I always felt lingering around me that only carried depression and insecurities.

After a couple of days, Oliver called me while I was at my shift. "Hi, do you have a minute?"

"Yes, I do." I wondered what he was up to this time.

"My mom called me yesterday, and she asked me if you like them. And I said yes, she said you guys are very sweet couple."

Really? My thoughts were actually the opposite. I thought she or they would say, "Well, Amelie is okay. She is nice" or whatever. But no. She was actually asking what I thought of them. Was she kidding me? I loved her. I loved the both of them.

"Amelie, my mom has a favorite French chair. She upholstered it, and she wants you to have it. There are two sets, and it's in her living room at their house. You know what, she never offered anything to my ex-wife. I am surprised she offered you her favorite chair. And not just that. Both my parents said that you can go through their other two houses and browse for more furniture to put in our new home. Anything you find there, you can have it."

I was very speechless. Was that not insane? Wait a minute. His parents were offering us furniture. I was curious though. Why was it that when I first went inside his house, there was just a sofa and a portable table in the kitchen and a portable chair? Like those party tables and chairs.

He was married, but why was that house empty? And his bedframe was bought from a secondhand store. According to him, his ex-wife never bought furniture to put in that house. She did not even buy a can of paint, yet she demanded him to sell the house and give her half of the worth of the home.

What really surprised me was that Agatha, the wicked witch, graduated with a degree in behavioral sciences. It's funny that she never applied it to herself. Wasn't that all about the discipline with human actions and other stuff? Maybe she only did that course to get a good position and for her to announce to everyone that she had good manners. I thought she needed to go back to school and refresh her memories with the courses. Maybe it would help her with communicating better with other people. I wondered if she even had any friends with the kind of attitude she had. But I wished her all the best in life, and maybe one day, if ever I ended up working at the massage parlor, I could send her my card and give her a free massage. I ruined her family and her relationship, according to her. Well, according to the internet, she actually filed a divorce against Oliver back in 2007. She walked out on him three times. So why was she even blaming me when I only came in lately?

Oliver was craving for some Filipino dishes and bunch of rice, so we went to this Filipino restaurant and bought some food to go and brought it to the new house. We did our first walk together and sat in the kitchen and ate our lunch there.

"Next time, we will bring our wine with us. To celebrate," Oliver said to me.

"I can't believe you are living with me in this house," I told him.

"You don't like it?" He was sad when he asked me this question.

"What do you mean, don't I like it? I love it. This house has more lighting. It's bright. And it's much cooler because it's by Lands' End. It's close to the beach, and it is uphill, and it gets foggy. And all our neighbors are Chinese. I love it so much. I am just speechless."

Oliver agreed and said that this was the reason why he loved me so much. Was this good karma? When you do good to people without asking for anything in return, the blessings come on their own. It was somewhat frightening because of every action we did, karma was right there. The consequences of every word we said and every move we made, it always had a comeback. I expected that Oliver and I would have to move to an apartment and would have to store all our furniture and most of our stuff in the storage. I guess that was not happening.

Could you imagine when I first moved to San Francisco? I was living in my car for at least two weeks with my five comforters and pillows. And after four years now, I had my own bedroom that Oliver and I shared with a queen-size bed and my very own kitchen that I could design with my own ideas. I was turning the kitchen floor from wood to Spanish tiles, like the ones I saw in Spain and Portugal. And we would order the kitchen cabinets. They would be a dark blue with gold handles and a white backsplash tile. The countertop would be white or beige granite. And the bathroom? It had a Jacuzzi. The only thing the bathroom needed was a glass of wine and a good-smelling candle with a cute robe.

What a life. I still had the hangover from our Greece trip, and it would be crazy with all the designs because Oliver and I both loved Greece and might copy a lot of stuff we had seen in that country to this house.

"Are you happy, Amelie?" I asked myself. There were times, once in a while, that I made sure that I was okay with my current situation. And yes, I was very happy. Now I could walk with my head up and say that I was with Oliver, and he was my partner.

He was calling. My phone was ringing. I answered it. "Hey. I have great news for us."

Another good news? I wondered what it is. He did sound excited. If he was in front of me, he would probably be jumping up and down with the way he sounded. I wish I could guess it. I wanted to see if I was really a psychic, if my premonitions came out right.

"I talked to my parents, and they said that there is a blueprint in the garage in our new home for us to install a unit downstairs. Do you want a unit downstairs? We can rent it out, and we will have income coming in, or we can Airbnb it. What do you think? It will be a three-bedroom downstairs and a bathroom and kitchen."

For him to ask me for my ideas made me flattered. We were not even married yet, but he acted like I was his wife. He had been doing this since last year.

"Do you think everything that is happening right now has an affect from our previous trip, by visiting the Greek gods? Because right now, the blessings to you are just overflowing. It's like a broken faucet. The water is unstoppable." That was a good way to put it.

"Amelie, this is us. We are being blessed. This is not just me. It's your house. It's both ours. We are starting fresh, my love. Oh, my parents said that they will help us with the unit downstairs. The construction downstairs will start in two to three months."

That fast? That was amazing. Before Christmas this year, everything should be all fixed, and we should be settled.

"When you get off work this weekend, can you help me organize the house and clear everything out? The broker and Agatha were coming in the afternoon. Can you go to the other house and wait for me? I just don't want any conflict. I want everything to go smoothly with the walk through with the broker."

What could I say? "Yes!"

That day did come. Where was Oliver? I thought today, the broker would come in. He texted and said that he wouldn't be home until 2:00 p.m. Seriously? What should I do now? There were twenty boxes behind the front door. I started opening them and putting duct tape at the bottom. I started in the living room. I organized everything and made sure there were no cups and blanket. I set it up according to the magazine I saw with the busts we bought from Greece and scented candles. Now the next room was the master bedroom. I had three boxes. I dumped all our clothes on the chair and the ones that were on the edge of the bed inside the box without folding any of it. I only had two hours left before Oliver came home. It was not that I was trying to impress him, but somehow, I was trying to impress him. He was exhausted with life and with everything else that was happening at the moment. I just wanted to help him.

Next was the middle room. I stripped the bedsheet and took all the pillows out and put them in the box because it didn't look presentable. Last was the kitchen. The bathroom was quite clean and ready to go. So that left the kitchen. I put the pots and pans in the box and cleared the countertop where the sink was. And the kitchen table that is full of food, I dump it all in the plastic bag and threw it all in the box.

I did it. I was happy with everything, except the dining room. I left the table full of our knickknacks. I could not do it anymore. I was tired. And the entire time I was cleaning, I was also talking to Oliver. He kept calling every minute to say he loved me and missed me. I felt like I would faint from exhaustion. And finally, he was banging at the door for me to open. It had been three days since we saw each other, and he was sweating from climbing the tree to cut it. The muscles he had on both arms were just unimaginable. He grabbed my arms and pulled me toward him and hugged me tight.

My head was lying on top of his left shoulder as he said to me, "I love you so much, Amelie. Thank you for being by my side. Thank you so much for everything." His arms were around my back.

I pushed him away. "Come on, we have so many things to do. I made two cups of coffee for us. I need us to sit and have a cup of coffee for a short time."

Oliver looked around, speechless that I was able to pull everything off within two to three hours. "I need to shower after I drink this coffee."

I actually put his clothes in the bathroom so he didn't have to look around. Every time he would come home, he was always sweaty, and I demanded him to always go straight to the bathroom for a shower.

"Wow, Amelie. Thank you, really."

We put everything in the truck. I put everything in a box earlier so I could take it to the other house that was twenty minutes away from this house. So the witch and I didn't have to encounter each other. I left right away. When I got to the other house, I couldn't open it because it had two locks, and Oliver only gave me one. I had to wait until he was done with his meeting. I parked outside and rested. Good thing I brought the coffee with me. I had something to sip. I just hoped this neighborhood would bring us good karma, that everything would be okay. And hopefully, it was also safe.

Oliver got us a house at the corner of the street, which made that the biggest house in the street because it was a corner house. Oliver was done with the broker, and they just left. I started heading back. I parked in front of the house and moved to the passenger seat. He jumped inside the driver's seat and started driving back to the new house. "How did it go?"

He looked at me and smiled. "Amelie, thank you so much for all your help. The broker listed the house at a good price. There are two interior designers who will get the house ready to sell, but they told me that it looks staged, and everything there is amazing, and they want to use it for staging, except that the law is they cannot use it because of the pandemic, the COVID issue we have. They cannot use it. But you really did good, love."

Wow. Really? That was surprising and shocking. I mean, hello? An interior designer left a comment about what I did. That was big. I always wanted to do interior designing, except that I never believed in myself. This might be the beginning, don't you think? The new home we were moving in to would need a lot of fixing. I could definitely put my own designs into practice.

We sat on the sofa in the new house. Oliver wrapped his arms around me and was so thankful. He put his head on my neck, asking me, "Are you happy, Amelie?"

"Yes, I am very happy, Oliver."

We lay down for a while before we went back to the old house. I mean, haunted house. That was what I called it.

CHAPTER 13

End

Two months later, we completely moved all our stuff from the old house to the new one. A new family bought Oliver's home. We finished painting and setting up the dining area and living room to how we wanted it. Actually, to how I wanted it. Oliver gave me that bookshelf that I had been dreaming of and a fireplace with a bunch of wood on the side, ready for a fire. I got my Spanish tiles in the kitchen floors and a granite countertop with blue cabinet with gold handle bars, just the way I wanted it. I was able to frame our Santorini painting and hang it in the kitchen for the finishing item of my design.

The unit downstairs was almost done. They put three bedrooms, and we ended up having one garage. Oliver put his old 1970s vintage car and parked the other truck in the driveway. We bought another car, a small one to use for work. Oliver made the balcony outside the kitchen much bigger. He put the rocking chair there for me and a table for our coffee. It was my new spot for reading. I loved reading with my coffee in the morning. I was almost finished with my very first story, perhaps a novel. I hoped that somehow, it would be turn into a book, and some readers would love it. That would be a great achievement in this lifetime of mine. If ever that was accepted and published, I would definitely write another one. I could not imagine myself being an author, but that would be a dream come true.

Oliver asked me, "Amelie, do you want to get married?" Was he trying to piss me off?

"No." Why would you ask someone if they want to get married? Shouldn't he be saying, "Amelie, let's get married" or "Amelie, will you marry me?" Seriously.

He started laughing hard with my response and said to me, "Oh no, Amelie, will you go with me to the courthouse? Will you marry in the courthouse? Then later on, we can do the kind of wedding you want. Do you love me?"

I definitely loved Oliver. He was very sweet, and like everyone else and me, he made mistakes and forgot a lot of things. He got into an accident before when he was young. He was riding his bicycle so fast, and he was hit really hard at a metro bus stop that he lost consciousness. He was unconscious for a month in the hospital. According to him, he didn't remember every single thing you told him. It was really difficult, and patience was a must. For two years, I always wanted to beat him up because he didn't remember details of what I told him. He would say yes, but after a couple of minutes, he would ask you the same question. Fascinating, wasn't it? But a lot of times, we ended up just laughing at it, after I got super irritated and explained five times what I just told him. But yes, I did want to marry Oliver. I loved him and I loved his soul, most especially his kind heart.

"I don't really mind where we get married, Oliver. It's actually much better if we elope, just the two of us, then use the rest of the money to buy flooring for the house. We can get the real hardwood floor. That would be a treat," I said to him.

He replied, "You know what, Amelie? I like your idea. If that is what you really want, then we will do it. Just make sure it's what you want. We can go somewhere for our honeymoon, wherever you want. I will pay for it."

Hey, how about Maldives? If Oliver and I went to our next international trip, it had to match the first trip we did a couple of months ago in Santorini. But this time, I would make sure that we disappeared for a week and not two. And I had to bring extra medication for his lower back.

Oliver and I went to the government office to get the marriage license. He had to bring his divorce papers, proof that he was not married by law, and an identification card from both of us. Oliver and I eloped. We hired an officiant. Just him and me, no one else. And we went back home in Oliver's Chevrolet Impala Coupe 1974. I set our dinner table with beautiful expensive dinnerware and silverware. We put out candlesticks, and we bought a bunch of flowers from the flower mart and took our own wedding pictures by setting the timer. We had our meal delivered to us.

"Hey, the catering is here," Oliver said while laughing, but it was the food delivery online. What I loved about our wedding was it was just me and him. We cherished every moment of being together, and by nightfall, I put my nightgown on, and Oliver put his pajamas on. He threw a log into the fireplace, and we had red wine.

"Are you happy, Amelie?" Oliver asked me.

"Yes, I am happy, Oliver. Very happy. Thank you!" I replied.

The next day, a postman had something for us in a box, and it was very heavy. It was for me. Oliver helped me bring it upstairs. We looked at each other, and I removed the scotch tape on the box. I opened it, and there they were, my books. My self-published books that I worked hard on for six months. I finally turned it into a book. Oliver helped me distribute it around San Francisco City. He helped me get back on track with school and continue my education. Everything was consistent, and everything was at peace. Oliver gave me the best gift in my entire life, which was family.

Was I happy? Yes. I was very happy.

About the Author

Clara Poppy Gallot is thirty-three years old. She resides in San Francisco City. She loves to hike with her partner and reads novels and writes in her spare time. She likes to travel, and she dreams of retiring in Scotland, in a small brick home with a cabbage patch garden.

Hannah Casey